Seeing is Believing

The Crumbs Mysteries Book 1

Marilyn Boardman

ISBN: 9798857284179

Cover design by: Art Painter
Library of Congress Control Number: 2018675309
Printed in the United States of America

To life, the giving of love and the receiving of love, both here and from above.

Contents

Chapter One

Everything in my blackout curtained bedroom appeared to be normal, not that I can see much more than the outlines of my furniture and my bed. It's not a big room so it's thankfully quite easily done without moving my head far, but something isn't right. The darkness in my brain begins to clear as I lie listening, for what I'm not entirely sure of for a moment and then it strikes me. Not only is there no snoring and other disgusting manly noises (I won't elaborate as you could be dunking your favourite chocolate biscuit whilst reading this) but I am in the middle of the bed with all the duvet! He's shuffled off, finally departed after only one week of knowing the dreaded truth. Now I am alone, totally alone and at last I feel at peace, I smile which turns into a big stupid grin and stretch my legs even further into "his area" feeling totally and blissfully free!

24 hours earlier

Alright I know, many of you ladies including my mother will want to say, "I told you so" and believe me if I only rang her or answered her phone calls she would, joyously, but too late, that's life. I didn't listen or want to see the signs all those years ago, physical or spiritual. Well, I've grown up fast, the hard way. In the space of two weeks, I have lost the person I loved most, no not my husband, my godmother Rose, been made redundant (a blessing) and now have just watched my husband of five years pack his belongings and drive off in his BMW sports car to live with a blonde bimbo who works in McDonald's! Incredible. Should I be crying? Hitting the bottle? I did all that when the devastating news of Rose first came through and there's no way I'm doing it for him. At times like this I need to calm down and think carefully, do what Rose taught me. I'll put the kettle on and take it from there.

I'm feeling strangely very calm to say the so-called love of my life has just gone, maybe it's the rose tea I'm sipping in between sniffing, no not because of tears, it's the gentle sweet aroma of roses and herbs I love. Matt hates anything that fills the air with overpowering smells. I can't have my scented candles, potpourri, he even objects to my herbal teas. Odd really, that's what first made me suspect all those "covering away matches" (he's a 35-year-old sports journalist for the Yorkshire Post) and extra fitness regimes to keep up with the sporty types when he eventually got back home. He had a glow and cheap pong around him, a Superdrug special by Britney Spears. Now I'm free to do exactly as I want, and I will.

Ten minutes later and my minimalistic lounge

which I've always wanted to "warm up" but which I wasn't allowed to, is glowing like Santa's Grotto. All the beautiful candles my friends have bought me as pressies over the years and were tucked away in my wardrobe are now lighting up the open plan lounge/diner kitchen area. I'm glowing with happiness, it's never taken much for me, something Matt has never understood. Wow, there's some heat coming from them, it's great. I'll just open up the patio doors out onto our tiny balcony. Outside it's getting dark but it's beautiful for an early May evening. Our home, an apartment overlooking the river Aire in Leeds, is very nice but not at all what I'd wanted. Laughter and the voices of people walking over the bridge to the restaurants and bars near the Royal Armouries is drifting in. The night is just beginning for all those wanting to look good and be seen in the right setting, "the beautiful people" as I call them. I've never wanted to be part of it, I'm far more of a homely person at heart, this was Matt's idea and sadly I just went along with the life plan like a fool. Why do we do it?

"Stop it Kate, shake yourself free, no negative thoughts now". I'm saying the words out loud but it's almost as though Rose, my godmother, is saying them to me except she always called me Kitty. She would have done, she was a very spiritual lady and besides my beloved Gran, her best friend in life, they were the nicest people I ever knew. Hopefully both are now reunited in the blue beyond to continue their giggling schoolgirl antics. Both were spiritual, well Gran thought she was, she did know what I was up to when I didn't want her to, but Rose certainly was and I loved her dearly, correction-them both, with all my heart.

"Chocolate, I need chocolate, and cake". Staple diet of any female with problems to work on, no more tears I promised myself, but these were for Rose and Gran. Like someone possessed, my tiny ever so neatly stacked cupboards are thrown open and ingredients, cake tins, utensils and the mixer are spread across the gleaming, "show home" surfaces. Whenever I'm down I bake, it is about the only thing I feel comfortable with. It's creative and totally mind blowingly soothing on my soul plus the end results are yummy.

"Eat your heart out Matt the Rat, no more special recipes, home cooked meals, cosy dinner parties for your up their backsides friends. It's quarter pounders abound from now on!" Boy, am I starting to feel good.

The thing about baking, like doing the ironing, is that you know what you're doing, and your mind can wander. Only slightly though. Well for me baking is like breathing and boy does my mind wander! The last five and a half years are flashing fast forward as I beat the brains out of my organic free-range eggs.

"How could I have been so stupid? Love is blind, too right it is, we should petition for our rights. Get compensation; maybe get issued with parking stickers. Prime Minister and co watch out, there's a lot of us could march on your new pad and wreak havoc!" Well. He looks so smug and smooth faced and I'm going into a hating men phase so don't stop me.

As I reach for the organic self-raising flour and the Fairtrade cocoa powder everything is suddenly crystal clear, shame it had taken so long. Better late than never!

My life hadn't been too bad, just what many other kids went through all over the country. My mum hadn't really wanted me, well she was only 18 and on her first holiday with her pal, all packed up and ready to experience everything that Butlins in Blackpool had to offer for the week. She did and more besides, resulting in little me. Cute as I was, baby puke and poo were not top of her list with Santa. Gran was left holding the baby in her little cottage in Headingley whilst "Mum", or Carol as I had to call her, got herself a job on the cruise ships, conveniently jumping from one to another and rarely coming home.

"Her loss the selfish..."

"Now, now stop yourself there Kitty."

I'm spinning around now whilst trying to sift the cocoa and flour into the mixing bowl, a dangerous act and I mustn't lose any. It's Rose's voice again in my head.

"I'm sorry Rose, well I did have some great clothes from her but that's about all. Come on, concentrate on what you're making Kate, you're letting your mind really take over now." Although the sound of my own voice is very convincing, I shake the voice out of my head and carry on beating in the ingredients, maybe a glass of something stronger will be needed later, a large glass.

So, for years it was Gran and me, oh and Rose of course who lived next door and had done since both girls had got married. Close friends, sadly both were widowed whilst still young so shared the rough times and happy times together. As Gran only had Carol and Rose had no children, she became my "Fairy" Godmother. We had fun together, gardening, baking, that's where my love of it started and when money was sent home from Carol's trips all three of us shared caravan holidays on the East Coast. Happy days of sandcastles, fish and chips, campsite bingo nights and sing-a-longs with whoever was on at the club. Rose and Gran shared something else which I wasn't allowed to talk about at school as it was a Catholic one (Gran being Catholic she brought me up the same) and that was Spiritualism.

Leeds has a good Spiritualist Church and that's where we walked to twice a week down from Headingley past the University. We also walked to "proper" Church on Sunday to St Anne's. I seemed to spend my time during Mass looking at the congregation and dreaming about floating down the aisle in a Cinderella wedding dress. How wrong I was.

Not being remotely academic, even though the nuns and teachers at Notre Dame School tried their hardest before giving up, I left school defeated and got a job. All my working life I'd been a receptionist at the Ramada Jarvis Hotel at Lawnswood or the Parkway as it had been called. I had found my calling. They were my other family; I belonged there and loved it till the Rat walked in and took over my life.

"Hang on, steady now Kitty, don't forget the three bangs and shakes."

There it is again, that voice, sorry not any voice, it's Rose, how she used to talk to me as we baked together in her small, neat kitchen.

"It's the stress isn't it; I'm hearing things?" Now I'm talking out loud to myself as I'm banging the two filled cake tins and shaking them to settle the mixture, our little bit of "magic" as I was taught by Rose. Perhaps the act was a bit ferocious, but the chocolatey mixture reminds me of his head-brown hair and lots of it.

"There, in the oven they go, and I'll eat the lot of it if I want to!" That's a bit stupid as I know I will, let's face it who am I going to share it with? My thoughts return as I clean up the mess and drips I've made whilst being overzealous with the beating.

He'd walked into my life and totally taken over my body and soul like an alien from outer space. Reorganised my wardrobe, my hair (ok so I needed it), and my life. Gone were most of my friends as he made me see they were losers and then in came his. He said when and where we were to marry and the type of dresses he thought would suit me. He even went to look at them with me. I thought it was so romantic, he cared, my Gok Wan of Leeds. Rose never passed comment except to say that his aura was all wrong. Gran agreed, but I thought she didn't want to be left out! I refused to listen, he had charmed the pants off me, literally and that's how I ended up married after 6 months, in an apartment at Turlow Court overlooking the water, living a life totally controlled by a water rat! Rose had only said, "Don't live by the water, it's bad vibrationally". "Piffle" I'd said behind her back.

Strangely enough the constant loud flow of water as it tumbled over the small weir just to the right of our apartment had never bothered me. But now with the patio doors open it's as though I'm hearing the river Aire for the first time as it roars past deafeningly. That's what love and a control freak does for you. Blind and deaf, what other senses did he kill? Certainly not my smell, yummy chocolatey wafts are coming out of the oven.

"Ten minutes girl, then a little bit of heaven will be in my hands."

I've decided to go all the way. Chocolate buttercream and melted dark, rich chocolate for the top plus dark chocolate swirls to decorate.

By the time my perfect cakes are out and cooling on the rack I'm off the tea and on to a glass of rosé. Michael Bublé might as well keep me company, no one else will.

"What the hell am I supposed to do now?" I'm starting to crumble, I know I am. Five and a half years of being told what to do and now it's hitting me big time. All through my life changes have hit me hard.

"Pick yourself up, shake yourself down and start all over again" sings in my head.

"It's there again, who's that? Is it you Rose?" No answer. I'll probably wet myself if there is, not that I expect one. I'm sitting on our sofa facing the water roaring past, hell it's so uncomfortable, whatever possessed us to buy this? It looks good but feels like a dentist's waiting room chair, cold and tense. Tears are now mixing with my rosé, and I don't do watered down drinks. Strictly a no ice girl.

"Life's a pig!"

I'm not good with changes in my life. Change had sent me in a spin at the dangerous age of thirteen. I'd got used to being "different", no mother, well just Carol and her rare visits. At school everyone loved my two "Grannies" as they called them, mainly because when they called at my house there was always something delicious to eat. It was good and cosy, comforting like my childhood blanket with the satin trim hanging in shreds from so much snuggling with it. Then suddenly my life was shredding too. Rose announced she was thinking of buying a small café in Wetherby that a friend was selling. A pretty market town halfway between Leeds and Harrogate with nice walks, the river Wharfe running through and fantastic fish and chips but a long way from us. Rose and her husband George had done their courting on a Saturday there and it was a special place for her.

In time Gran got used to it and together we helped Rose out on a weekend and in the school holidays. Secretly Gran loved it. It was so Rose, filled with quaintness, fresh flowers and delicious smells.

That's where I've been for the last six weeks, I had to, and Rose needed me. Gran suddenly died after I married leaving me devastated and with a small inheritance as her cottage was rented. The money all went on this flat; it just got swallowed up in dreadful designer furniture. Gran's heart gave up quickly, but Rose had cancer and needed me. Work said they understood and gave me leave to nurse Rose; Matt pouted like a spoilt brat. I spent my days looking after Rose, dealing with the café and dashing home every evening for a couple of hours to see to him! What an idiot I have been! I was washing and ironing his favourite shirts for him to go and take the blonde bimbo, who probably has five gold stars awarded for services rendered on her McDonald's uniform, out for slap up meals and rumpy pumpy dessert!

He couldn't even make the funeral; an emergency came up in London with an overnight stay. I'd come back to this place four days ago, drained both physically and mentally and an empty shell inside a bigger empty shell. He'd come back glowing and with scratch marks on his back.

I just knew, I didn't even ask. Six weeks of watching a truly lovely person fading away, trying right to the end not to cause too much pain for others when who knows what pain she was enduring had made me numb.

Work called me in for a meeting, Redundancies, cutbacks and a load of meaningless pleasantries, forced smiles and apologies later I left with my few belongings in a Tesco carrier bag. Matt took it badly, ranted and raved about money and what problems me being jobless at my age would cause him. HIM! Not me, for better or worse. That's when all the pent-up anger in me burst out, louder than the roaring river Aire. Today he packed and left but not before giving me the low down on how Miss McDonald's satisfies his hunger.

The phone is ringing again and my mum's voice, equally piercing, is shouting my name from the answering machine.

"Kate, are you there darling? Do pick up, Lawrence and Mummy are very worried about you, I'll keep ringing until you do." Then silence.

"Oh God why do I deserve this?" but in my heart I know she is all I have left now. My mother and her husband Lawrence. He is a banker she met on a cruise and married fifteen years ago. He's nice and keeps her happy and away from me, they live in Geneva. Her garage is bigger than my apartment and she disliked Matt after only two meetings in five years.

"Kate, I'm still here, pick up darling, speak to Mummy."

Mummy! She has never been "Mummy" to me, not even "Mum". Carol yes, "Mother" for school purposes but "Mummy", that's banking Geneva beautiful people talk.

"Hello, I'm here." I can't bring myself to say the "M" word.

"Darling, how are you, are you eating, sleeping, being cuddled?"

Maybe it's because she actually flew over for Rose when I hadn't expected her to that made me reach for the phone and talk. The last time had been Gran's funeral and before that my wedding. Neither time had been particularly warm and friendly. Gran's funeral I can understand, but my wedding? She was dressed in a designer creation in off white. White, on my day! The only colour was from the huge sapphires and diamonds around her neck and dripping from her ears. Memories of that tense day still haunt me,

"No," was all I could say.

"What do you mean no? Where's...that husband of yours? He should be looking after you."

Oh, what the hell, my mouth opens and spills forth all the gunge before I realise it's done. Well, the therapists would be pleased if I'd had to use one. Who knows maybe I will. There is silence on the phone.

"Aren't you going to comment?"

"No, your Gran and Rose did that."

I can't believe it, what's my world going so topsy turvy for? Now Carol acting out of character, maybe it is the menopause, or she's nicely pickled with her constant round of cocktail parties?

"Okay." I'm speechless.

"First take time to think carefully, stand up for your beliefs. You're strong enough, you always were. Ask Gran and Rose for a little help, I'll call in a couple of days, please answer the phone for me. Goodbye darling, take care." Then she was gone.

I'm left staring at the receiver in a daze. I don't think I can take too many more shocks. She hates spiritual things, wouldn't listen to Gran and her rantings. Why the sudden change? She was too restrained, too nice; it's not normal or fair. I like knowing where I am with people, I don't like change.

I can't be bothered waiting for the chocolate topping to set, I need chocolate and cake now! Two huge portions of chocolate heaven and most of the bottle of rosé later I manage to turn off the music, lock the patio doors and stumble into my bedroom.

My one obsession, well maybe not my only one but to me it is important, is clean skin. No matter how late or what state I am in the face must be cleansed of all make up. Not like Carol with her magic pricey pots of goo, good old-fashioned soap and water for me. The appearance of two zits at a tender age because of laziness was enough to cure me.

Somewhere between hanging onto the moving sink and rinsing my face with cold water a familiar voice is coaxing me gently.

“Come on Kitty, time for bed, tomorrow’s another day.”

“Okay, night night Rose,” I answer.

Chapter Two

The sun is streaming through my bedroom window onto the right side of my face, warm and inviting. It's my fault for leaving the curtains open but I like it, the feeling of sunbathing on a beach before it gets too hot in the afternoon. "Afternoon!" suddenly I'm brought abruptly out of my daydreams. The sun doesn't come around this side of the river till after 11:00 AM. I'm panicking now looking around for Matt, the time, my clothes, then it hits me as well as the pounding on the top of my head. I'm alone, I'm redundant and I've got a hangover, something unknown since my illicit teenage drinking days.

"Make the best of it whilst it lasts girl, another half an hour isn't going to matter now is it." I've talked myself into it and am just moving further over onto his side which is nearer to the window and sun when the phone interrupts my luxurious movement.

"If that's "Mummy" she can..." strange, I've never needed to swear. Gran detested it and drilled it into me so why change now. My senses are picking up on a male voice but it's too deep for the Rat.

"Mrs Philips? Please could you call me at Ison

Harrison's Solicitors as soon as it is convenient, oh yes and my name is Oliver Barton. Thank you."

A sudden panic and dread of the future had stopped me from picking up the phone. I'm next to it in my Take That t-shirt I wear to bed when I'm on my own, which has been a lot recently, but I'm numb again.

"How could he move so fast? The Rat had it all planned, all worked out with that bimbo. Strewth he only left yesterday what a ..." My mouth is open, my brain is thinking the word, but I can't. I can't say what others find so easy to express.

"Oh Gran, Rose, just let me shout and scream it out, just once, you left me, now he's left me." I'm choking, not on the tears streaming down my face but because I've got hold of the front of my t-shirt and I've been screwing the material in both hands into a tight ball at the front. Gone are the gorgeous faces of my dream men and the neckline is suffocatingly tight, almost garrotting me. My bits and pieces are also now being flashed in front of the patio doors! A youth with a can of Coke to his lips is motionless and staring up to my first floor, the can of Coke getting squeezed harder and harder, his eyes on springs.

"My God, he thinks I'm a nutcase or, oh no, a flasher! Me, a pervert!"

"Pull yourself together and move away from the window. Look on the bright side, you did shave your legs if nothing else," the voice is saying.

"I'm going mad, I'm hearing things as well, I've

got to stay calm, one thing at a time. This isn't happening, it's just stress. Kettle, water, tea bag. No, I'll make coffee, I need it good and strong. Now I'm talking to myself. It's got to stop. It will, won't it?" No answer.

Two beakers of coffee, two hot buttered slices of toast and a thick wedge of chocolate cake later, well it's 12.50 PM so it's breakfast and lunch together, and I'm psyching myself up to ring the solicitors. My mind keeps going to the youth's face, pimples and all. What if he brings back his grotty pals and they hang around for a repeat performance? I'll get some nets so he can't see in, but I may not be staying. Better ring and get it over with.

"Oliver Barton here."

Nice voice, not too posh for a solicitor, a slight accent, maybe Scottish but not so you'd pin it on him. Thirtyish, no older than forty. My ears have had plenty of telephone training with my work. It's a game I play when people ring up for bookings, visualise and then check them out on arrival. I'm usually not far off the mark, or was. Suddenly my bubble pops and I'm aware I will not be playing the game anymore.

"Hello, is anyone there?"

"Yes, sorry, the pan was boiling over." Well, when on the spot, improvise. "You rang and left a message, I'm Kate Philips."

"Oh Mrs Philips, that's right now I wonder if you could call in to see me perhaps 4.15 PM today if you're free?"

"May I ask why?" My knees are feeling weak now and I'm in danger of passing out with the sudden reality of it all, so I do the next best thing and sit on the floor. The cool wood on my bare backside soon jolts me back to earth.

"It's best we discuss matters in my office, is it convenient for you?"

A weak "Yes" escapes my lips.

"Good, very good, I'll see you at 4.15 PM then."

I put the phone down before either of us says goodbye. It's rude but I'm not feeling good and need to lie down fully. As I'm on the floor already that's the best place to stay, legs stretched out for a while, and I don't care if anyone can see me. My pounding head is back, I feel deadly.

Nice office, small but nice, light and airy not like I imagined all dark wood and files piled on the desk and floor, well that's what they portray on the television. I'm right about the age I'd say mid-thirties, tall, dark hair with beautiful grey eyes and seriously long lashes for a man. His mouth curves into a warm smile as he talks, I can't take my eyes off it.

"Kitty, concentrate, shame on you."

"No!" I shout. "Not again!"

"Pardon, are you saying no you don't want it?"

"No! I mean yes, sorry it's complicated."

"What is?"

By this time, I really don't understand anything let alone what he's just said to me. My hands are flying all over the place like somebody demented.

"Please can you just repeat everything for me, I'm really sorry it's just so much is happening, I'm not myself at the moment, I don't know what I'm hearing and what I'm not." Well, that part's fine anyway.

"Perhaps some tea or coffee?"

"As long as you don't mind if I spill any, I'm a bit unsteady at the moment." He's looking at me seriously now I can see him wondering if he should press his panic button or whatever they do when faced with weirdos.

"It's shock, my husband's just walked out, I could be made homeless, jobless and penniless all on top of losing Rose. I'm sorry it's all so much at once."

As though by magic his homely looking secretary appears with a tray holding two cups of tea, a milk jug and wow, those dinky sugar cubes in a bowl complete with sugar tongs and a plate of Bourbon biscuits. Bourbons, I love them, and Rose always gave me them, she used to let me take the top off and lick the delicious filling as long as I didn't tell Gran.

Now it's really getting to me, I can't even remember if I thanked her before she left the room, I'm so emotional and my eyes are about to overflow. Too late, they are and are taking my mascara with them.

"Have a tissue, it's a very delicate time for you, I do understand." A massive box of Kleenex is under my nose. Boy, this man is prepared. Panda eyes are not phasing him, He's still got that sensuous smile and I'm drawn to it again as I dab away feeling weirdly attracted to him until suddenly, I'm catching sight of a glistening wedding band holding onto the box of tissues.

"I did try to tell you my dear you're really going to have to start listening to me sooner or later. Just be a good girl and let the nice man talk," Rose's voice is in my ear again.

"Thank you, I'm ready to listen now, sorry for the blubbing. "My eyes are scanning around him and the parts of his office in view, but I can't see Rose. Maybe I should book in at the doctors.

"Mrs Philips, Mrs Philips, have your tea whilst I tell you."

Like a good girl I'm listening as I'm told unfortunately, I realise too late that the top is off the Bourbon and I'm licking it! Oh well, in for a penny in for a pound. I might as well carry on and enjoy the biscuit.

I don't remember walking back along Wellington Street, through City Square and up into town but here I am sitting outside Pret drinking a coffee whilst everybody rushes past. A lovely girl I've seen before is busking just opposite me outside WHSmith and she's really good, but I hadn't even heard her until now. I look up at her and she smiles, belting out "I will survive, ooh ooooh I will survive". Before I know it, I'm singing along and clapping like an over excited seal at the Sea Life Sanctuary.

"Thank you Rose and Gran, I will survive now with your help." This time my eyes are clear in more ways than one. In my bag, clutched firmly between my feet on the floor, is an envelope with all the documents needed as the new owner of "Crumbs", Rose's café in Wetherby. So much has happened, and I've had so much to take in, but I know everything will be alright. I've also got an appointment to start divorce proceedings. Well at least the card in my handbag tells me I have although it's all a bit blurry.

"Tomorrow's another day and I'm going to use every minute of it." I'm toasting the sky with my paper cup, and I don't care who thinks I'm potty. It's time to celebrate.

"Another cappuccino please and heavy on the chocolate." Well, why not.

It's not easy going back to the home of someone you loved dearly who died there. So many memories come flooding back. It's the second time I've had to clear personal items out and seeing someone's life packed up in bin bags for the charity shops cuts deeply into your heart. This time I don't have to do so many trips for one thing. Rose wasn't such a hoarder as Gran and for another I need most of it for living here. I've given myself the weekend to settle in, do what's got to be done in the living room and then I'm opening up the café again on Monday. Matt is keeping the apartment and paying me my share of everything. The cheating coward is getting off too lightly, it all seems so straightforward and civilised, but I just don't care anymore, I can make a new life for myself and that means a lot to me.

Last night, my first in my new home, I just had to sleep with the light on, like a child afraid of the dark even though I was in the spare bedroom, the one I've slept in since being thirteen. It's small and pink with Laura Ashley rose print curtains and cushions I chose and helped to make. Sewing was something I loved in my teens. The living area above the café is not big, one good sized bedroom at the front over the café, a larger than average bathroom recently converted with a shower cabinet and my bedroom at the back overlooking the garden, which is a nice, manageable size with a couple of apple trees at the bottom. Of course, there are rose bushes, good old fashioned English roses with large, full blooms, velvety petals and heady scents. Summer evenings in the garden drinking home brewed drinks with Gran and Rose, playing cards and looking at the stars. It was wonderful, well to me it was but not to any "normal" teenager. Don't get me wrong, I did have my moments, granted not many, but the few parties and booze sessions I later took part in were just to try and fit in with my school friends. I wasn't good at it; Gran saw through the excuses, and I felt guilty on top of the hangovers and soon gave up.

The lingering smell of Rose's Chanel No.5 hits me as I open her bedroom to clean it although there's very little to do as she was so particular right up to the end. I'm smiling at how she bossed me around when she finally gave into her bed. For the six weeks I lived with her I cleaned harder than I had ever done before. I realise now it was Rose's way of putting her house "in order". At 73 she had always been fit and strong, so it hit us both hard to know how little time there was left, and it was used wisely.

It's a very pretty room full of sun in the morning until lunchtime and the pale lemon theme glows. All the floors and landing are wood with rugs in the bedrooms by the beds. The bed frame is what Rose had when she got married and now is back in fashion, all metal, very fancy and a devil to dust! The only thing I'm changing is the mattress, well I have to, Rose will understand. That's why I'm in here to strip the bed ready for the delivery. The doorbell is breaking through my thoughts.

"What's the matter with delivery people, they tell you a time then come two hours earlier!"

The best I can do is grab everything and throw it into a chair over by the dressing table before running down to open the shop door.

"Sorry we're early love, upstairs which way?"

"Turn right at the top of the stairs, the room at the front."

"Ta, we'll get rid of the old mattress first then come back with the new. Better just move a couple of your tables to the side to make room first. Don't want to damage anything." Winking he set to with his helper to move a space. As Crumbs had originally been a house the café area is in what was the front room with the large kitchen at the back and a downstairs toilet. Rose had a door put on the bottom of the stairs up to the living area and had it locked during opening times. I'm staying downstairs out of the way as there's not enough room on the landing to stand about and watch.

Everything in this room reflects Rose's charm and personality. There are eight round, wooden tables each with four balloon shaped backed wooden chairs, it's pretty, ladylike, genteel. The walls are covered in a small print floral wallpaper with the lilac and pink taken out of it for the seat cushions. When set, the tables have white tablecloths which Rose was very particular about, completed with small lilac or pink ones on the top. She always had fresh flowers in little vases in the centre. Neatly folded serviettes are served with the cups of tea and cake on rose bud printed crockery. Only tea from the best tea leaves is served here with silver tea strainers in their own stands. The shelves in the kitchen are lined with teapots, coffee pots, water jugs, milk jugs and sugar basins, cake stands and crockery. All the utensils in the kitchen and cutlery in the drawers are gleaming. My eyes rest on the shelf with her beloved cookery books. The ones I grew up with and used. The large hardback Sonia Allison from the 1970s was our favourite for baking. I tell you I have tried lots of recipes over the last five years but the ones I have written down from this book never fail me. Tears are welling up in my eyes now as I touch her books. They're mine but I have no little ones to pass all of my knowledge onto.

Locked in my memories of loving lessons given by Gran and Rose the floodgates have opened, too late, I can't stop the flow. I'm lost in my sorrow and fear of the future.

"Now, now love, everyone gets attached to furniture. Had some good times in it did you? Come on love, think of how many more you'll have in this one." Winking that manly, know it all way to his mate as he thrusts the delivery papers and a pen into my hand.

"Sign here love and then we'll be gone."

I can see the paper though a big, salty blob has dropped where I'm supposed to sign, turning the delivery note a fawny colour and making it like tissue paper. I manage to scrawl something as my nose is now about to drip and that is pulling me to my senses. Tears and snot. NO!

"God, I tell you mate, I've seen some sights, this one's as nutty as the cakes she sells. All that tea and not a cuppa in sight!"

They've gone and I'm left with a reputation before I even reopen Crumbs, and a bed wrapped in plastic and nobody to share it with.

Outside the market square that Crumbs faces onto is busy. People rushing around getting what's needed for the weekend. Wetherby is a market town but there's only a market on Thursdays with stalls all around the square with the Town Hall stuck in the middle. It's changed over the last few years with a big Morrisons and even a Marks and Spencer. Coach loads of people get dropped off in summer for walks by the river and to browse the charity shops. Saturday is always busy. I can see the yummy mummies in their big vehicles driving around the square wanting a parking space, preferably right outside the shop they need.

"Why can't they go down to the big car park by the river, it's free? Blocking the roads with those monsters, they don't know what it is to bus it and drag their shopping home!"

Wow! I sound like my Gran, but I mean it. As a driver of a modest but well loved, elderly Clio parked in the small space at the back of Crumbs, I get outraged in car parks. The yummy mummies park alongside you, swinging their doors into your car, oblivious to any damage they cause or the fact that you can't see properly and if it is even safe to move out. I'd have special designated parking lots just for them. No! I'd ban them altogether. Maybe I should stand for election in the future. Yes, that's it; I'm a businesswoman now. A person of standing in the community, believe me when I get a bee in my bonnet I buzz.

"That's right you're a businesswoman now, so get to business, there's cakes to bake and a business to run, chop chop."

The voice is there again, I can hear Rose loud and clear, well I think I'm hearing her. It's as though it's in my head and my ears at the same time. Sticking my fingers in my ears doesn't make any difference, she's still there.

"Rose, I can hear you, but I can't see you, am I going mad? Please show me, anything, just so I know I'm sane."

Okay, I know that's a tall order as I've always been a bit "wobbly" at times, but I know I'm basically normal. PMS can play havoc with anyone, but this situation is new to me.

"You're going to have to help me out more here Rose, I didn't take that much notice at the Spiritualist Church, I only went for the tea and biscuits at the end. You and Gran were the ones taking part remember. I don't know that I even believe in it all so come on, prove me wrong."

Maybe that was a bit cruel after all they did for me but I'm actually starting to get a little spooked by it all. Do I need some counselling? But I haven't registered at the doctors yet, surely they will take me on, of course they will and certify me straight away.

I stand shouting, well not exactly shouting, more calling out a little louder in between the tables looking around Crumbs for signs. There's nothing obvious happening. No scraping on the wooden floor of chairs being moved. No knocking three times for yes on the tabletops. Everything in the kitchen area is still in place and nothing is floating. I'd be the first, well the only one, to run out of the café door into the market square if anything does happen.

Relieved but also slightly disappointed I'm grinning with my arms spread out, blowing my kiss as I always did to them both as I got into my car after a visit.

"Alright, I'm now officially mad but I love you both, bye for now, I've a bed to make up and shopping to do for the baking tomorrow if I can decide what to make."

Suddenly the air around me is thick with the beautiful fragrance of freesias. I know I can smell it. My nose is clear after a good blowing session as the delivery men left. It's even near the door up to the living quarters, getting so strong that Zoflora could bottle it. Rose loved all flowers like my Gran did but her husband had often bought her the highly perfumed, delicate blooms so she bought them whenever she could. To me the smell is real but there's nobody who can reassure me. It's not something I'll be able to talk to Carol about, she's said enough over the years about our trips to the local Spiritual Church and Gran's delving into the unknown. One thing is jerking back into my mind. Spirit, particularly female loved ones, when gathering close to us can bring the smell of flowers, the males surrounding us with tobacco or gardening smells to trigger fond memories.

"So, I did learn something after all but seeing is believing, only please don't scare me. You could always make the bed or do the baking; now that would be good and very helpful. Well, you can't blame me for asking."

It's strange but the smell of the freesias has brought a more peaceful feeling around me. As I make up the new mattress with clean lemon sheets and Rose's favourite duvet cover, white with dainty bunches of lemon embroidered flowers with pale green stalks and leaves, it suddenly feels so right to be here where I belong, in this room, running Crumbs, being me.

Chapter Three

It seems the most natural thing in the world to be waking up in this sunny room. The breeze from the open window is playing with the net curtain and the birds are twittering and calling to each other from the roof tops. It's spring with summer around the corner. I can always feel it, that tingle of excitement, a bit like Christmas only better, it promises new things, blue skies, holidays and strolls along the sand.

"No, no, no, not anymore it doesn't, I've got a business to take over, baking to do, huge amounts of baking, oh my God it's down to me!" Suddenly my sunny world is spinning, there's a sickly feeling rising up into my throat and I'm desperate for the loo. No, I'm not pregnant, just scared.

Yesterday had been hectic. After checking all the stock, ironing tablecloths I'd rewashed and answering the phone several times there was shopping at Morrisons to do. The kitchen now has pink post it notes everywhere, reminders of what has to be done today. A notice for part time staff is on the kitchen work surface waiting for me to put it in the window when it's been cleaned to Rose's standards. Thank heavens I've got Sally coming back to work tomorrow. She's lovely, cuddly and bubbly. Sally is in her late thirties, married to Chris with three children now all at school. Customers love her; she's worked for Rose for the last three years and is the best advert for cake you could wish to have, even more than me. She's a local girl who knows everyone and everything, nothing passes by her ears but she's never malicious, more concerned for people's wellbeing. A real mother hen bless her.

Carol, my mum, was part to blame for the red-hot telephone. She kept ringing with advice from both her and Lawrence on how to run Crumbs. I was trying to, but she kept interrupting me. She means well but after the fourth call I'm afraid I was tempted to unplug the phone. She stopped ringing after the fifth time as her hairdresser and beautician were arriving to prepare her for the Ambassador's Ball. It's a hard life being idle and rich.

Quickly washing and splashing cold water on my face to rinse it thoroughly and close the pores, that's my beauty treatment and it costs nowt as we say in Yorkshire. My shower can wait till later, my tum is still feeling gippy. When I'm nervous my stomach suffers, always has right through school and exams. Rose and Gran decided it was because I'm a Gemini and prone to these things. Me, I just reckon it's because I never have enough confidence in myself, time will tell.

Breakfast, I need food. I love Weetabix but I have to pour hot milk over it and make it into a sort of mushy pudding. Anything milky like puddings or custard I lap up. The more in the dish the better. Blame it on my two Grans or maybe I was a cat in a past life. Sitting at the back table nearest to the kitchen, the table we always used for meals when the shop was closed, I have the full view of my empire and out onto the street. I'm visualising all the tables full, chatter and laughter, cake stands with afternoon tea, small triangles of sandwiches and slices of cake, delicious warm scones with jam and thicker cream. As long as I stick to a system as Rose did then I know I can do it. Behind me is a low wall which also serves as a counter with the till at one end and order pads and pens lined up ready for the day's work. To the right of me is the door to upstairs and next to it, what used to be a walk-in pantry is now the loo for the customers. The kitchen door to the back garden is also there just through the kitchen, we open it for a well needed breeze in summer.

Rose had never wanted to put tables in the garden, saying she had enough to cope with but I'm going to, it's big enough for five and it's pretty. My mind's on the flowers in the garden as I spread my croissant with plenty of Nutella, another weakness; well, most food is my weakness.

"Flowers! Flowers, that's what's missing!" How could I forget, Rose never had. The small crystal vases are clean and lined up on the windowsill, empty.

"Morrisons first, baking later or should I do it

the other way round?" Nobody can give me an answer, so I don't know why I am even talking out loud. If it were not for health reasons a cat would be the solution but blimey, that's sad, alone and talking to a cat. No! Well, what about a dog? That's better, a dog, something I've always wanted and couldn't have. Yes, I like it and there's the garden and...

A deafeningly loud bang followed by the sounds of cutlery falling and crockery breaking on the floor makes me jump, tilting my chair backwards at a dangerous angle and sends my arm automatically flying out sideways spilling the rest of my coffee all over the floor. The counter directly behind me is wedging me in and prevents a nasty fall and possibly a broken chair. I honestly thought the shelf with all the crockery on had given way and everything was about to come crashing down. Pound signs had flashed before my eyes.

"What the hell is going on?" I'm really shaken but not wanting to turn round and count the cost of replacements then I'm totally confused at the sights before me. Only my empty dish from the Weetabix was on the floor broken into pieces and the spoon I'd used was upside down near the oven. What made me chill to the bone and have goosebumps the size of gobstoppers was my, well Rose's favourite cookbook open on the worktop surface as though ready for baking. "The Love of Cooking" by Sonia Allison is lying open on page 212, recipes on the left-hand page and a full colour page on the right of the cherry cake, farmhouse cake, Danish almond cake, orange layer torte and sand cake. All simple, good recipes we'd baked together endless times. Favourites of ours which are proving to be very popular with the customers. My mouth is drying up faster than the Sahara Desert. It's also wide open along with my eyes.

"Do close your mouth Kitty, it's really quite unbecoming. Chop chop, get busy now, time is money as they say."

"Yes Rose, I will, which one are you baking first?" The question is out of my mouth before I realise.

"No, my dear Kitty, you're on your own now, don't forget to turn the oven on to warm first, the flowers will arrive soon."

"What? How?" Suddenly I'm back to my senses having turned to talk to her and all I can see is my broken dish and spoon. "This isn't happening, it can't be, it can't." I feel so cold and shaky.

Frantic knocking on the shop's glass door is suddenly breaking through my numbed state. I'm at the door without feeling my feet move.

"Morning love, thought you wouldn't remember the flowers, so I got some whilst getting a few bits at Morrisons. What's the matter, seen a ghost? It's only me love, Sally, hey now I know I'm a bit of a mess without my polyfilla but surely not that bad. My Chris still fancies me the devil, too much at times but that's men for you, always are when spring arrives! Must be the animal in them, what do you think love?"

Typically, Sally breezes in full of life and energy, bunches of pink spray carnations and white gip in one hand, two bags of shopping in the other. Her dark curly hair, usually tied back neatly for work with a pink or lilac ribbon, is giving Tina Turner a good rival.

"Good Lord love, I'll get the kettle on, something tells me you've a story to tell and I'm parched and need an excuse to stay out of the house a bit longer."

Huddling over beakers of strong, hot, builder's tea with, on Sally's insistence, sugars for the shock, I poured out everything, not just my spiritual events, I mean everything! Sally hadn't known about Matt's infidelity; I wasn't suspecting him myself the last time we worked together. I'd been here for Rose and been worked off my feet with the café to run as well. Part of me wants to be cautious but I just feel relieved telling her, wanting her to understand and reassure me that I'm not going mad. She's not commenting just looking at me with her big doe like eyes over the rim of her beaker as she sips her tea. I'm feeling sick again now, that panicky feeling deep down. I've blown it! She's going to hand in her notice in a few days. She won't want to work with an emotional wreck who hears voices! I can see her searching for some kind of words to get her out of the situation.

"So have you not seen Rose or your Gran yet?"

Here we go, she's testing me, weighing up how

certified I'll become.

"No and so far, it's only Rose I've heard, I don't think I could cope with anything else yet!" My voice doesn't even sound mine; it's like a child's in front of a teacher waiting for the punishment to come.

Sally isn't replying, she's just looking at me, straight into my eyes, it's quite unnerving really. In another life she'd make a good policeman. Stop it, stop saying all this spiritual nonsense, I'm telling myself.

"You will, mark my words love, you will. Rose is too strong a character to float around on clouds all day. She'll be down here bossing around and checking up on everything as soon as she can."

I'm amazed a tide of relief washes over me; I certainly didn't expect Sally to understand. She may be a mother hen but what I've seen of her in action she doesn't suffer fools either. Sally puts people in their place in such a way that they don't know it has happened and nobody takes offence.

"It's alright love, don't worry about me I don't think you're bonkers. Good Lord, Rose has helped me out more than once with her special gift. My Chris swore by her readings. Didn't she ever tell you love?"

"No." It sounds weak and pathetic.

"Strewth, she's been round my house many times. It's thanks to Rose that my Chris landed on his feet again after he was made redundant. My mum and his sister had readings too. I bet half of

Wetherby saw her."

Her kind, rounded face is glowing with the fond memories of Rose and I'm now understanding why so many people had packed the church for her funeral service. I'd thought at the time it was because of Crumbs, apparently not. I wonder if the Vicar knew. Maybe he was an "in the closet" spiritualist, that brought a smile to my face. Vicars sneaking around here in the dark. Sally has soon dunked all the chocolate McVities biscuits bar the one I'm still holding untouched with chocolate melting fast between my fingers.

"Chop chop as Rose would say, you've baking to do. Do you still want an apple pie and a cherry pie this week as usual?"

For a lady with such warmth radiating from her she makes the best pastry in Yorkshire, supplying us with two pies a week to help us vary the menu. We serve the delicious pies with cream or Cornish ice cream as Wednesday's and Saturday's treats.

"Yes please, I'm not changing much just bringing in a few different cakes but ones from Rose's books that we used to bake together."

"That's good, Crumbs has a good reputation built on proper old-fashioned recipes. It worked for Rose, it'll work for you love, now come on I'll clean up the mess and you get cracking."

In true Sally style everything is gleaming in minutes.

"I'll let myself out love, see you tomorrow after I've dropped my lot off at school, have the kettle on."

Hugging Sally is like hugging a warm, cuddly bear that smells as fresh as a field of daffodils in the rain. She positively glows.

Ten seconds later the penny drops.

"Oh, my giddy Aunt, or should it be godmother. Rose, Gran, she glowed! All golden around her head and shoulders." I don't know if I'm shocked, scared or happy but I know what I saw in that split-second was real, not in my head. Gran used to check people's auras out wherever we went, and I just let her ramble to keep her happy. Am I now seeing auras?

"Kitty get those cakes made, tomorrow's another day," Rose is twittering.

Whatever is happening around me I know those words are right even if it's my own head thinking them.

"Ok, I'm on the job so stop nagging, will one chocolate cake, one coffee and walnut cake, two cherry loaf cakes, the coconut loaf I baked and put in the freezer and fresh scones in the morning do you?"

The freezer is full of what Rose called her "stand bys" brought out if stock was running low. There are some scones but Rose always made a fresh batch each morning. English muffins and currant teacakes for toasting and the bread for the sandwiches all ordered from the bakery and delivered by 7.30 AM each morning. Eggs from the farm and home cooked ham from Mick the butcher organised and all that can be ticked off my list.

Monday tends to be a bit quieter than the rest of the week so I'm planning to bake whilst Sally serves, helping her in between. At least I'm used to it all and not being thrown in at the deep end. Mick the butcher will drop the roast ham and fresh eggs from his farm off for the sandwiches and everything else is in the fridge or cupboards. As long as I work out each night what's what for the next day, I reckon I'll be alright, well I hope so, time will tell.

Music, I need music whilst I create, no not Queen that's good for pounding dough to, some Corinne Bailey Rae will do nicely. A "local lass" as Gran would say, two local lasses making a name for themselves, well me in a small way for now but who knows, this time next year I could be owning a string of Crumbs cafés.

"Just bake Kitty!" Rose sounds cross now.

Hectic, manic at times is how I would describe my first week. Monday was the worst! It felt as though the whole of Wetherby came in that day, I'm not sure if it was for support or downright Yorkshire nosiness. It doesn't really matter to me; business is busy and my feet and dark rings under my eyes from baking at night and early morning are proof enough. Hopefully next week will be easier now I've got two part timers to help at the weekends and in the school holidays. Simon and

Charlotte, or Charlotte as she prefers to be called, seem good, clean, intelligent kids, well I think so, they were the only ones who didn't have piercings, tattoos or swore when I interviewed them. It's difficult not to judge wrongly when you're looking into a face full of metal, the whole experience has left me feeling old, even a little drab. I'm finding myself checking my short blonde hair in the mirror on a morning for grey hairs. At this rate I'll be sporting a full-grown head by the time I'm thirty.

"Thirty!"

"What's up love? Have you burnt yourself?" Sally's dropped her mop and is by my side, her face bless her, full of concern.

"No, it's alright, no it isn't."

"Well, which is it love? You can't have it both ways."

"The sponges are in the oven, but something has just hit me."

Sally's eyes light up and her head starts spinning around looking at the tables with the chairs upturned on top of them.

"Where? I thought it'd been too quiet; I've not said anything 'cos you've been so busy. What's she thrown at you then love? There's nothing on the floor."

"Thrown at me? When?"

"Now, just now, Rose."

"No. No, it's nothing spooky; it's something that's just dawned on me. Sally I'm thirty next month, soon about to be divorced, no time for anything but this and I'm sure I'm going grey!"

"Good Lord above love, is that all?! Age is a number, it's not printed on you for the world to see, it's in here." She's tapping her head with two plump fingers. "It's up to you to keep it a mystery to others by acting how you feel in here. Keep young and mysterious love, there's always Nice'n Easy to cover the greys, my Chris does it for me, likes to rub it in and wash it off." A new, deeper pink tinge on her cheeks is breaking out.

"Enough!" My hands go up to stop her and I can see the light shining in her eyes as her romantic moments flash before them. "Too much information for a lonely divorcee to be. I'll take your advice but there's nobody but me to do the Nice'n Easy bit."

"Give it time love; you've enough to cope with at the moment. If you're that lonely I'll send the kids round for a bit, you'll soon change your mind or get yourself a cat. Not one for them myself but my sister's got one, big hairy thing, says it's therapeutic stroking its ears."

I am almost chocking on my biscuit, a new recipe I'm trying that Rose had circled in her book for the future.

"Not good, eh? Let's see, I'm a good tester for Crumbs' baking." Taking a big bite out of her sample, Sally's face is in raptures.

"Sally the biscuits are great it's your words that need tweaking a bit."

"What did I say now?"

"Nothing Sally, just keep making me laugh will you, it does get a bit lonely at night, I did think about a dog, maybe a small one. I've got the garden out the back and the walks around here are lovely."

"Lovely idea, a dog's better love, go to that Dogs Trust place on the York Road there. Get one of them rehoused ones."

"Rescue Sally, they're called rescue dogs." She's looking blank again and reaching for another sample biscuit. "Never mind, you're right as well, a little Jack Russell would be just big enough for me and upstairs."

"Oh, Rose wouldn't mind what size you have, it's up to you now, it's your home."

"Not upstairs as in the big café area in the sky, I mean my living quarters!" At least she's made me smile again. I don't want life to be all serious and no fun.

"Well, that's me done love; don't go baking all night, the freezer's bulging. At least have a lie in tomorrow, it being Sunday. You've no excuse, wait till three kids are pounding on your bedroom door from early on, do it now whilst you can love, that's my advice."

"Thanks, I'll try, maybe the paperwork I'm tackling tonight will knock me out, it's so mind numbingly boring. Here take home these biscuits for the kids and Chris, I'm starting to eat far too much and am not doing enough exercise."

"Thanks love, do you reckon I could pass them

off as mine? His mother is coming tonight for her tea and her roots need touching up."

"Chris isn't doing them, is he?" My mind is starting to turn weird thoughts around.

"Lord no love, it's his night out with his pals down the pub, reckons he deserves it after looking after the kids on a Saturday, tit for tat he says. See you Monday love, you'd better lock the back door after me, the front's all bolted, ta ra."

Hugs, kisses and the sight of Sally's cheery wave from the garden gate suddenly make me feel so alone. If it's fine tomorrow I'm going to tackle some of this garden. Looking at the grass and bushes they look as though they are also ready for some tender touches.

"Stop it Kate, don't start getting yourself all moody and pathetic." I'm hugging myself standing on the back doorstep and the only thing listening is a blackbird digging away in between my roses. After a frozen stare from its beady eye, it's had enough of me and gone, just like Matt the Rat.

Door bolted, that's me in for the night. Getting a lasagne for one out of the fridge I'm tempted to do some chips with it but decide on just a load of mixed salad and a low-fat yoghurt for afters. I can wash everything up together; the cakes are still cooling on the racks. Sally's right, the freezer is bulging but I want to be ready for all emergencies and it's the Spring Bank Holiday weekend next week. I've started making a plan for a month, what to use each day of the week for cakes and sandwiches, something Rose never did. My mind wanders back to those happy holidays and weekends working here with Rose and Gran. It seems so long ago, and she was so easy going apart from her insistence on fresh scones and produce for the sandwiches it was all decided on the morning whilst she filled the kitchen with delicious fruity smells. Sitting down at our table looking through my plan Gran's words "it wouldn't do for us all to be the same" spring into my head. How right she was.

Eating alone doesn't take long, let's face it there's only so much chewing you can do. This is getting ridiculous I've even started to count with some mouthful of the lasagne but I'm wanting to swallow it after fifteen chews. For company I've got my Michael Bublé on only tonight for some reason it's not working, his gorgeous velvety voice is making me feel even lonelier. I'm almost on the verge of ringing Carol, this is bad, now I know I've got to do something to make an effort, join a class, do anything that's not too sporty or intellectual. Wetherby High School will do classes. There we are that's sorted. I'm feeling better now I've come up with a semi determined action plan. That's fine but me and schooling, well deep down I'm not holding out too much hope, but I've got to give it a go.

There's something interfering with my thoughts and Michael's singing, in the background, there it is again. My ears are straining through his dulcet tones, I can hear it again, sort of scratchy. It's not the CD I'm so careful with my precious discs, unlike Matt. The oven's definitely turned off.

"Sorry Michael, I need to knock you off mid flow so I can hear it better. My God it's mice!" It sounds like scratching and scuffling coming from behind the kitchen units. This is really scary for me, we once had them in the cottage at Headingley. Gran set traps everywhere and even battered one with a shovel, ugh! The sight was so disgusting I didn't dare go to sleep at night.

Why me? Why now? What if it's not mice but a rat! The river's only down the road and there's plenty of pubs and restaurants with tasty leftovers in the bins. Rats are gross! I know, I married one. Oh hell, what do I do now? Maybe Sally's Chris will sort it out for me, I'm not sure I can, it's getting louder. The scratching seems to be coming from the back door area. There's no way I'm looking outside, visions of a black rat with a long tail and big teeth eating through the wooden door or skirting board are rushing through my mind. There's never just one. Gran had said they breed fast; "Running Wick" was how she'd described the cottage and its mice. I can't cope with mice or rats running wick. They'll close Crumbs down.

It's definitely coming from the door. Where's the shovel when I need it? Not the blue plastic dustpan from Morrisons, Gran's metal one with the wooden handle she shovelled up the coal on for our fire. Who am I trying to kid, I couldn't use it even if I had one. Suddenly the noise has stopped, all I can hear is my heart and heavy breathing. Where's it gone? They don't just give up and go next door because they didn't get invited in, but it has, no scratching and scraping, just silence. This is ridiculous, I'm a grown woman standing on her own two feet, strong, well trying to be. I've managed to stand up to one rat and walk away, yes albeit I did get help there but I took up the challenge instead of selling Crumbs and moving to some sun-soaked island. That's it, I'm angry now, nothing is going to spoil what I have and intend to work hard for. My inheritance is my life past, present and future with no more rats getting a foot in, or is it paw? What do they call a rat's foot?

"Do get on with it Kitty, just open the door." Rose is twittering again which strangely makes me cross.

"Don't you start Rose, if you want to help you should be here not floating around giving the orders." Tears of fear and frustration are welling up in my eyes. The best thing I can do is batter it with the long handle brush standing by the door.

"That's it, scare it off, whack it on the nose and it will scuttle back down to the river. Here goes, wish me luck Gran."

It's not easy to hold the brush, yank the door open and step outside grabbing the brush in both hands again, ready for action but it's open, I'm fighting mad now like a regular Scrappy Doo, swinging my lethal weapon. All my pent-up anger from the past weeks is travelling like a surge of electricity down the handle into the brush head ready to whack the rat senseless.

Chapter Four

"Well, you made a right pig's ear out of that didn't you? Pick yourself up Kitty, the neighbours will think you're drunk." Rose's voice is still in my ear.

"What neighbours? Nobody else lives here, it's a good job isn't it; they'd think I was mad throwing myself out of a door onto a path and then talking to NOBODY," I'm shouting into the quiet evening.

I can't help it; tears are streaming down my face now. My black trousers probably have holes in them, and my knees could be seeping blood all over the path, but I don't care. Suddenly my world feels empty and as hard as the ground I'm sprawled on. This is just all too much for me. I'm giving in, long hours and sleepless nights. I can feel the soft springy grass under my right hand and all I want to do is be on it. Shuffling sideways is making me realise nothing is broken so to hell with it I'm going to just lie here at least it's softer. The smell and feel of the grass on my face is so good I haven't done this for years, since my hot sunny days in the back garden in Headingley. Gran would weed and see to the veggie patch; Rose would come from next door with cakes and a jug of lemonade. They'd both sit in striped deckchairs reminiscing about their childhood summers before getting down to telling the latest bits of news about people they knew, insisting it wasn't gossiping just a healthy interest in others, whilst I sprawled on the grass on a blanket listening. It was fun, I was happy and felt safe but now those days are long gone.

It's a good job the day was so warm, and the sun has been in the back garden all afternoon, the grass is so pleasant, just another five minutes, I need this time to feel me, young, happy and carefree again. Nobody is here, all the shops either side are closed, and the owners have gone home to enjoy the evening with their loved ones, eating, laughing, loving. This is pathetic, I look pathetic but who cares, right at this moment I want to be the pathetic me with tears watering the grass, alone with my thoughts. I want to go back to those days in Headingley sprawling on the grass listening to my two Grans and the traffic on Headingley's main, busy road in the background.

I am almost there in my tearful but happy bubble, the smell of fish and chips even wafting across on the light breeze from Bryan's Fish Shop two streets away. Heaven! Any moment now Gran and Rose will have the same light-hearted ribbing of each other when Rose decides to have curry sauce instead of the traditional mushy peas with her fish and chips for tea. Gran will get her big brown leather purse out of her handbag she carries everywhere with her, even to the loo.

"Too many foreigners and students in Leeds, can't trust them," she used to say.

"Live and let live Kathleen," Rose would answer.

Rose would have her purse in her pocket and "cough up" as Gran used to say, grinning and holding her hand out for Rose's money. Neither was mean, just careful and kindness itself, Rose would pass through the gap in our fence back to her cottage and return with a plate of homemade white bread, spread thickly with butter. I could never slice it evenly, not like my two Grans.

"Go on Kitty, nip to Bryan's and don't forget to ask for plenty of scraps on top of the chips, and well-done fish mind." Rose liked her scraps on top, lovely little golden bits of crunchy batter that had fallen off the fish whilst being fried.

In my beautiful, hazy tear drenched bubble of nostalgia I'm on the grass and we're eating the delicious Saturday treat, out of the paper of course, the only way. Something Matt disapproves of, that and the smell of course, maybe I'll do it again, here, not now if only I hadn't had that lasagne. It can't ever be as good though, can it? Not without Gran and Rose. Suddenly my bubble is being burst and I'm jolting out of it faster than a sprinter at the Olympics.

I daren't move. Something warm but wet is against my cheek, I can feel it breathing on me, I'm rigid with fear. Hells bells the brush is too far away where it flew when I fell, I can't reach it. I'm going to wet myself I just know I am. No, no, I won't be caught with wet pants when the police arrive, hold on you idiot, do some pelvic clenching, I can't I'm too petrified, oh hell!

Bravery has never been on my list of assets, my reasoning being that the man in my life should be my protector, my Galahad, but now it's me, just me. Counting to three the long way I'm steeling myself to open my left eye, I don't dare move my right cheek off the grass or roll over onto my back as the rat might go for my throat. They do don't they, rats? Well, I think I've read that somewhere, shut up Kate, stop being a wimp, face the animal.

I swear my heart has just leapt over to the other side, or have I? No, I can still feel the grass on my cheek so I'm still alive and kicking, God it's huge! Its nostrils are level with my now open left eye, dark holes opening and closing as it breathes in my garlicky fear. It's a monster from the deep river Wharfe! Now I know how Little Red Riding Hood felt, here comes its tongue! My one visual aid has automatically shut down, maybe if I keep still it will move on, it's my only hope, keep calm, breathe, don't forget to breathe you idiot. Grass is starting to get sucked into my right nostril as I'm breathing like a bull fighting for its life in a bullring. I'm going to sneeze, and I can't stop it.

"Achooooo!" Tears bring with them snot which I'm ashamed to say has now sprayed out, but my reflexes have jerked into action, and I've rolled over and over away to the right like a commando on a mission. Not quite, but at least I'm now kneeling and ready to face the thing, secretly hoping that my loud sneeze scared it away.

Still rooted to the spot is the thing but it's cute, so adorable, head on one side with its left front paw mid-air, fixing me with its big browny blue eyes, weighing me up, almost apologising for scaring me.

"You're a big ninny aren't you Kitty? How can a cute little thing like this ever hurt you?" Rose's voice is there again and I'm trying to look around for her but keep my eyes forward at the same time.

"Alright, I know I'm pathetic, a real wuss, don't rub it in." Why am I even bothering to talk to thin air, this is getting to be a habit, a very bad one.

"Meet Flossie, a little friend for you."

"Flossie?"

At the sound of her name my cute nightmare has padded across to me and is licking my hand, her big, browny blue eyes appealing to me to return her show of affection. Who could resist? I can't. I'm falling under her spell, her little white face tilted to one side with one brown ear up and one white one flopping over. Her beautiful eyes are staring straight into mine unblinking, pleading with me to love her and suddenly I can feel my whole body tingling. I'm consumed with this warm maternal instinct of love and protection for this little creature sitting at my feet. It's a totally strange but wonderful feeling, more powerful than young love. This is devotion and, in an instant, I know I don't want to be parted from my vulnerable, small friend lifting its paw for me to take.

"Hello, um, Flossie?" I'm gently holding her warm little white paw; her hair is so soft it's not as I expected at all.

"Woof."

"So that is your name then."

"Woof."

Flossie is gently licking my hand and I have to stop myself from scooping this cute white and brown patched fur ball into my arms to cuddle. I may scare her; she could run away back to where she belongs.

"Flossie, where have you come from darling, you've no collar? I bet some little boy or girl is out looking for you crying their eyes out thinking they've lost you."

She's looking straight into my eyes again and shaking her head. Crikey! She's saying "No" I'm sure she is. It's not possible; it's just me wanting it to be like that. No dog is that clever, I've met plenty of humans lacking in the intelligence department, but a dog could never outrank them. Ok, I'll try something else.

"Flossie, would you like something to eat? I've got some sausages."

"Woof."

"Maybe you'd eat some lasagne, there's another one." Flossie's shaking her head again. "No?" a very vigorous shake is almost moving her whole body and it's so funny I can't help laughing.

"Ok I get the message, sausages it is then; will you wait here whilst I get them?"

"Woof."

Wow, what's going on, I hear and talk to my invisible godmother Rose and now to a dog that I think talks back. This is getting spooky, I'm too young for a mid-life crisis, I'm not depressed, much too busy for that, what is it?

All sorts of questions are going through my head as I get out the leftover cooked sausages from the fridge. Of course, I'll have to ring Wetherby Police station; someone could have reported a missing dog. A hundred and one things are racing around my head but most of them are related to what I need to buy to keep her! She might have vanished into thin air again by the time I take this lot outside so why am I worrying? Get a grip girl, she's not yours. My heart is giving a twirl as I step back outside with the sausages.

"Flossie, you waited, here you are girl, tuck in and then feel free to go back home when you want to."

Flossie is licking my hand as I put the bowl down then looking at me straight in the eyes with her browny blue ones as she shakes her head slowly from side to side as a "No" again. I can't speak, I'll cry if I do.

My days are fuller than ever now, from the moment Flossie wakes me up with her sloppy kiss to our last stroll around the garden before bed. We've settled into a comfortable routine, and I'm dreading the phone call or visit from the police to say she's been claimed. Flossie steals the heart of everyone she meets; maybe I should take some lessons from her, especially as the local vet who gave her a thorough check up is certainly well worth rolling over for. It's a shame we don't have to go back for anything else, wow He's really something, oozing with male hormones but oblivious to any human attractions. I'm tempted to grow my hair and see if it makes a difference but come off it; my hair could never look long and sleek like a horse's mane. Something tells me animals are his only love. Actually, my source is Sally and no he isn't gay, just dedicated, pity.

Now I have a reason to get out of Crumbs and into the fresh air I'm loving it. Walking around and playing ball with Flossie means a whole new world has been opened up to me and dog walkers are all so friendly. Whilst Flossie does her sniff and greet routine with her four-legged friends I get to have a chat with so many people and it's great, alright they may all be retired or thereabouts, but I live in hope.

Bit by bit the garden is starting to look good. The patio is nearly finished which should hold at least five tables with umbrellas, there's still enough garden for lawns either side of the path with flower beds and roses down to the gate. Next week is the Spring Bank Holiday weekend and Crumbs will be able to open its garden to customers. I'm really excited, this is important to me as so much has happened in the last few months that was wrong, negative energies Rose would say but now it's changed.

One thing is puzzling me. Since Flossie's arrival I haven't really heard Rose's voice which is only proving to me that grief was playing tricks with me. How come it didn't happen when Gran died, I loved her more than anything. Ah! I had the Rat as I continue to call him. Pandering to his every need must have stemmed all that for me; hey this is clever for me, all this self-analysis.

"Woof."

"What are you now, a mind reader?"

"Woof."

"Come on then, where shall I put this tub of petunias, here or here? Hurry up Flossie, this tub is heavy make your mind up, stop looking over there and concentrate."

"Woof."

"That's better. A firm decision and you're right, nobody will bump into the tub here and it looks good from the patio."

The patio isn't my only change. Hanging baskets full of trailing pink begonias and mixed lobelia now adorn both the front and the back of Crumbs. Wherever possible I've got tubs of brightly coloured petunias and geraniums of every colour including some burnt orange ones and nonstop flowering begonias. All the flowers we used to have at Headingley, Gran loved her garden with lots of colour and of course I have roses, sweet smelling, the older varieties Rose planted either side of the garden path. I know it will be more work for me but it's going to be worth it. Stepping back and looking around I'm happy, it's going to be as pretty as a picture when they are all in full flower.

"Woof."

"Come on it's been a long day and we can't do anymore tonight, tomorrow we can get the tables and chairs out of the shed and put your bed in there for during the day, will that suit you Madame?"

"Woof."

The new shed right at the bottom of the garden was a good idea of Sally's. A storage place for the tables, chairs and umbrellas at the end of the good weather and a place for Flossie to keep out of the sun. During the day she plays in the garden and the only time she's allowed over the threshold is to be taken upstairs to sleep. She knows the rules and sticks to them. Actually, when I think about it, I never had to set them, she did. Any customers with dogs will be welcome but only in the garden unless they have a Guide Dog and that goes without saying of course, Flossie understands that.

My two new part timers Simon and Charlotte have settled in very nicely, well after a few broken plates, not from Simon, He's a natural at waiting on tables, Charlotte has learnt the hard way. I have a feeling young romance is blossoming between them, they both seem very eager to work the extra shifts together over the holiday weekend, it suits me as long as I don't catch them slobbering in the shed. Ugh! Now I do feel old.

"97.2 Stray FM weather for Harrogate, Wetherby, Ripon and Boroughbridge," the DJ is about to announce today's, Sunday's and fingers crossed, Bank Holiday Monday's weather forecasts. It's just after 7:00 AM and I don't usually take any notice of the news, my head's always in and out of the oven taking out the day's batch of fresh scones. Today is different as it's Saturday, my "open day" for the garden and I really need some good weather.

"Please everyone upstairs, blow the rain and clouds away, over the farmers' fields that's it, they always need rain for their crops." My reckoning is that at least it won't be wasted.

My head is cocked just like Flossie's, do I usually do that? Not a good sign I'd better watch that, they say owners start to look like their dogs, that's worrying. Here it comes.

"Today after an early spot of drizzle the clouds will clear to bring sun and a high of 18 degrees. Sunday and Bank Holiday Monday will be fine during the day with rain coming in for the evenings, highs of 16 to 18 degrees. Enjoy the weekend.......Stray FM."

Thank you that will do for my opening. "Ow this tray's hot!" I'm too distracted with the weather forecast, I should know better. At this time of a morning, it's all systems go getting the scones done and out to cool before the deliveries of bread arrive, before double checking everything on my plan for the day then it's a quick break for our breakfast, walk Flossie, shower and get the cakes out into the glass cabinet and be ready to open at 9:00 AM. I must be mad to give up my Sundays and open from now on, well let's just see how the summer goes, 10:00 AM-4:00 PM isn't too bad but for now I'm clocking up a full seven days a week. Keep calm, it will all pan out, that's it, breathe in, out, slowly, my sudden panic starts to cease. Food, I need food to start the day, right, "Come on Flossie, breakfast!"

"Woof!"

Chapter Five

It's funny how you get used to your regulars and worry if they don't turn up on their usual days. People are creatures of habit; well at least the older ones tend to be, doing bits of shopping two or three times a week, going to the library, meeting up with a friend. Some of them I've known for years and what they like to eat and drink.

Glancing around Crumbs I can see Sally taking Mr Potter's order although he usually has the same one, just as he always likes to sit in the window to look out onto the market square waving to neighbours and friends. He's been a widower for the last ten years and keeps himself very smartly dressed, still has a good head of thick white hair, I bet he was not short of admirers in his day. Mr Potter retired from the Halifax building society branch in Wetherby so like Sally he knows a lot of local people. I try not to ask personal questions, but I have a feeling he's getting lonelier as his years advance. Dear Mr Potter is a four times a week customer, a pleasure to serve and one of the "Gentlemen" of this world, God love him.

"Pot of Earl Grey, scone, jam and cream is it Mr Potter?" Sally is beaming at him, her curls already trying to escape her ponytail. Sally only has to go over to a table with that warm, sensitive smile of hers, big brown eyes open widely and even the most obnoxious customer melts under her charm. She treats everyone the same, men and women, it took me a while to realise she is totally unaware of her effect on people. She's my secret ace card.

"Do you mind if I have a change of order?" Mr Potter seems apologetic and slightly distracted today, his voice hasn't any depth to it, and he has such a pleasant, well-spoken voice.

"Good Lord love, you can have whatever you want. A little bit of what you fancy does you good my Chris always says."

Laughing to myself as I cut the cherry pie into sections ready for the refrigerated glass case, that's just the sort of thing Sally's Chris would say as for him it has another meaning. Jealous? No, well just a little bit, hell a lot!

"Now there's chocolate cake, mandarin orange gateau, Madeira cake or cherry pie love or of course your toasted muffins and currant teacakes. Anything take your fancy love?"

Mr Potter still seemed distracted.

"You alright love? Do you want to sit in the garden? It's open now, a lot of sun and fresh air to cheer you up?"

"Cheer me up? Oh no, sorry, I'm a little out of sorts today, Sally, the cherry pie sounds good, but I'll stay here for now, perhaps next time I'll try the garden thank you."

"Well, we're open tomorrow if you fancy a

change of scenery, Sundays from now on till 4:00 PM, my Chris can take the kids swimming, I'm working this one then off the next."

"He's a good chap, you're lucky, a good partner and family are precious."

Poor Mr Potter, what's wrong with him today? He's usually so cheerful, he happily talks to everyone who stops by his table, this really is so unlike him.

Between taking Mrs Dyson's order that Charlotte has just brought to me and wiping down some trays it's starting to bother me. Music, that's what is missing. We always have some on just in the background, just low enough not to disturb our customers. Rose always played tracks she felt were appropriate for the type of customer in at the time, couples like to talk but single customers sometimes feel uncomfortable, even awkward and too "on view". Rose would look around, use her "gift" and always chose what was perfect for them. You could see their shoulders relax, tension disappearing as the gentle melodies floated around them.

"Come on Rose, I need a little help please." I'm looking up as I whisper, nothing, absolutely nothing is coming back. Well, that's just lovely! I'm on my tod. "Don't blame me if I get it wrong, you had your chance."

The cupboard under the counter has a stack of CDs on the shelf, all in alphabetical order. Rose used to get cross if we didn't put them back in the right place. Smiling at the memory of her telling me off on a regular basis, well I'm not so particular but something tells me I'll be just the same as her now. Bending down for a better look I can see one is sticking out more from the neat rows of them standing side by side on the shelf. It's a CD Gran bought Rose one Christmas, songs by Vonda Shepherd from a TV series called Ally McBeal. I remember how the two of them loved it. Rose would be watching it in Wetherby, Gran and I in our pyjamas cuddled up together on the sofa in Headingley with more often than not, me falling asleep. Next day one of them would always ring the other, depending on whose turn it was and spend half an hour dissecting the programme. Gran lived for it.

The dulcet tones of Vonda Shepherd start gently to fill the atmosphere, "See the pyramids across the Nile......." She's got a very unusual voice but it's soothing, strange though, I could have sworn that track isn't until later in the CD. Maybe it's slipping, or I am.

"Hello Miss Taylor, nice day, isn't it? We've got a table in the garden if you would like to go through. Let me know if you want the umbrella up. Simon see to Miss Taylor's order would you please, don't rush her, she likes time to decide and if she wants lemon for her tea put three slices in a small glass dish with a cake fork on the side, got that?"

"Yes boss, will do."

Simon's a nice lad, dark haired, blue eyes and not

a pimple in sight. No wonder Charlotte's smitten, I would be if I was fifteen years younger, oh that's so pervy of me, stop it, I'm just getting old, and boy do I feel it!

Charlotte is starting to come out of her shell too. She was so shy at first, blushing whenever the customers talked to her, or she dropped something which I've noticed thankfully isn't so often now. Her pretty face is clear of makeup, and she has naturally blonde hair and marmalade brown eyes. I bet given a year or two and more confidence and she will be a stunner. Both want to go to university; both want to be doctors and save the world. Let's hope they do.

"Here Kate, do you reckon Mr Potter's alright? Look at him; He's gone all funny, sort of frozen. You don't reckon He's having a stroke, do you?" Sally has come to behind the counter and is trying her best to keep her voice low. Vonda is still crooning away, "You belong to me..."

This is tricky. I've seen the adverts on the TV about how to spot the signs of a stroke. I suppose it could happen here in Crumbs and any of our customers could suffer heart attacks or anything really. In that split-second my mind is registering that I should check on First Aid training for us all, but this is the here and now.

I'm by his side and he doesn't even know it. This is worse than I thought.

"Mr Potter?"

Nothing. Just watery grey eyes staring straight

ahead. He's not even blinking. His face hasn't dropped, can he lift his arms? I think that's what you test, that and his speech. I'm aware of Sally trying to distract the nearest two tables bless her, nattering away about the weather and my garden.

"Mr Potter, can I help you with anything?" Well what else can I say? I'm really not prepared for this sort of thing, it's scary.

"Peggy?"

He's talking, that's good, no drooping visible but he's confused and that's still not a good sign.

"No, I'm Kate, Mr Potter, you're having a drink in Crumbs, are you alright?"

As he turns to me, I can see his eyes are filled with tears. Wow, what can I say, come on think fast girl.

"Oh, I am sorry, is your tea not right? I'll get you a fresh pot." My hands are reaching for the teapot when his soft, warm hand covers mine.

"No, my dear, your tea is perfect as usual, please don't concern yourself, I'm just a silly old fool who just had a jolt down memory lane with your good music, not good at my age."

I'm trying not to show my sudden surge of relief and immediately feel pangs of sympathy and selfishness at the same time.

"Good memories I hope."

"Very good, too good and a lot of regrets."

"Why don't you go into the garden and get some fresh air whilst I bring your tea and cherry pie."

"You're very kind, I think I will, she's gone

forever and there's no sense looking for her."

His words are a bit puzzling, but I haven't got time to ponder over them as more people are coming through the door. Ignoring his refusal of fresh tea, I replaced his teapot of Earl Grey with a new one. Charlotte took it out to him, coming back in smiling.

"Mr Potter says thank you for everything, He's lovely. I think I could adopt him as my granddad."

"As long as he's alright, just keep an eye on him, will you? Use your medical eyes."

"Sure."

Sally has come to my side of the counter to toast some currant teacakes.

"Is he alright now? Fair gave me a funny turn he did."

"He's fine, it was the music set him off down memory lane. Poor soul, you can tell he's still pining for his wife. He must have doted on Peggy."

"Peggy? You've got it wrong there love, she was called Esther and a right stuck-up nasty cow, sorry love "woman", she was. Miserable, mean, sour faced, no matter what he did for her it was never enough. My mum knew her. Peggy, who was Peggy then?"

"No idea, watch that toaster it's heating up too fast and we need a new one."

"Will do."

I've decided to check on Mr Potter myself and make sure Flossie is alright at the same time. I didn't need to worry about her, she's in her bed just inside the open doorway of the shed, dreaming away, oblivious to the chatter of a patio full of customers. Even Mr Potter is joining in with the ladies at the next table. That's a good sign. This is just what I imagined it would be like, a miniature garden party. "Keep the customers happy and they will keep coming back" was Rose's motto and she was right.

"We're running out of Madeira cake love; shall I get the farmhouse and ginger cakes out?" Sally's breaking into my daydreaming.

"Yes, and the box of cherry shortbread biscuits is under the counter, we're being eaten out of house and home Sally."

"Sounds like my house love with my three tykes, well four with my Chris, He's the biggest tyke of all," she chuckled, sashaying her way back inside.

Thank God for Sally, she's a worker alright. I don't know where she gets all her energy from but I'm also aware that if trade continues like this through summer it could be too much for her with the school holidays. Holidays! What I'd give to be able to go and sprawl by a pool or on a beach. Don't talk daft girl! What's the fun in doing it by yourself anyway and what about Flossie? I can't help smiling looking at her dreaming away on her bed, I just know she's mine and here to stay.

"Kate?" Sally's calling for help, it sounds like the lunchtime rush is upon us.

"Coming!"

By early afternoon Crumbs usually has a lull. Today has so far been the busiest Saturday morning for a long time. Simon and Charlotte had their lunch breaks together in the garden, laughing and teasing each other as they sat further away towards the gate on a tartan rug spread on the grass. Flossie revelled in the attention and even got a quick walk down to the river. As usual I snatched five minutes to eat a sandwich in between customers. My staff deserve their breaks and I need to keep them happy at all costs.

"Come on love have a drink and a sit down, these love birds can hold the fort for a little surely." It's Sally's turn to eat; her face is looking very pink with all the rushing around. "I need to cool off love, and no don't even think it, I'm not that age yet." She's fanning her face with a menu.

"Just a few moments then."

It's still a beautiful day and the sun is just right, pleasantly warming after such a long, cold winter. So far, the umbrellas have not been put up, everyone's just happy to feel the warmth on their faces. We head to the furthest part of the garden which is now going to be termed as the "staff area". Flossie's shed is next to us and she's jumping up and down as we spread the blanket on the grass.

"Steady on Flossie, don't spill my tea."

Flossie shakes her head and dutifully settles between Sally and I on the blanket. I can't help stroking her ears, they're so cute and it's very relaxing for both of us. Looking up I can see the three tables occupied. I don't recognise the couple on the furthest table to my left at table 1, tucking into an early Afternoon Tea from the two-tier cake stand. Probably day trippers. Miss Taylor sitting at table 3 is a regular customer, she comes in every Saturday afternoon, has done for as long as I have known Crumbs. She's delicate looking, neat, slightly greying hair cut short in a no-nonsense bob, but it suits her, and she is always well dressed. Looking very stylish in a navy linen trouser suit and a pretty white top underneath, trimmed with navy and red, she obviously has her nautical look but it's so her. If I were to put an age on her it would be mid-fifties, maybe I'm wrong but she can't be older as she still works at the library. Today she's not alone which I've also never known, not that she's a loner, far from it. Miss Taylor is always pleasant to anybody who greets her but is never here with a friend. I'm trying not to stare but it's odd.

Table 5 to the right side of her has "the twins" as we call them, seated and with prim little fingers arched as they drink their tea and eat scones. They are also regulars. Identical twins they may be but they're certainly not identical in their natures. Why in this day and age do they still dress alike? Pink twin sets and pearls, blue and pink pleated skirts and sensible Footglove shoes from M&S. To me it's bonkers, cute for 3-year-olds but surely not at 60ish.

The Miss Passmores are well known in Wetherby. They were born and bred here. Dorothea always worked at the doctor's surgery working for old Dr Ackroyd until his retirement and major changes were made. She currently reigns supreme as receptionist/practice manager at the new medical centre and by what Sally says, she makes you feel guilty for daring to be ill.

Florence, when at her job in the Wetherby One Stop Council office, is friendly in a refined, ladylike manner. At least she smiles and tries to help people even if you come away not really sure if what you have said actually registered with her. Surely it must or she wouldn't be working there. Florence always appears to be in a dreamlike state or as some locals unkindly say, "not quite right in her head". Dorothea is certainly the dominant one, she decides on the cake, does the ordering but I have noticed she makes Florence come to the till and pay but I bet Dorothea holds the purse strings tightly shut. Watching them only having the odd word to say to each other as they cut their scone into delicate pieces, a sad feeling comes over me. These three ladies all grew up here, never married and are still here, is this how I will be? No, well not quite at the moment I am still tied to Matt the Rat, but not for much longer.

"What you reckon then love, has our Miss Taylor got herself a toy boy? Those shoulders are quite broad in that beige jacket and look at his meaty thighs bulging in his jeans. I like a fit man, nice shoes; he's got style like her. Bet he goes to the gym." Sally's comments draw me out of my moment of gloom.

"Shh, they'll hear you, if his front is as good as his back, he gets my vote."

"Naughty, naughty love but I'm with you on this one."

"I didn't mean anything like that Sally! I just meant his looks and everything."

"Whoa stop right there love, let an old married woman have her moment, will you? Come on, let's get back in before we drool all over the blanket, bye Flossie, get his number for me," Sally laughed, stroking Flossie's shiny coat then gathered our cups and wiggled passed the hunk's table inside back to work. Her curves did not go unnoticed, his dark head turned momentarily, giving me a glimpse of his profile as I followed her, all I can say is wow! It was brief and only half a face but very tanned and handsome with dark hair and long lashes framing a dark, smouldering eye, no ring on his tanned left hand conveniently on view, interesting.

Rinsing and drying my hands before starting work again his image keeps coming back into my head. "Come on girl, you're not ready yet or that desperate, pull yourself together," I'm trying to convince myself, but I can't understand why I feel so odd.

"Sally, have you ever seen the hunk before?"

"No but I'm sure willing and able love, anytime," she winks in her cheeky way.

"And Chris wouldn't mind?"

"Don't spoil my private fantasy love, that and a bit of your mandarin gateau later are the perks of working here."

Just at that moment Miss Taylor came back in to pay her bill. Both of us are looking behind her expecting a proper viewing of the hunk but he isn't appearing. He's gone back through the gate the way he came in, shame. Sally's quick to the till.

"You look a bit peeky love, not had too much sun, have you? We could have put the umbrella up if you'd asked."

"No, it's perfectly fine thank you, nice to feel the sun for a change." She certainly doesn't look fine, blanched and edgy is how she looks to me.

"Well, your young man looks as though he likes it."

"Young man?"

"The one at your table, came in to sit with you, did he?" Sally is trying hard and getting no results, poor Miss Taylor is starting to look flustered. Please don't pass out on me, two scares in one day are two too many.

Miss Taylor isn't answering; in fact, she's turning and rushing to the door.

"Your change love, don't forget your change it was a £20 note," Sally calls out and several customers are looking now to see what's happening.

"Put it to the side with her receipt, I'll take it to her when I take Flossie for her walk tonight."

"Oh yes, so you can meet the hunk, is it? I want to know everything tomorrow, all the hot details, it'll make my day. Yes love, what can I get you?" Sally carries on serving whilst I need to clear the tables outside ready for the next customers.

A family are just sitting themselves down at table 1 and the young girl is asking her dad if she can play with Flossie.

"Is it safe for our Laura to stroke your dog? She's used to animals back home."

"Flossie loves people Laura; you can play ball with Flossie at the bottom of the garden away from the tables." Smiling at her and hoping she listens, it's up to Laura's parents to control her but as I'm watching Flossie, I can see there won't be a problem, my little dog has found a new friend.

Smiling at the family, Laura's mum smiles back, happy her little girl is occupied for a few moments. I don't get the chance to take their orders; Simon has sprung out of the doorway and is busy chatting away with them. The Miss Passmores look ready to leave, Dorothea's top lip is curled up and there's no disguising the look of disgust on her face. It's a blessing she never married; she clearly doesn't like Laura's childish squeals of delight coming from the bottom end of the garden. Well tough! My garden is for everyone.

"Everything alright Miss Passmore? It's such a glorious start to the holiday weekend, isn't it?" My words are for Dingy Dora, as she's known around here but I'm smiling at Foggy Flora, she has a timid but far away, vacant look as she nods back.

"It was till now, come on Florence, we have things to do." Dorothea is patting the corners of her mouth with the paper serviette and I'm really having to control the urge to cram it into her sour mouth. To stop myself reacting I'll clear Miss Taylor's table, that woman could curdle the milk with one stare.

"Goodbye and thank you," Florence's meek voice is drifting over my shoulder.

"Goodbye Miss Passmore, call again, we're now open on Sundays through the summer at least."

Florence nods nervously, brushing some crumbs from her twin set.

"Florence, pay the bill and hurry up!" Dorothea barks from the doorway making poor Florence jump slightly. I'm sure her eyes have suddenly darkened liked clouds covering the sun, maybe I'm wrong. The couple at table 1 are smiling across at me but I'm not going to comment, after all they are my regulars and Rose wouldn't approve of me gossiping about them with strangers.

I was right, the handsome hunk did not drink anything at Miss Taylor's table, there's only her crockery to clear. Stacking her teapot, small silver tea strainer, milk jug and empty plate onto my tray my right hand reaches for her cup and saucer. I'm drawn to the amount of tea leaves in the bottom. Miss Taylor hadn't used her tea strainer and the leaves are clumped in shapes even going up the side of the cup she drank from. What's going on? No, no, no! I don't want this; I can feel my body tightening again like a charge of electricity going down to my toes. My eyes feel as though they're bulging out of my head, and I feel freezing cold again. Flossie is by my side barking, but my eyes are glued to the cup and I can't move.

"Oh for goodness sake Kitty, calm down, don't upset your customers, just look in the cup will you?"

"Rose, you're back, why?" I don't know if I'm thinking the words or if I'm actually speaking, either way it's disturbing and a sure way to get rid of people. No, I am speaking, I know I am. "Hells bells, what's happening?"

"Language Kate!" Rose sounds stern, she seldom used my name. What am I thinking? Rose isn't here; she's gone, as in gone forever. "Just look at the cup will you, I'm not doing it for you, goodness it's taken long enough to get this far, why do you think I left you alone for a while?"

I'm whispering now, trying not to attract any attention. "I don't know."

"Because you were acting like a schoolgirl and refusing to believe. The business needed dealing with first, which you have done and splendidly I must say but now this won't wait so hurry up before it's too late. Look will you, clear your mind, read the leaves."

"What on earth are you talking about? Me read

the leaves? You know I can't, that was your job." This is barmy, why am I doing this?

"Well now it's yours so get on with it, I've places to go, people to see. Remember what I used to tell you, concentrate and you can do it."

"Woof!" Flossie agreed.

Partly because I am curious but mainly because there is only so much wiping of the table I can do before looking as though I have a bad OCD problem or worse, the cup is in my hand and I'm staring at the leaves. At first it is just a load of mush to me but suddenly it's like a veil has been lifted, the leaves are now clear shapes and I know the meanings, it's horrible, spine chillingly scary.

"My God Rose, Miss Taylor's in terrible danger, what am I going to do?" My voice is a panicky whisper, but Rose isn't answering me, she's gone again.

I feel so helpless, what if this hocus pocus delve into the supernatural is wrong? Who can I go to? Not the police, they'll only laugh at me. Looking back at the leaves my heart is pounding. "Please let me be wrong, please," I silently pray.

Flossie is shaking her head as I drop the cup scattering the leaves onto the patio as it breaks. They may have splattered to the ground, but the meaning remains intact, staring up at me, telling of Miss Taylor's danger and sudden death.

Chapter Six

Sally brings me a cup of chamomile tea and is fussing over me as she knows how to with her family. Finding me in a state of shock in the garden after Flossie ran into Crumbs barking and pulling at her black skirt, I'm now forced to lie on my bed and rest. I feel absolutely dreadful; my mind is racing and thinking of all the ways I could be wrong. Just when I'm totally convinced I am it's like a million watt light bulb switches on in my head showing the leaves again. All I keep hearing is "the leaves cannot lie". Why can't they? Who says they can't? I'm the only one who saw them so could I be lying? Of course not, why would I? All I did was clear the table, what's it got to do with me?

"Rose! Don't you go gallivanting off leaving me with all this, it isn't fair, do you hear me! I don't want this!" I'm aware my voice is getting higher.

"Now, now love, I can hear you and so can all the customers. Come on, drink this chamomile tea and it will help to calm you down." Sally's come in just as I'm ranting; she's going to want an explanation. Well at least she's a believer, perhaps she can make some sense of all this because I can't.

After quite a lot of gentle coaxing from Sally, I've eventually got it off my chest as they say. For me it's been the hardest thing since having to tell Sister Annunciata at school in the middle of Maths that I'd just started my period. Well, it was my first time, made even worse by some girls clapping me as we hurried out of the classroom. Strangely enough I was more popular after that, anything for a break from Maths.

Sally is deep in thought so I don't know what else to do but sip my tea. Flossie is sitting at the side of my bed looking at me with her big browny blue eyes.

"Am I right Flossie?"

"Woof."

No offence but it's only a dog's word or bark should I say, and I've never heard of a bark holding much credibility in the law's eyes.

"Right love, it seems to me I know what I knows love."

My heart's sinking fast; it isn't the most encouraging of answers. "Yes, and that is?" I can't help it if I sound rude; I'm drowning here in desperate need of a lifeline. Sally just gives me a sideways glance, putting me in my place.

"Rose knew a thing or two about spiritual goings on, everyone respected her."

"Yes, but that was Rose, nobody knows me."

"It stands to reason love, whether you realise it or not Rose must have taught you well over the years."

"So?"

"So, don't doubt what you saw, you can't take a

chance on someone's life can you? Life is precious. Use your gift wisely."

How many times did I hear Rose and Gran saying that? Rose would always say "Only use the spiritual gift for the good of others Kitty, it isn't a party game, use it wisely."

I never really listened; I wasn't interested then but the words are all so clear to me now. In a flash my plan of action is strategically worked out.

"OK Sally, thank you but it will have to wait till tonight when I take Flossie for her usual walk. There's the change from Miss Taylor's £20 note to give back to her and that can be my genuine reason for calling by her house."

"You know where she lives don't you love?"

"It's the first bungalow on York Road, isn't it?"

"No love, the second one, the bungalow after the dentists. Number 54."

"Right, thanks, it's a good job you asked."

"Woof."

The rest of the afternoon, although extremely busy, just seems to have dragged. My mind has been filled with my mission ahead of me and not on my work. Sally, bless her, has worked doubly hard at her people skills, not that it doesn't come naturally to her. She must have said something to Simon and Charlotte because I've not had to ask them to do one single thing, they've all been fantastic. I'm a firm believer in giving credit where credit is due and all three deserved the chat and bonus given to them after closing. Tomorrow's another day and I don't know how it's going to be right now; I just can't think past tonight.

It's no use, my food is sticking in my throat, I've never been a food freak and my philosophy is "a little bit of what you fancy and everything in moderation" but I can't go without my veg and that's down to Gran. Looking down at my plate of chicken, roast potatoes (OK so they're frozen-it's easier when it's just for one) and three different veg with gravy it has suddenly lost its appeal and I really can't manage it. Judging by the doggie chomping noises, Flossie doesn't seem to be affected in any way; I can hear her eating heartily behind me. Scraping my plate and putting everything in the dishwasher I know there's still so much to do in preparation for my first Sunday opening but it's now or never, it's making me feel queasy in the pit of my stomach. A glass of water, that will do the trick, right stop stalling girl, go for it, lead, handbag, keys.

"Come on Flossie; let's do this before I chicken out."

Flossie is looking at me with her head on one side.

"OK wrong choice of words tonight, let's go before I change your name to Sherlock or Watson." Flossie is sitting shaking her head. "So, you approve of Flossie and you're happy staying here to look after me?"

"Woof!"

It's such a beautiful evening, one I would normally have enjoyed but it's as though I'm just walking the route on autopilot. The pubs and restaurants are starting to get busy although it's still fairly early yet. Sunshine brings out the best in people. We relax more, smile more, become more sociable, and embrace all the outdoor activities we've been denied through the winter months. Walking through the garden gate and along our usual route down to the river it's clear that the good residents of Wetherby and its surrounding villages want to soak up every last ray of sunshine they can.

Mick the butcher, who owns Wilson's Butchers two shops down from Crumbs, is walking towards us alongside the river, Flossie and his boxer dog Chops are good pals now. As they happily do their "sniff and greet" routine I just laugh to myself, grateful I only have to smile and chat, not all that weird routine that dogs do, well I am new to all this.

"Glorious day Mick and it's still quite warm. Everybody wants to be outdoors tonight; the pubs will do a roaring trade. Have you been busy, or doesn't anybody want a Sunday joint in this weather?"

"It's been busy but more for barbecue food, the great British pastime. Let's hope this weather keeps up for them, it always rains when we have a barbecue."

“Don’t you dare fire yours up then, it’s supposed to be good all the holiday weekend and a lot of people seem set to enjoy it.”

“Just wait till later Kate, this lot when tanked up with real ale and their fancy wines will turn this place into Beirut.”

“Oh, you’re just getting old and cynical Mick!”

“Maybe, maybe not. What you see in people is not always what you get. Bye Kate, have a peaceful night. Come on Chops, let’s be getting back lad.”

“Bye Mick.”

Having that conversation with Mick has only unnerved me more. All these underlying currents running through this pretty place I have now made my home. Surely he’s wrong and my silly mind and all this hocus pocus is wrong too.

“Time to check on Miss Taylor Flossie, no more dawdling. I’ll feel better when I prove it all to be false,” but Flossie is shaking her head whilst I’m clipping her pink lead onto her collar. Does she mean no, I won’t feel better or no, I won’t find it to be false? Next time Rose, leave me out of any mysteries please. I have had enough drama recently to last me a long time.

Miss Taylor’s bungalow is the second bungalow in a row of four. Detached, solid properties probably built in the 1960s when houses each had a good sized garden to separate them from their neighbours. The detached brick garage to the right has its door closed and there’s no car parked on the drive but that doesn’t help as I don’t know if she drives. Neat, very white, pleated net curtains hanging in each window either side of the wooden front door are making it very difficult for me to see if she's in either of the rooms. I can hardly stick my nose up to the glass; I'd die if Miss Taylor was looking straight back at me.

"Oh, crikey Flossie, I feel a real idiot, this is a bad idea, come on let's go home." I'm still pressing the doorbell and I can hear it echoing through the bungalow, but nobody is answering it.

"She could be out visiting friends, having a meal with them." But Flossie is rooted to the path and refuses to move. "Oh, come on Flossie, don't go all stubborn like a toddler, I'm looking stupid standing here."

Flossie is shaking her head. For a little dog she is very forceful at times. I'm starting to feel jittery. I get like it when I'm stressed, I really don't want to find Miss Taylor, I mean I do but not dead, as in dead to the world. My knees are feeling wobbly and I'm going to end up puking in her flower bed I just know what I get like. Reaching into my dog walking jacket pocket my hand is on the bank's clear plastic bag with Miss Taylor's change in it, there should be some sweets in there somewhere. Flossie is looking up wagging her little tail; it's the rustle of her treats bag exciting her.

"Where are they? Not yours Flossie, mine."

It's creeping over me more now, it's like the sea when its waves rush up and then slowly drain away. In desperation my hand grabs at Flossie's choccie drops and before I can give myself time to refuse, two are in my mouth. Hard at first but slowly giving way under my teeth crunching them up. Not bad, but not good, well not your Green and Black's anyway. There's a lot of whining going on down below, bringing me slowly back to life, not noises from my stomach but from Flossie who's looking at me in a strange way.

"Well, what was I supposed to do? Flake out on the doorstep? Needs must Flossie, here you are, have a couple yourself and don't worry I'm not going to raid your choccie drops again in a hurry. I live for my chocolate fix, but I'll pass on these thank you. Here's the deal, I'll try once more then we're going. Don't you shake your head at me young lady. I'm not cut out to be doing this."

Inside the bungalow it's as quiet as a graveyard. This is doing serious things to my body, my bladder is now objecting, I've seen that on television, victims so scared they wet themselves, no, no, not me, it can't happen to me! What if it is all true and Miss Taylor is in there lying in a pool of blood, lifeless. Her neat bungalow looking like something straight out of CSI. Desperation and the fear of a huge wet patch on my beige trousers are spurring me on to bang loudly on the door. This is crackers, total madness, I'm never looking in a cup again, why couldn't she just have used the stupid tea strainer like everyone else? Flossie is pulling me between the garage and bungalow. This is it; this is the stuff nightmares are made of.

"Hello Kate, what are you doing here?"

I swear my heart can't take this, I've jumped so high you could award me a gold medal, well a bronze then, worse than that it's happened, just a tiny drop but I'm aware it's there. It's true then!

"Miss Taylor, thank goodness you're here."

"Sorry dear, I had my earphones in listening to the radio as I finished a spot of weeding."

To say Miss Taylor is gardening she looks a lot smarter than Gran used to, right down to her flowery gardening gloves but better than that, she is alive!

"Are you alright Kate, you look very pale? Has it been a long day dear, maybe you're doing too much? I can make us tea and wait on you for a change if you'd like some."

My bladder couldn't stand any more pressure from tea and nerves. I need to get home and change, to feel relaxed and safe again.

"Thank you but the baking won't get done if I do; it's my first Sunday opening tomorrow, pop along if you're out for a walk."

"Tomorrow I'm rather busy but perhaps on Monday, yes Monday I may be in need of a friendly face."

That's a strange thing to say and warning bells are ringing in my head. This Miss Marple mystery business is starting to get to me. Don't be stupid Kate it's only a phrase, something people say, don't go overboard with all this. I'm trying to convince myself but I'm failing miserably.

"What's the matter, what do you mean?" That's right, no beating about the bush, I need to know.

Miss Taylor is definitely looking uneasy, I can tell. There's a slight pink flush creeping up her throat. Poirot eat your heart out! Tut, what a horrible saying! I'm getting worse.

"Oh, nothing my dear, only family and you know how trying it can be sometimes, well you'd better get back to your baking then."

The change in her attitude is remarkable. One minute she's practically begging me to stay, well not quite but anyway very friendly and the next she's marching me down the path.

"Come on Flossie, home time. Gosh I nearly forgot what I came for Miss Taylor," I'm calling to her back as she strides ahead of me and opens the gate. I'm sure I can see deep anxiety in her eyes; her face looks strained, almost pinched and slightly older.

"Yes."

"It's about today when you left in a hurry."

Now it's Miss Taylor's turn to go a shade paler and she's reaching for the gate again to steady herself, even her voice is different, almost harsh.

"What about it, what do you mean?"

"You left your change." I'm holding out the bag with her money in it but she's just looking at it without really registering what is in my hand.

"Your change from your tea and cake, you left a £20 note."

"Did I? That is kind of you to come all this way,

thank you my dear."

Don't push it Kate, I'm telling myself. Miss Taylor is showing very clearly in her face how relieved she is. Even a fool could detect that from her expression and her body language. Miss Taylor's pinched face has smoothed out again with her now trying to force a smile and her tensed up shoulders have visibly dropped a couple of inches. Leave now Kate, quickly, don't let her see you know something's wrong, keep it pleasant. This talking to myself is my new release valve in these situations. It could be a lot worse, Rose could be here, strange how she's always missing when I need her most.

That's it then, what a fool I've made of myself, she's perfectly well, alive and kicking is the expression, where on earth does that one come from but in this case it's very true, seeing as she almost kicked me out of her garden. Miss Taylor is certainly alive but there's definitely something upsetting her all I can do now is hope to goodness she comes into Crumbs over the Bank Holiday as I've no other reasons for visiting her.

"Come on Flossie, two minutes and we'll be home. You can play in the garden whilst I bake for tomorrow and then it's a long bubbly soak for me and bed."

"Woof."

Baking soothes me; all my thoughts have to be

pushed to one side and all my heart and soul given to what I am creating. Gran always taught me, "You only get out what you put in", meaning use the best ingredients possible mixed with a huge amount of love and respect. Knowing when to beat or when to fold mixtures with a gentle turn of the spoon before carefully smoothing them into the well-prepared tins and into a correctly heated oven. It's an art form to me and a labour of love. I know how much people enjoy a good piece of home baking, not by all the compliments, which of course is wonderful, but by the silence. That first mouthful is the giveaway, sometimes I watch to make sure and when I see the dream like expression my heart is cheered no end.

Ten o'clock, what a day it's been. There are only the butterfly buns to finish in the morning whilst my scones are cooling and everything is ready to serve. I've gone for easy options but that's not to say they're inferior. Sitting in neatly stacked boxes for tomorrow are "Choccie Rockies"-my own version of rock buns but with dark chocolate chips instead of currants, young and old love them. Then there are raspberry buns, two marmalade loaf cakes one to use and one for the freezer, and plenty of rectangular shaped portions of light sponge cake, some with white icing, a few sprinkles and a cherry on top and others with chocolate or coffee icing with chocolate sprinkles. They are the simplest cakes you could ever whip up and look so attractive. A basic sponge cake mixture into a rectangular cake tin and when it's cooked it can be iced and cut into a good number of portions. Never skimp on a portion! That's a strict rule of mine, being a chocoholic and a cakeaholic has its draw backs and I would never give to others what I wouldn't have myself. My thighs are proof of that, and my bum.

"Bedtime Flossie, come on girl you can watch the telly whilst I soak."

Flossie is in the doorway with her little nose twitching at all the delicious smells. Baking does tend to penetrate everywhere with its aromas, my hair always smells until my morning shower but at least this isn't a curry house. Yuck!

One thing I've started to notice is that when Flossie comes into my bedroom she always goes to the chair and sits with her head to one side looking at it. Sometimes her tail dusts the floor for me, I'm ashamed to say it's beginning to leave marks where she does it but there just aren't enough hours in the day for me and who's going to see upstairs anyway? Tonight that's where she's heading. Maybe it's her routine, we all have them and mine is putting hand cream on my feet. Well, it keeps my hooves soft; don't knock it until you've tried it.

"Flossie you're missing your 10 o'clock news, come on girl."

Reluctantly she's plodding to her doggie bed with full view of the telly. After a few prods and pushes with her nose, a few circular turns in the bed, she's sitting in her usual carefree pose, head on her paws hanging over the front, eyes glued to the telly.

Bubbles up to my neck candles on the windowsill glowing, this is heaven and if I'm not careful that's where I'll end up. More than once I've started to nod off whilst soaking in luxury, well at least all my bits and pieces will be clean! A girl I worked with at the hotel a zillion years ago who is larger than life in all ways decided to fill her bath with lighted floating candles once. Dangerous perhaps but heaven to her until the perfumed bubbles entered her nose. One sneeze and a tidal wave later all the candles were out, she never tried it again, but the memory stays with me and makes me chuckle every time I think of her. This is so nice and cosy, mmm just a few more minutes.

"Kitty you're drifting again, get out and go to bed, now! Before we have two bodies in Wetherby!"

"What!" My toe has almost gone up the tap with the shock of Rose's voice breaking through my sleepy, euphoric, floating state. "What the hell do you think you're doing to me, you nearly drowned me, Rose."

"Firstly, my dear don't use that kind of language when you have a position to withhold and second, I just stopped you from drowning yourself."

She's sounding very indignant, this new bodiless Rose. My head's spinning, looking in all the corners of the bathroom, even the ceiling. Well, they float, don't they?

"No use looking for me, you're not ready yet so stop imitating a hen."

"Then just tell me where you are, oh for God's sake this is ridiculous!" I'm getting angry now and getting ready to jump out of the bath when it occurs to me Rose will see me, I mean all of me. Modesty is suddenly taking over as I slide back under the bubbles.

"Kate!"

"Sorry."

"Very well, I'm sitting on the loo but it's no use, you won't see me."

"You're not, you know, no you can't be."

"What, can't be here? Well, I assure you I am, for now anyway, oh I understand. No, my dear girl, such bodily necessities are now obsolete, such a blessing."

"Then why are you checking up on me?"

"I'm not, call it more guidance, I'm here to guide and reassure but don't get too used to it, I do have other things to do with my time."

"Such as?" I can't believe I'm talking to a toilet.

"A few of us are just nipping over to Venice for the evening, that's quite an achievement for a learner; we don't have long so listen to me."

I'm just too gobsmacked to argue, how can you argue with something that's not visual, physically in front of you, a solid mass.

"Close your mouth Kate and by the way, watch that tooth right at the back on the left, the double one, you need a filling. Please don't interrupt I said

I don't have long, you've no idea how draining all this is for me. Spiritually you're not ready yet, oh it's there alright but you're putting up barriers so you will just have to learn the hard way. Gran agrees and before you ask, she's fine, having a wonderful time flitting around with your granddad, so it's up to me to sort you out."

"Charming."

"I asked you to listen, that's what you have to work on. Read the leaves of which you're more than capable and listen to what you are being told. Don't doubt what you hear when concentrating on them. If you doubt you will have lost the true meanings. Are you following me so far?"

All I can do is nod.

"Good well I'm not saying anymore for now, just don't doubt what you saw and do your best to help. That's it, my time is up. Just believe Kitty, just believe."

"Rose don't go, I need to ask you things please don't tell me half a tale I'm in need of help here, please." I can't believe I'm actually pleading with thin air, what else can I do, this is scary stuff for me. I can almost feel them measuring me up for a straitjacket!

The water is now only lukewarm, and my skin has developed the prune effect which is a sure sign it has soaked up all it can take so why am I still lying in it? Because I don't quite know what else to do and I keep hoping Rose will come back from Venice. How absolutely ridiculous. I'm raving bonkers! Get a grip Kate, get washed, there's only my face left to do.

I'm cleaning my teeth and remembering what Rose said about the tooth, that will prove if I'm going bonkers or not, yes that's it. Just that little test suddenly makes me feel better, all of 20 seconds better, it's like a stupid double-edged sword, I'm either bonkers or stuck with hearing voices forever! My next dilemma is can I use the loo?

Chapter Seven

Even if the alarm clock were not set or didn't work properly, Flossie's alarm does. My morning has started brightly enough helped by the sunshine, two paracetamols and several cups of tea. The scones are cooling, butterfly buns are looking delectable with ample fillings of creamy vanilla buttercream, well placed wings dusted with icing sugar and a glace cherry gracing the centre. I'm not a lover of the new trendy cupcakes, all mounds of buttercream disguising the fact that there's no sponge in the bun case. As my Gran used to say, "All fur coat and no knickers". I loved her sayings, still do and that's why I quote them.

Putting a selection of cakes and scones in the glass display cabinet I can't help but feel proud, my babies look good enough for any posh place. Sally is bringing a Yorkshire curd tart as she's the pastry Queen and another pie for Bank Holiday Monday. My new Sunday opening isn't until 10:00 AM and I'm not expecting such a rush so early but it's better to be prepared. When Simon and Charlotte arrive, they can start on preparing the salad for the sandwiches and washing down the tables outside, I really need to fill Sally in on all last night's "happenings", it just feels so unreal.

"Come on Flossie, it's got to be a quick walk today so try not to stop at every corner, it's hard I know but just do this for me today will you?"

"Woof."

As good as her "woof" we are back in record time, maybe I should ask her to do that every day. It's really difficult going into my bathroom without expecting Rose to "pop up" somewhere, it's killing me, I'm not cut out to live with "spirits", not this kind of spirit. I'm not adverse to the alcoholic ones, in bottles that is. What's also bothering me, and this is too deep thinking for my ordinary, easy going, happy go lucky, cakeaholic personality, is what if there's more of them everywhere, sitting in Crumbs, walking the market square? Wow!

"Morning love, one pie, one Yorkshire curd tart, where shall I put them?" Sally, her usual bright self is efficient as always.

"Curd tart in the glass cabinet please Sally and the pie in the fridge. Let's hope we can have some left for tomorrow. Thanks Sally, they look perfect as usual, your pies should win prizes."

"They wouldn't last long enough to get to the competition love; I've had to double up on these so my Chris and the kids have some seeing as I'm working today."

"Does Chris mind, it is good of you to help out on your day together as a family."

"Mind? Lord no love, He's palmed them off onto his mum so he can go fishing with his pal, no the tarts are a thank you to his Mum though I daresay he'll get back in time to scoff them. Before you worry love the money is going to come in handy, we're thinking of buying a caravan or one of those motor homes. Plenty of time to go off in it later on, freedom for the kids."

She's got a faraway dreamy look in her face, and I feel better knowing I'm helping to make her dream come true. If it's a good weekend there should be enough for some extra money for them all, well I hardly need it I'm not going anywhere.

"Tea love? Before we open, there's a good 40 minutes yet and by the look on your face you've a tale to tell."

"Better make it coffee Sally, I need something stronger, do you fancy a croissant? There are some almond ones in the cupboard."

"Best offer of the day, well no that's not true but I've put my Chris on hold, told him He's on a promise for tonight if he makes the tea. I'm learning love, everything comes with a price tag and I ain't cheap!"

She always cheers me up, but I can't help feeling a twinge of envy at her loving, easy-going relationship with Chris. The wonderful smell of good ground coffee is wafting towards me, jolting me back into action. Two almond croissants each and an empty cafetière later Sally has listened to all the events of last night. Smiling broadly when I recalled the bathroom incident.

"It's great love; wait till my Chris hears about

this. He loved Rose and her spiritual gift, quite shook up he was when she died."

"But what about Miss Taylor?"

"All we can do love is wait and see if she comes in and then take it from there, don't worry I'm sure she'll be in for her tea and scone, she never misses her Saturday scone, jam and cream treat."

"But Sally, Saturday was yesterday, I can't wait a whole week it'll kill me, no I didn't mean that, oh you know what I mean don't you."

"Point taken love, but short of rushing round there every hour with a different excuse you don't have much choice, do you? Come on, time to open up and feed the hungry travellers and bored residents of Wetherby."

Goodness knows where everyone had come from; Crumbs just never seemed to have emptied all day. It's now just after 3:00 PM and still no Miss Taylor but it's very nice to see Mr Potter back again looking very summery in his light grey, perfectly pressed trousers, pale pink shirt and a black and white small checked jacket. For the first time I notice he isn't wearing a tie, it makes him look so much younger, more relaxed.

"Hello Mr Potter, nice day, isn't it? What will you have this afternoon?"

Flossie has come closer to the table but is just sitting looking at the empty chair next to Mr Potter. She knows the rules, her end of the garden whilst I'm working and as if Mr Potter is reading my mind he breaks through my thoughts.

"My cream tea please Kate, with Earl Grey tea, no don't send Flossie away, she's a very welcome companion."

"I'm afraid I can't let her come any nearer, my other customers may not like it Mr Potter. Flossie, you know what to do, go on that's a good gal."

Flossie looks at me with her browny blue eyes, cocks her head to one side as though weighing up the situation and promptly lies, sprawled out on the grass, her head on her front paws and eyes glued to Mr Potter's table.

"Flossie, don't you come any closer, do you understand?"

"Woof."

"Thank you, Kate, I'm sure she does understand, as long as I can talk to her that's fine."

"Woof."

"Looks like you've got yourself a companion then but don't let her fool you with those big eyes, we do feed her, she will eat anything on offer if we don't stop her. No nibbling at any dropped cake do you hear Flossie? Or it will be Weight Watchers for you." This time Flossie just huffed like a teenager, who knows, she could be I suppose.

Each time I come into the garden I'm trying not to look like a mother checking up on her child, but I am, so far she's behaving. Mr Potter is staying far longer than usual not only talking to Flossie but to all who sit at his table and around.

"Can I trouble you for another pot of Earl Grey please Kate?"

"Of course you can, just tea is it?"

"Yes please," Mr Potter is patting his stomach which looks fine to me, "or I'll be accompanying Flossie to her diet class, I don't get the exercise I used to now I've moved into the apartments by the river. We had quite a large garden with our house, but it all seemed so silly just me, rattling around in it when my wife died."

"They're lovely overlooking the weir, I lived in a similar one when I was married but mine was in Leeds, not quite so lovely for me though."

Mr Potter only gives me a knowing smile. News travels fast in small towns. Reaching forward to clean his crockery I'm being overwhelmed again by the heady perfume of freesias, wow should I tell him to go steady on the conditioner he puts in his washing? In a split-second I also register how my right arm and right side of my body feel as though they're delving into the freezer compartment of my fridge, no! I'm screaming inside "go away!"

"Kitty don't let Mr Potter see you having a tantrum it's not good for business my dear."

Trying not to be so obvious I'm doing my best bit of acting turning to the empty chair on the right and pretending to swat away a fly. "Go away," my mouth silently hisses, hoping Rose will oblige.

"Look at your left hand, look deeply."

"No, go away; Mr Potter is lovely I don't want him scared!" I'm now screaming the words in my brain.

"I know He's lovely, my dear I would let him stir up my cake any day."

"Rose!"

Mr Potter is leaning forward full of concern now. "Are you alright my dear? It's only a fly."

"Ah yes, sorry it's the, the er, rose bushes perhaps you can come one day and check them for me, I don't know what I'm supposed to do with them, and they were a favourite of Rose's."

Mr Potter is beaming his dashing smile at me, "That will be my pleasure Kate, now if you don't mind me saying that cup is in danger of being crushed in your hand, you're gripping it so hard."

"Cup?" My attention is suddenly downwards to the cup in my left hand, and the leaves, again those flaming leaves!

"Go on then, get a grip of yourself and focus my girl." Rose is twittering to my right.

My eyes are looking deeply into the leaves; I don't have much choice do I except I'm absolutely terrified of a repeat of Miss Taylor's situation. Gran used to say, "Every picture tells a story". As this one is unfurling before my eyes this time I can't help but smile. Before I know what's happening my mouth has taken control and I can hear myself saying "Mr Potter, don't go looking for love, for love will find you."

That's it, now I've gone and done it, I've never been totally in control of my mouth, but this is too much. My face is as red as my glace cherries on the butterfly buns, this is just awful and all I can do is look at Mr Potter's stunned face, jibber my apologies and escape back into the kitchen.

"Simon, can you take Mr Potter his tea and his bill out to him please, I need to pop upstairs whilst it's quiet."

"Sure thing."

Simon hasn't noticed my red face and I'm taking the stairs two at a time, up to my sanctuary only it's not, is it? Rose could be there ahead of me.

Splashing cold water over my burning face helps but it's not washing away the words I spoke which are now banging around in my head. I'm so angry, how could I have fallen for it again?

"Oh, get over yourself, you can't stop what's meant to be so you will just have to get used to it."

My hands are covering my face but it's not working. "Rose, stop it, please stop this. I'm grateful for all you've done for me but please not this, I don't even know if it is you or just me going through a psychological blip."

"Poppycock!"

"Then let me see you then I will believe what you're saying."

"Oh, you will, believe me, all in good time Kitty, all in good time."

"All in good time? How can you say that to me, it's, it's..." I'm fighting to find the right words to express my deep frustration and growing anger. "It's like telling a child in an oversized school uniform that they'll grow into it, that means nothing to a child who's feeling totally sick inside them for fear of being bullied!" I feel a pulse beating at the side of my head; at this rate I'll be joining Rose sooner than expected!

"Oh, grow up Kate; you've got it so use it for the good of others."

"I am grown up, and what good is it doing me? At this rate we'll have gone through all of our customers, they'll be dead or too terrified to come into Crumbs."

"Well, that's up to you to handle it correctly. You're a little green yet but you will learn my dear, now come on pull yourself together I can't hang around here all day sorting you out."

"That's very reassuring, please don't let me stop you, go on, float away or whatever it is you do, go on."

"You're getting very childish Kitty; I'm leaving before you have a tantrum. Just calm down and go back to your customers you have a lot to do today. Remember my dear I can't do it for you, I can only guide you through it. Toodle pip."

"Toodle pip! Since when did you start talking like that?" Silence is around me, she's gone, well at least I'm presuming she has, nobody is answering my question whether it be Rose or my own subconscious thing-a-me-gig. Hells bells, this is potty I'll just have to go back downstairs and face the music. My main concern hasn't shown her face yet, I swear I'll go grey overnight with all this worry about Miss Taylor.

Mr Potter has paid his bill and gone. The feeling of relief floods through my body till my brain abruptly stops it. He's coming back to look at the roses sometime soon Simon is telling me, all I can do is nod.

"Kate, Kate, can you hear me, ooh our Sally what's going on, Kate looks all peculiar, trance like?"

"Ugh, oh sorry yes Julie, a coffee to go, is it?"

Julie has popped in from Needles and Pins, her sewing and craft shop. She's another born and bred, never moved away Wetherby girl and her shop is sandwiched between Mick Wilson's butcher's shop and Crumbs.

"You look like you've seen a ghost sweetie. No, you're not, are you? Ooh what a shock."

My mind is racing, has Sally told her? Julie is Sally's husband Chris's cousin, just one of many. I swear half of Wetherby is related! I'm just giving Sally one of my looks but it's falling flat, she's giggling and talking away to a dishy young man whose girlfriend is starting to mark her territory.

"Am I what?"

"Preggers sweetie, making it a baker's dozen with the old buns."

Thank God for the Wetherby simple mentality!

"Oh no Julie, don't go spreading that around the square, it's just the heat and lack of food, my blood sugar feels low."

"Grab yourself a slice of our Sally's pie and a big dollop of cream sweetie before you drop on the floor. Doesn't look good for business sweetie looking like Mike the mortician's next client. Anyways I came in for some change but go on, you've twisted my arm, I'll have two coffees white no sugar and two Choccie Rockie buns and change for a tenner if you can do it sweetie, please."

"Will do, are pound coins OK? I'll get Charlotte to pop the coffees and buns next door in a minute."

Satisfied, she's paid and gone back to Needles and Pins next door. Charlotte is quite happy to get out and do a delivery for me leaving me to brood over my worries, time is ticking away and there's only two more hours left and then Crumbs will be closed for the day. If Miss Taylor doesn't come in soon, I swear Julie will be right, I'll give birth to something!

Every inch of Crumbs is sparkling; I've scrubbed it so much. That's another thing I tend to do when I'm stressed is clean everything in sight. Sally is my ideal cleaning partner she sweeps and I mop, she sprays and I wash off. We'd be great on a TV show, the Morecambe and Wise of grime and grease. Simon and Charlotte have done the outside tables, watered the pots and hanging baskets and are now using Flossie as an excuse to walk together by the river, that's fine by me, my nerves are shot to pieces, and I need to have a chat with Sally now we've finished everything.

"Come on then love I know you want to tell me

things, it's written all over your face."

"Have you got time; it's been a long day for you? I'm really confused Sally, first Miss Taylor now Mr Potter, I don't know if I'm cut out for all this spooky stuff."

"Just take it nice and easy love, Rose wouldn't let you get into something she didn't think you weren't capable of working through. Sit down I'll get us a drink, what do you want love, hot or cold?"

"I could really drink a long cool shandy, there's some cans in the fridge and ice in the freezer."

"Won't be a tick love, get your feet up outside, you need some fresh air."

Talking to Sally is like going to a therapist without the expensive bill at the end of the session. I'm sitting quietly looking down the garden at nothing in particular. Sally is just thinking through one of my problems. Apart from not wanting to be involved at all I have to think of a good enough reason to call on Miss Taylor again and risk her getting even more agitated. Sally's face is screwed up, her lips tightly pursed, and her eyes closed deeply, lost in thought. What the hell am I doing this for? I'm involving a friend too and why? Because I think I've seen danger in her tea leaves, that's too much thinking for me and not enough proof to back it up. Just because Miss Taylor was with a stranger and seemed to be anxious and then funny with me doesn't add up to blue murder, does it? My whole body is suddenly feeling cold, and a shudder is going through me from head to toe. As Gran would say, "Someone just walked over my grave."

"Got it! Brilliant, just brilliant."

"Phew, keep still my beating heart, Sally shocks like that can kill! Oh for pity's sake I've got it on the brain."

"Listen love it's simple. You should win her over with this one." Sally's face is flushed; she's getting so excited with herself.

"I'm listening."

"All you have to do is appeal to her love of gardening, don't look like that, this will work I promise you. She's got fruit bushes and fruit trees, she used to enter at the Flower Show and win too."

"I'll take your word for it but now how does it all fit in with my visit?"

"You're going to tell her you want to do a little "Use local produce" campaign for your pies and have been told of her wonderful apples, plums and fruits. You want to do a little business with her, get my drift? Keep up Kate love; we've not got much time left before I have to go home."

"Sorry, tell me a bit more, you're the brains here."

"Spin her a line about looking for a local source, helping the community and all that."

"Well, I do like to with my salads and bread and eggs so why not with my fruit, it's genius Sally and not a bad idea. I could say we want to do speciality pies, seasonal and fresh fruit flans, great I like it, thanks you're a real friend."

“What’s up now love? I’ve given you the reason so get to it.”

“It isn’t that,” my stomach is starting to do somersaults because it’s crunch time and terrifying thoughts are creeping in. “What if when I get there it’s too late, only you know the truth, nobody’s going to believe me are they.”

“Now stop it, you’ll be fine, Miss Taylor will be alive and kicking so stop worrying love, now I’ve got to be off, call me later.”

“Thanks Sally I will.” Well, that’s it, as soon as Flossie is back and I’ve locked up we’ll walk to Miss Taylor’s, only five minutes’ walk and then it will all be over, just hold that thought I’m telling myself.

Chapter Eight

Standing rigid in Miss Taylor's long back garden silly words are catapulting into my brain. "Alive and kicking". "It will all be over." Miss Taylor is far from "alive" and by the look of her leg could have "kicked" her last and it's certainly "all over" for her. Most definitely. Her neat bob of hair is splayed out at the sides like a fan floating on the water with her face deeply submerged in her ornamental pond. Flossie is sitting by her side looking at Miss Taylor's body and then at me, shaking her head like an old woman.

"Woof."

Her bark cuts through my sheer terror, this is my first dead body, I didn't even see my Gran or Rose afterwards, I'm too much of a coward. I can't take my eyes off her head, the red, sticky looking mass at the back that flies keep landing on. Oh God this is awful, my stomach's doing a bungee jump, up, up and...out all over the grass.

"Sorry, I couldn't help it," I'm apologising but who the hell's going to hear or care? Pull yourself together Kate. My phone is in my hand and my shaking fingers are only just managing to tap out 999. It's done, I've got to move away, get back away from her body, the flies. I need to sit down before I fall down. Sally, I need to ring Sally. As I somehow say the words to her, sirens are screeching in my ears and the pounding of feet and voices calling out break through my tearful phone call.

I can't stop crying and shaking, everyone's doing their job as they've probably done hundreds of times. Crime scenes on the television look so real but when you're in the middle of one it's unbelievable. I know they need answers and fast, but I'm reduced to a shaking, snotty, blotchy faced jellyfish. My tissues have run out and the last one is starting to shred in my hands. Please don't offer me a beautifully folded white hankie I'm thinking as the tall, dark haired detective in front of me starts to look concerned at me twisting and pulling. I just can't blow my nose on a cotton hankie, it's wrong; it makes me feel dirty, yucky. They always do that in films, and I hate it! He's reaching into his suit jacket pocket, oh Lord what do I say?

"Here have some tissues Mrs Philips."

"Thank you."

It's strange what rushes into your mind at times of stress but all I can think is what lovely, kind eyes he has, warm nutty brown coloured with a hint of blue, very much like Flossie's, this is mad. I want to go home, I feel dirty, smelly, from puking. The embarrassing memory is making me colour up.

"I'm sorry, I was sick, over by Miss Taylor's bod..." I can't say the word and I can feel my eyes filling up again.

"I'm Detective Sergeant Benson, do you feel up to answering a few questions and then a policewoman will take you home?"

"Benson?"

"Yes."

"As in Sally Benson?"

"Well yes, but I'm from Chris's side, his cousin actually."

I'm nodding, of course he is, dummy and another stupid thing is rattling around my head.

"Is Wetherby full of Bensons?" Before I realise it, the words are out, me and my big mouth again.

"Pretty much so, we're a biggish clan."

"Right Benson, who's bagging up this puke, do we know if it's dog or human?" A big, broad Irishman is calling over and all I want to do is crawl home rather than admit it's mine.

"Human sir, I'll get PC Roberts to do it."

The brusque Irishman is now towering above me, boring through me with his piercing, icy blue eyes. "Detective Chief Inspector O'Donoghue and you are?"

"Kate Philips sir, the owner of Crumbs. Mrs Philips found the body," Sergeant Benson answers for me, leaving me with my mouth sagging half open.

"Do you know who she was, or do you always take a shortcut through someone's back garden?"

My God he's rude! I'm not taking this from him I'm going to...burst into tears again! Rose where the hell are you?

Suddenly my anger both at this incredibly rude policeman and at my desertion by Rose when I need her most has fired my whole being. Standing up hasn't made too much of a difference, this bully of a man is like Goliath, but Gran always said, "Stand up and face your enemies". Well, I'm trying Gran, honestly it's not easy. Looking up a long way I scowl back at him, well he deserves it the arrogant pig!

"I'm not in the habit of strolling through stranger's gardens unless they have invited me." I'm trying desperately to sound strong and articulate. "The "LADY" is called Miss Taylor, I came to chat with her and "the puke" is mine, my apologies but I wasn't expecting to find her anything but fully alive. Now if you have no objections I'm going home to clean up. You know where I live and you can finish my interrogation there, come on Flossie."

The big ape just nods. My God how did I do it? My knees feel wobbly, but I'm determined to walk away with my head held high, how dare he speak to me like that. Cars, policeman and figures clad from head to toe in white are piling into poor Miss Taylor's garden. Blue and white tape is being stretched out around the bungalow. Just let me get home please before I collapse!

Nothing has sunk in yet, I keep expecting to suddenly feel weak and pathetic, but I haven't, it's that uncivilised Barbarian that's fired me up. Every time I think of "it" his massive, arrogant bulk blocks out the pictures, maybe I should be grateful to him. No! Poor Flossie, she keeps coming up to me and snuggling against my leg to comfort me, but I am fine. I'm washed, changed, I've fed Flossie and I'm now making some beans on toast, it's food, comfort food and I'm just considering whether to put some cheese on top and grill it, but my door is being hammered on. Typical!

Looking through my glass door is Sergeant Benson; at least he's giving a little wave and a smile as I walk towards him. Here we go, let's get it over with, big breath and try to look calm and...

"Hello Sergeant come in." Ooh! His warm eyes are friendly, that's better. "I'm just going to eat; do you want anything?" Please say yes then I can eat without being scrutinised!

"Well, a coffee would be great and anything else you have to go with it is a bonus, thank you."

Right, that's it he's having some of my beans on toast whether he wants it or not.

"Please sit down it'll be ready in a tick. Your boss isn't likely to barge in, is he?"

"No don't worry, he's had to go to Harrogate, sorry about earlier but it's always difficult at the start of an investigation, my boss is a force not to be reckoned with but a good one."

"Are you allowed to eat with a suspect? Well, I take it I am one, your only one so far. Beans on toast could be seen to be a bribe by some individuals."

His eyes are twinkling; gosh his teeth are beautifully straight, real pearly whites! Glancing at his watch he's looking straight at me, smiling and my cheese could bubble under the warmth of his eyes. I can see the little creases in the corners as they crinkle up slightly and he mutters something about teatime and hospitality.

"Right, cheesy beans on toast it is, coming right up sir."

Concentrate Kate, that's it, fork beans and toast up to your mouth, chew, no don't look up, wait till it's safe. Phew done it! He's eating, that's a relief, not talking but it's giving me the chance to take sneaky peaks at him from time to time, nice, very tasty.

"More coffee?" I'm doing my hostess job but am very aware it's time to get down to the real reason he's here, He's probably married or spoken for or a serial womaniser. Life's full of them.

"Mrs Philips thank you for the food, but I really need to start getting your statement."

I noticed his eyes look towards my hand when he said my name, stripped of rings from the day after Matt had left.

"Right yes, fire away."

"No need to ask about you and this," his arm is gesturing around Crumbs, "I know of your circumstances, talk me through this afternoon and why you went to see Miss Taylor please."

He's now got his policeman's hat on so to

speak and I'm starting to feel edgy. I know my face is a pinky shade and I can feel it getting hotter. "Keep cool you fool, you've done nothing wrong," I'm repeating in my head. Here goes. Nothing happened concerning Miss Taylor this afternoon; tell him that, it's the truth. Yesterday, don't talk about yesterday. My mouth's open but I'm suddenly as dry as a bone. He's looking at me, waiting.

"Nothing happened this afternoon I just..."

"Kitty that's not true, now my dear something did happen."

My head has suddenly jerked all the way round to the counter behind me where Rose's voice is coming from.

"Now you decide to turn up, when it's all over!" I'm spitting it out and I've now jumped up from my seat. I'm blazing mad, it's all the stress, how dare she, this is all her fault!

"Mrs Philips could you sit down please."

"Why?"

"The statement." He's tapping his pad with his pen. "Or if you're not comfortable here I could take you to the station."

I daren't look at his face, mine is now traffic light red. If Rose were not dead, I'd kill her, honestly I would, how on earth can I get out of this one?

"Sorry, I'm not myself at the moment."

"Really? And why is that?"

"Careful my dear, you've watched enough Midsomer Murders with me, trick question time coming up," Rose is twittering behind me.

"Shut up, go away, haven't you got a haunting to go to?" I've turned around again and I'm mouthing it as silently as I can.

"Pardon? Mrs Philips please can we get on." He's not exactly stern but certainly sounding more forceful, under different circumstances I'd say quite yummy. I'm sure I detected something in his eyes just then, but I'm hardly coming across as a sensible, reliable witness so what was it? Oh, so he's just realised he has another loony in front of him, all the signs are certainly there.

"Mrs Philips I'll ask you again, why did you go to Miss Taylor's, it's not your usual walk is it?"

"Told you my dear, watch it." Rose sounds excited; she's damned well enjoying this!

"Sometimes I go that way."

His eyebrows have just arched and he's fixing me with those warm brown eyes.

"I wanted to talk to her about using her fruit in my summer baking." Sally, I could kiss you! That sounded good to me.

"Tut, tut, tut liar, liar, pants on fire," Rose is chanting now from just to the left alongside him. I can't help but glare, my face screwing up as I do. Nothing passes him by, He's written something on his pad, but my skills don't stretch to reading upside down.

"And what did Miss Taylor say?"

"What do you mean? How could she say anything when she was dead?"

"Dead when you got there, how do you know, did you feel for a pulse? Touch her?"

"Told you my dear, careful now," Rose is warning.

Trying to control my temper and my nerves I'm jumping up and getting some water. Sergeant Benson is just sitting, watching and waiting.

"I didn't touch her, I couldn't, her head was in the water, her hair floating and flies, lots of flies, her head."

The full horror is being shown to me again and I'm suddenly feeling the beans on the march upwards.

"Sit down, drink some water, that's it," his hand is on my arm, and he guides me back to the table.

"I just knew she was dead; I knew it."

"Did you know of anyone who would want to harm her?"

"No, I don't know much about her, other than she was a librarian and a regular customer here."

"You do!" Rose is shouting. "Tell him about the man and the leaves go on, you have to."

"No!"

"No what?" His eyebrows are up again.

"Nothing, I mean I just don't know much else that's all."

"Right, we'll leave it for now; I'll probably be back tomorrow. Do you have anyone who can be with you tonight?"

"No, I'm alright, I've got Flossie, she's my dog."

Flossie as usual knowing she's not allowed in

the café must have been on the stairs behind the closed door listening. "Woof" can be heard in reply.

"Goodbye Mrs Philips."

"Goodbye." My hands can hardly turn the locks on the door I'm shaking so much but at least it's over for now.

"Well, that was a waste of time, wasn't it?"

"Just what do you mean by that Rose? Don't you get me into any more trouble with your remarks and butting in and anyway, why weren't you here when I really needed you huh?"

"Kitty I'm not talking to you if you're taking that tone of voice with me."

"Good, then please leave; go on, off on one of your trips. Go do some haunting in someone else's home and leave me alone!" I'm screaming into thin air; I can't help it.

"Silence is golden" is just another thing my beloved Gran used to say when our lovely cottage at Headingley was still and peaceful. How I wish I could be transported back to those days, this time with appreciation not teenage boredom. Tonight I don't want silence, I don't want time to think, right that's it, Queen to the rescue, not our sovereign no better than that, QUEEN and Freddie Mercury as loud as my eardrums can manage. That will get rid of any remnants of thoughts and Rose!

Dancing between the tables in Crumbs isn't so easy, well not the way I dance but at least my energetic arm and leg movements are starting to disperse the images in my head. With a flower behind each ear and a bottle of water for a microphone and my eyes tightly shut with the glare from the stage lights I'm the great Freddie Mercury harmonising with him.

"We are the champions; we are the champions, no time for losers".

BANG, BANG.

"Cos we are the champions..."

BANG, BANG, BANG.

My eyes are wide open now, what's going on? Startled, my first thought is Rose, she's throwing the furniture around or maybe one of her "heavier friends" is. No, I'm wrong; everything is still around me, a bit skew-whiff from my dancing but still there. Freddie is still belting it out without me, and two shapes are belting it out on my glass door! It's one of those moments where you don't know what to do first, music off or door open, music off won.

"Ah, it warms my heart to see you have recovered from your shocking experience Mrs Philips, may we come in there are a few more details needing to be cleared up." His Irish voice is holding more than a hint of sarcasm. Detective Chief Inspector O'Donoghue's big bulk is filling my doorway, but I can see to the side a dark haired, shorter figure and a glimpse of a blue shirt that is familiar. Hell's bells! Why isn't he in Harrogate? He must have seen Sergeant Benson leaving Crumbs.

"Come in." To cover my embarrassment, I am walking to the kitchen area. "Can I get you a drink?"

"No thank you I think we had better crack on, sure there's a lot more we need to cover." He's looking straight into my eyes with his icy blue ones. "Now you've had time to...shall we say "think", there will be more you can fill in the gaps with." DCI O'Donoghue's broad hand is gesturing towards a chair he's pulled out. Sergeant Benson is sitting next to him, I can't even look into those icy blue eyes, but I can feel them penetrating my whole being, scouring my brain for any untruths. In a flash, memories of our times at the Spiritual Churches are playing out before me. Lessons on how to protect yourself, surrounding the whole body in a golden light of protection. It may be hypocritical, but my options are pretty thin right now so here goes.

Chapter Nine

Sergeant Benson had hardly turned the car out of the market square when Sally was rattling the door handle.

"I thought our Cameron and Doughnut were never leaving love, it's a long time since I hung round street corners. Don't look like that I mean as a kid love."

Actually, it was the name that made me look, it's a nice strong name it suits his dark looks. Sally is hugging me tightly, rocking me gently as if I were one of her children.

"News spreads fast love, our Amy, my niece, lives further along in the council houses; she spotted our Cameron arriving and watched it all. Her Mum rang my Chris, and I hot footed it round here, was it awful love? Come on that's it, sit down love let's have a brew, you're looking very pale, he can be a bit tough old Doughnut can."

"Old Doughnut?"

"Chief Inspector O'Donoghue, that's what they call him at the station. Our Annie cleans there, has done for over twenty years. Apparently, the lads and lasses there call him that, not to his face of course. Don't get me wrong love they all have a lot of respect for him, they say he's tough but fair and can be a real Irish charmer at times. Was he tough on you?"

"No but I have a feeling it's yet to come."

"Well drink this you'll feel better and tell me everything, two heads are better than one love."

Now how many times have I heard that before but it's often true.

Sally's an excellent listener, that's probably why she knows so much, people open up to her and she pours out tea and sympathy. Her eyes have widened at times, but she has listened without commenting just sipping her tea, crunching on her biscuit and nodding occasionally.

"Right," she's brushing fallen crumbs into a little pile on the tablecloth then onto her plate. "You need to write down everything that's happened whilst it's fresh in your mind love then tell our Cameron. I mean everything."

"I can't do that, they already think I'm involved somehow and then seeing me in here dancing around, no I just can't, nobody will take me seriously, "Oh yes Chief Inspector I knew she was in trouble because her tea leaves indicated it and my dead godmother told me". I'll just dig a deeper hole for myself if I do."

"But you can't withhold evidence."

"What evidence? It got washed away."

"Point taken love, but you can't change what happened, get some paper and a pen and let's crack on and do it together; you can keep it just in case."

To please her I get a pen and some paper. I

suppose in a way, deep down, it's the sensible thing to do it whilst it's fresh in my mind but now it's in black and white it looks even more unbelievable. The hate is deepening.

"What now?"

"Nothing, just wait, the police will be back. If you won't tell our Cameron then stick to what you told them, it's the truth apart from the reasons behind it. Don't worry love. Now what about tomorrow's cakes, have you got plenty in the freezer? If today's been anything to go by it will be a bumper Bank Holiday Monday, the gossips will be clambering to have tea and cakes here, wait and see love." She's looking quite pleased with herself, I'm not quite sure if I like the idea of a load of ghouls in my tearoom. "There's nothing like a catastrophe or a good murder to bring the good folk of Wetherby out for a good nosy and seeing as the Post Office is closed then where else but here love? Right are you sure I can't help you with anything?"

"No thanks Sally, you've been wonderful, see you tomorrow."

Where would I be without my wonderful freezer, baking till gone midnight that's where. Taking a cheesecake, two sponge cakes, a chocolate cake and a box of Fat Rascals out to defrost I'm hoping the week doesn't carry on like this or my freezer will be almost empty, I know I have enough cream, raspberries and strawberries in the fridge because I bought extra yesterday. Great that's the two sponges sorted. I can whip up some chocolate buttercream in the morning when I do the scones and there's a tin of black cherries in the cupboard for the decoration, now should I put oranges on top of the cheesecake? Yes, alright. I'm sorted now everything is mentally arranged and I feel a little easier knowing that Crumbs will still be able to meet with the demands Sally is predicting. Personally, I'm dreading it, I'm on show and I don't want to be.

"Come on down Flossie let's have a quick walk and a bag of chips before bed."

"Woof."

Flossie is down in a flash, tail wagging, her pink lead in her mouth. She's so cute and she's my little dog now, who would have believed just over a month ago that all this would be mine and I'd be a number one murder suspect as well? For a moment the mild evening air feels chilly. Standing on the patio I can still see Miss Taylor sitting there looking anxious as the dark stranger talked to her. I can't shake the feeling that I've met him before but when I only saw him side on how sure can I be? A little shiver is running right through my body and suddenly I just want to get away from here and walk.

"Just chips is it love?" Madge is one of my customers and works evenings in the Wetherby Whaler fish and chip shop.

"Oh, go on Madge put a haddock on as well please, if I'm going to be bad I may as well be downright wicked."

It's the smell, once you're in the shop those enticing vinegary smells play with your inner strength and weaken you.

"Mushy peas?" she's laughing now.

"Ooh naughty, yes please but no scraps." I've got to be strong somewhere along the line. "Thanks Madge, see you."

"Bye love, I've put you a broken fish in for Flossie."

"You're a gem Madge."

Next time she comes into Crumbs I'll make sure she gets a treat from me. People can be so kind. I love Yorkshire folk; they may tell it as it is, but they can be kindness itself.

Feeling full of good thoughts with the box of hot, delicious, well salted and vinegared delights in my hand, my pace is quicker heading for a bench overlooking the river. Too much steam inside the box can ruin the crispy batter.

"Bliss Flossie, what more could we want girl?"

Neither Flossie or I can deny that sitting here as it's growing dark but still warm eating fish and chips in the open air is anything but heavenly.

"Great minds think alike. May I join you?" a voice says somewhere behind me. It's Cameron, Sergeant Benson complete with a box of fish and chips. He's got curry sauce on his. That's a man thing, curry sauce, although I do occasionally sway that way myself. Looking into his eyes wow, I could sway given the chance!

"Good evening officer, you've caught me red-handed."

Totally cringeworthy but I can't help mocking a little, I know it's unkind of me but in a way it's a test. If he replies in a friendly way then I know he's a good one, if he gives me a "Doughnut scowl" then I'll be on my guard. He's smiling but with his warm brown eyes as well. Not bad, not bad at all. Let him eat, it's giving me the chance to watch him again, twice in one night, not bad, He's a strictly no messing, just get on with it sort, never mind the small wooden fork he is straight in with his fingers, another man thing, A psychologist would have some deep and meaningful rot to say but I'm reading into it that he just likes his food in a down to earth way, I likey! Flossie, having no airs and graces herself, is just the same only noisier.

"Kate?" He suddenly stops eating and turns slightly on the bench. You could knock me down with a feather I'm so in shock from that one word. "Kate, this is strictly between us and maybe I'm sticking my neck out here, but Sally has hinted you could tell me more."

"What did she say?" I'm shrinking back against the bench.

"It's what she wouldn't say that is ringing bells." The eyes are searching mine but I can't look back. "Look we all knew and respected Rose, I'm not sure how much I can go with all that stuff, but Chris certainly does and plenty more of my lot come to think of it. If you're hiding anything back it won't look good for you, my Chief has a reputation and a nose for anything not quite right and it's starting to twitch."

So that's it! Nicey, nicey get me to squeal then wham! I'm back in there guilty as hell! I'm starting to get annoyed now, forget the chemistry building up around me; he's a man watching his own back, wanting a lead to look good in Doughnut's eyes. Typical.

"Oh, get off your high horse and tell him Kitty, get on with it I've better things to do than worry over you."

Mentally I'm trying to scream at Rose to tell her to stop interfering but it's impossible, I can say the words slowly but there's no way anyone can put enough power into it through the mind. As usual she's ignoring me.

"Tell him about the leaves and the man, you think you know him."

"I've told him about the man, he wasn't there long enough to see him." Oh lord that wasn't in my thoughts, that was out loud.

"Yes, you mentioned the man, we've checked with the Miss Passmores, they've never seen him before, nobody else took much notice of him. I just get the feeling your reasons for going to see her were completely different to your statement."

"Why should they be?"

"Sally's a bad liar, she's a wonderful, open person

and she's struggling."

"Liar, liar, pants on fire."

I'm turning towards the voice and glaring but what I need right now are the Ghostbusters. With a sigh he's closing his box up and wiping his mouth on a tissue. Standing in front of me and looking down into my face which I can feel is starting to redden. I'm forcing myself to look back and I can see a mixture of frustration and concern there.

"Please think about it, someone out there did a hideous crime to a lovely lady, and we will find them and anything else along the way."

His words "anything else along the way" stayed with me long after he had walked away.

"You fool; you should have told him my dear, what's wrong in saying what you saw?"

"Because Rose, I don't know how much I can believe in all this, don't you understand that? Hospitals are full of poor souls who talk to themselves, give me more proof Rose, show yourself or leave me alone."

She has left me alone and I feel dreadful, torn between anger, disbelief and hurt at my harsh words to someone I loved and owe so much to. I need to walk and think.

"Let's walk all those lovely but bad calories off Flossie, come on girl we'll go the long way around the riverside and down towards the Knaresborough Road."

Flossie is just looking at me without her usual reply. I have a feeling she would have settled for a night by the television, but I need to be outside, I can think better that way.

"No choice Flossie, I win."

"Woof."

There's a smell of grass in the warm evening air and the occasional waft of sausages and burgers from back garden barbecues. It's dusk but children are still enjoying the chance to play out in their gardens a bit later than usual. As Flossie and I cut through the streets from the river towards Wetherby High School the shrieks and childish laughter from the safety of their gardens is making me smile. Until it suddenly hits me, how safe are they? Miss Taylor was in the safety of her garden. Life goes on all around whatever tragedy has happened, tomorrow the people will be loading up their cars and doing the usual Bank Holiday trek to Scarborough or Bridlington, eager for a glimpse of the sea. The main road only a stone's throw away from here will be bumper to bumper. The sensible ones will stay at home and continue with the gardening or swamp the DIY stores, another Bank Holiday trend!

Smiling to myself has become another habit but what do you do when there's nobody to smile at, well apart from Flossie that is. Before I'd even realised which way my feet have taken me, I'm approaching the street running towards the back of Miss Taylor's bungalow, a route I've taken a couple of times since Flossie arrived. It's quieter around here and seems darker, no children's voices but then families don't usually buy bungalows, it's more a later stage in a couple's life known as "downsizing". These bungalows being so spacious don't really come into that exact estate agent category, but older couples snap them up at a hefty price. That's a point, who inherits Miss Taylor's bungalow? Sally should know if she had any family around here. There's tape across the back gate, the whole street just looks so quiet, curtains pulled tightly across windows with not so much as a chink of light escaping. A street in mourning, suddenly I feel so sad, and I just want to walk quickly to the corner ahead and cross over York Road to the Esso garage on the opposite side. That way I'm not walking directly past her front gate.

Without any warning a tall, dark figure suddenly charges around the corner smashing straight into my right shoulder knocking me backwards. I've dropped Flossie's lead and I'm desperately trying to steady myself from falling onto the pavement. In a flash two strong hands are grabbing my upper arms and pulling me towards what seems to be the dark tower that's crashed into me. Pain is searing through my shoulder and Flossie is going berserk at my feet, jumping up and adding more chaos. My face is brushing against something soft as in that split moment I'm saved from a nasty fall. In the dark I didn't see anyone as we both collided at the corner it was an accident, but it hurts like hell.

"Sorry I didn't see you," a voice is saying in the

dark.

Just as I'm looking up about to say something the hands are gone, my God he's legging it. The tall, dark haired figure is running down the street I've just walked up, boy he sure can run fast. Charming, why the hurry? I'm rubbing my shoulder, but Flossie is still going berserk.

"Flossie quieten down, I'm alright what's wrong with you?"

Something is not right; she never reacts like this, but I don't want any neighbours coming out so I'm trying to grab her lead and get going quickly. My whole arm is smarting, the pig! He couldn't even stop long enough to apologise properly, men again, everything they do in life is about them and their needs.

Flossie has suddenly decided to go sniffing along the pavement. I'm getting more used to the stop, start routine involved with dog walking but sometimes it still grates on me. Why can't dogs just walk and enjoy the freedom and exercise?

"Come on Sherlock, we're not going left, we're crossing the road here." But Flossie is on her trail and pulling me around the corner and down to Miss Taylor's bungalow.

Bunches of flowers in cellophane wrapping, many with bows and cards attached are lined up along Miss Taylor's wall. Standing straight like sentries guarding the home she loved and died in. Seeing how much others thought and cared for her is a very moving sight. I can feel my eyes filling up with tears, this is what I wanted to avoid, I have my own memories and sadly they're not all good.

"Flossie don't knock them down, come away, come on," pulling on her lead is doing no good plus she's shaking her head. "If you don't stop these tantrums, it's the vet for you madam!" That's the nearest I get to a "wait till your father comes home and I will tell him what you're like" threat. She's stopped at a bunch of pink roses, sniffing and wagging her tail, she's trying to bite the stalks, she'll destroy them if she doesn't stop.

"Flossie, stop!" That's my sternest voice without shouting loudly into the dark, still night. I'll just have to somehow get them out of her mouth. "Come on girl, that's right let me have them, preferably without all the slobber Flossie, yuck! That's it girl, you just redeemed yourself good girl."

Flossie has given in. Maybe she understands I mean business, that's good, one to me. I know I'm nosy, I can't help it but if people didn't want their private thoughts being read then they shouldn't put them on the cards. I can just about read them thanks to the streetlight outside the next bungalow. Turning towards the light I can see there's only one line written in the centre of the florist's card, "Just when I'd found you x"

Wow, that's pretty strong stuff, did she have a lover? It certainly looks like it, our quiet but pleasant librarian had found love and now it's all over, too late, that's so sad. I'd better stand them back up with the others, she deserves that.

Bending down to replace the roses suddenly sends a sharp pain shooting through my shoulder.

"Ouch that hurts, thanks a million I hope I bump into you one day, whoever you are, accidentally with a Morrisons trolley!" It's like the pain has activated a light switch in my brain, the card on the roses, the tearaway dark figure, was he the lover leaving them in the darkness and running? Ooh this is hot stuff!

"Come on Flossie, home girl, I've got something to do."

"Woof."

I've got into the habit of leaving some lights on in Crumbs when I walk Flossie at night. It never seemed to bother me when I was on my own back in Leeds but somehow here it does. Maybe because of the garden and the fact that nobody lives above the other shops either side of mine. Come to think of it, I'm the only person in the market square after closing time. The glow from the kitchen window is very welcoming as we walk up the path through the gate. Mental note to myself, remember to get some of those security lights put in.

Things are starting to bother me, little things but nagging all the same. The feeling I know Miss Taylor's young man is still there and tonight's strange happenings, do they all connect together? I need to sit down and look at the list again.

"OK girl think now, think about what happened tonight." I'm talking out loud again, so what it helps me to concentrate. "Think of what you sensed." Closing my eyes might help me work through it better.

"Visualise my dear like I used to try and teach you, that's it don't spoil it just listen to me, keep your eyes closed, that's right."

I was almost falling, he was tall, dark haired, something soft brushed against my cheek as he pulled me up, his fleece! But there's more, I know there's more.

"Now Kitty, feel the fleece, feel it against your cheek."

I'm doing as I'm told; let's face it she's back so I might as well let her help me.

"You've got it brushing you, now breathe in, what can you smell?"

"Can't you do this Rose; you can breathe in? Prove it, use your powers!"

"My dear I may be able to float around as you put it, but you are the one with the earthly senses, now please back to concentrating."

Is this for real? It had better be or I'm truly stumped...

"Gently now, steady, not too deeply you'll just fall asleep, that's nice, in and out, in and out, now zoom in on the fleece, good girl."

I'm zooming! Well, I think I am, in and out, in and out, just a split-second it was soft against my right cheek. He smells, not nice and not of any fabric conditioner either, no I'm wrong there is a slight whiff of lemon. Good I'm getting there! I can actually do this.

"Concentrate Kate! Don't let your mind wander or you will lose it." Rose is in her stern schoolmarm role, steering me back on track. "Think about the smell, is it strong? Familiar?"

"Familiar yes." It's in my nostrils now making me wrinkle my nose against the sharpness. "Bleach, it could be bleach."

"Keep calm, you're grasping at straws, think about it more carefully. Visualise bleaching the loo, is it that?"

"Not quite no, it's something else, I know it."

"In and out my dear, in and out." Rose is gently whispering like a midwife at a birth, gently but firmly encouraging calm and productivity.

Wham! It's there in front of me, Tuesday nights at Headingley and Gran dragging a soggy rolled up towel out of my Tesco carrier bag and my sopping wet swimming costume falling out of it onto the kitchen floor. The stench used to put me off my milk and biscuits!

"Swimming baths, that's it swimming bath water, what do you call it, that stuff they put in the water?" I'm really excited now; my hands are flapping up and down like a seal-another bad habit.

"Chlorine."

"That's it, chlorine, wow this is good, what do I do now? Rose? Rose? Nooooo!" she's gone again, was it really her or just me? "Thank you, thank you Rose," I whisper, just in case it was her. My heart's racing a little with the excitement, now's the time for a chamomile tea and another good think.

It's way past my bedtime but sleep wouldn't come to me even if I tried. The soothing chamomile tea has relaxed my body but allowed my brain to work. I'm not a sporty person; strewth I fell in a crumpled heap and cracked a rib the first time I did a headstand against the wall bars at school. No, my only sporty activities have been with Matt the Rat. Looking back in all honesty I don't think he would ever have got any medals either. Nasty but true, still his name is in big capitals on a fresh page of my notes. Underlined three times does not mean anything believe me other than he is the only way I could have had contact with anyone sporty. I've listed the events I attended with him as the dutiful but often bored wife the year before we split up or rather before he played away. The list to the left for daytime events which only has two and they don't seem very promising; one was a motorsport do at the Yorkshire Post and one a presentation at Moor Allerton Golf Club. Lovely people but none of the right age group are springing to mind. My eyes keep being drawn to the list on the right for the evening events and one event in particular. It was an evening do, a black-tie event. Matt always looks so handsome in his dinner suit, and I was wearing a full length strappy red dress I'd fallen in love with and spent a fortune on. It all seems so long ago now, and I can't imagine ever having the chance to dress up for a posh affair again.

"So, think girl, why is this one standing out? Who did I meet there?" The only way is to do a reconstruction in my mind just like they do on Crimewatch. Painful or not it is the only way.

Headingley Carnegie Stadium in Leeds, home of Yorkshire Cricket and Rugby is just down the road from where I lived with Gran and of course Rose next door. It's bang in the centre of Headingley and from the outside with its weird, modern shaped architecture and colours it looks to me more like a space age ride at Disneyland but then as I said, I'm not sporty. Its events room is very popular and apart from all the boring speeches and usual manly "nod nod, wink wink, ladies present" stupid jokes it was a thoroughly good evening. I'm always first to be on the dance floor, after sitting through all the speeches and after a few drinks who cares what the other stuck-up models parading as wives and girlfriends think. Half of them are usually hired for the night, nod nod, wink wink.

"Ok now do what Rose told you. Eyes closed and concentrate, picture the room." My hands are open resting on the table with my palms upwards. It's what Gran and Rose used to do when meditating and somehow it just feels right for me too.

"In and out, in and out" I'm telling myself as before when I thought Rose was instructing me. I can see various men standing at the front, no that's not him, no. I'm watching an action replay in my mind's eye of athletes and coaches receiving awards. Bla de bla de bla, lots of dull talk about the

Olympics and working towards golds. My bladder is reacting to all the water I'd drunk alongside the wine with our meal. That's interesting I can feel the symptoms, or maybe it's the chamomile tea I've just drunk.

Yes, I can recall how I drifted through for half an hour fidgeting in my chair trying to pluck up courage to move and relieve myself. Men were coming and going all the time but that's accepted, a lady and particularly one in a red dress is a bit more of a focal point.

After half an hour it was getting to be a touch and go situation. I chose to go. I can see myself suddenly pushing back my chair and banging straight into the chap at the back of me. That's the problem with speeches and tables of any shape; someone always has to turn around. He'd pulled his chair further out and was sitting sideways to watch.

"It's him, I'm sure it's him!" I'm so excited. "Come on concentrate more, where was he from? Did he get an award?" I'm trying hard to remember, willing myself to visualise more. Uri Geller eat your heart out! I recall the dark hair, spiked slightly at the front, around 35ish but that's all, I only saw his profile, the right side. In the garden I saw his left side, well that's almost all of him, two sides are better than one. There has to be something else but what? I'm sure as hell not ringing up the Rat to ask about tables. Will Headingley corporate events team still have a listing after all this time? I doubt it; we didn't keep them at the hotel. What else? Think, think, chair out, bump, me apologising but trying to get my skirt in one hand and control my chair with my other which was difficult when clutching onto an evening bag as well. He answered me! That's it, he said it was his fault and apologised. He spoke; I can hear him in that same soft Southern accent. I've done it, I've found him!

Just as I've reached a high, I'm catapulting back down again. "You haven't found him you clot; you've found a voice." I'm shouting at myself, disappointment filling my body.

Right, what now? I've got to think, did I overhear anything to do with the table behind me? Not sure.

Eureka! The Olympic bit, what's his name was mentioned, Sports Centres, university involvement, notes, all going over my head at the time. The bald-headed speaker with a red face and expanding waistline got over enthusiastic when he talked about fencing, I remember him lunging forward thrusting an imaginary foil nearly falling over. Too many whiskeys and too many free lunches made him look like one of those kiddies toys that wobble sideways but never actually fall over. I began to drift as he droned on about some big connections with Leeds University and he pointed beyond our table, and everyone clapped. There was only one table directly behind ours, some to the other side of it but no he pointed behind ours. My heart is pounding; I've done it I could have a lead at last wow!

Chapter Ten

The hands on the clock should be whizzing round we've been so run off our feet with customers but they're not. Spring Bank Holiday Monday this year is behaving itself and doing exactly what the weatherman forecast, the whole weekend has been sunny and mostly clear blue skies. Today there is a gentle hint of a breeze but it's warm and very welcoming. Simon and Charlotte have carried some of the tables and chairs from inside out onto the grass. Judging by how popular it is I'm going to have to fit another trip in to buy extra garden furniture but when?

Needless to say, I'm feeling very frustrated and all morning my mind has been drifting, going over and over my discovery last night. Sally knows I've had a breakthrough but there's been no chance to tell her yet, surely these people will want to move on soon. They are but more happy sightseers keep replacing them, just smile Kate I keep telling myself, smile wider.

"Hello Mr Potter, how lovely to see you. Have you been for a walk?"

"No not yet, it just gets so claustrophobic always in the apartment boxed in by four walls. Oh, never mind me my dear just a sit in your garden with tea and scones and I'll be tickety boo in no time."

Bless him and his gentlemanly ways, my smile is genuine now. "Let's find you a seat in the garden then, you may have to share though."

"What could be more perfect my dear than human contact."

Any more and I'll be adopting him or crying. A quick glance around tells me all the seats are taken, it's a similar case with inside. Poor Mr Potter he's standing next to me, and I swear I can feel his disappointment.

"Come on Rose, if you're around can you please whisper in someone's ear and get them to go please, now if it's possible thank you." I'm saying all this to myself but not expecting any miracles of course. The words have hardly left my over cluttered mind when the chair legs of a table in the corner to the left of me suddenly scrape across the patio flagstones. Bingo! It either worked through Rose or the couple just needed to move anyway, who cares I have a result but just in case I'm giving a quick thank you to Rose. There's an elderly couple still drinking and eating cake at the table but I'm sure they will share.

"Do you mind if this gentleman joins you?"

"Be our guest," the husband is actually pulling out a chair for Mr Potter, that's a good sign.

"I'll just clear the table and then take your order Mr Potter."

"Oh, my usual please my dear; this is just splendid thank you."

As I'm filling the teapot and another one with hot water, I suddenly have a brainwave which is good for me under the circumstances. Brilliant! This is something right up Mr Potter's street. Happy with my plans I'm going to take an extra pot of tea for the couple at the table by way of a thank you and in the hope they will stay and chat with Mr Potter a little longer.

Arriving at the table I'm a little surprised they're on first name terms already, surely it didn't take me that long to get everything together on the tray.

"Oh my dear I can't believe it, may I introduce Bob and Elizabeth Jenkins. Bob and I started working life together many many years ago in Leeds. Good days, oh yes good days. They've retired and are looking around these parts for property, wonderful just wonderful." Mr Potter is in his element, He's a lovely man perhaps I don't need to adopt him just yet, but I'll still put my plan to him later.

"That's nice; please have some more tea on the house as my welcoming to Wetherby." There it couldn't have been easier.

I'm walking away and I can hear Mr Potter saying, "Lovely girl Kate, I knew her godmother Rose, wonderful woman left her this place, wouldn't dream of going anywhere else. Got her godmother's touch with the baking for sure."

Aaw bless his well pressed pants, He's restored my faith in men, shame he's too old.

"Someone's cheered you up love, Kate I'm going to have to sit down soon love, my feet don't belong to me, and they need a good airing love, they're on fire."

"Sorry Sally, go now I'll manage, have love's young dream eaten yet?"

"They've snatched at some food like me love but I have a feeling they'd like to go together."

"Leave it to me, I'll get it sorted, you go down the garden it's bound to quieten down soon."

Sally left for the bottom of the garden with a ham, cheese and pickle baguette, salad on the side and a beaker of tea. Clearing some tables I can see she's happily munching away down by the shed talking to Flossie as she eats, sandals off her lovely legs and feet the only part of her in the sun. That's it Sally, get them tanned I wish I could. My legs are white from the winter's covering up. Come to think of it a quick deforestation wouldn't go amiss either, then perhaps I could put a skirt on. Another mental note into my cluttered brain. Shave my legs, all of them not just a circle around my ankles. Well, that's the only bit that shows if my trouser leg comes up in winter.

It's a miracle. Like the parting of the seas, it's slowed down; customers are busy elsewhere for now, this will give the kids a chance to be together. Ok so I'm a softie but everyone likes playing Cupid now and again.

"Off you go, half an hour then you can have another ten minutes later but it may not be together, OK?"

"Thanks Kate, see you," Simon's smiling.

"Make sure you have a break too Kate, you can't keep going without one." Charlotte's concern is touching.

"OK little mother, go on before it's too late."

Mother, oh no I suppose I should ring Carol soon; I've kept putting it off and now I'm just so busy. Surely she wouldn't hear all that way away about my involvement in the murder, no it's not possible. Now what can I eat, no not chicken I'm having that tonight with pasta. I'll just have a Sally special.

Snatching mouthfuls behind the counter doesn't look very professional but who cares, my stomach thinks my throat's been cut as Gran would say. Oh no! The Miss Passmores just passed by, please, please don't come in please.........too late they're back, I wonder why they did that? Theodora's face looks harder and sterner than usual; strewth she's a scary one alright. Poor Flora's face is slightly pink trailing in behind clutching her blue handbag with both hands as though someone's going to snatch it from her. Today they seem to be embracing the fine warm weather and wearing identical yellow dresses with little bunches of blue flowers on belts at the waist and with full skirts. Knitted blue cardigans in cable stitch and other intricate patterns I recognise from Gran's knitting days are both fastened at the neck with the top button. They're mad both of them, they must check each other before leaving the house, it's bordering on the obsessive to me. Smile Kate, without lettuce between your teeth that's it a quick swig of water, done.

"Good afternoon, ladies and a Happy Holiday to you." Why the hell did I say that? Because they make me nervous that's why.

"Happy Holiday? This isn't America, this is Wetherby, England." Dora's pinched; stern face is making me blush. "Never mind all that rubbish is there a seat in the garden? We only want the garden."

Her authoritative voice is making my customers sitting around stop mid drinking and eating to glance at the obnoxious female. The sight of this pair dressed alike is enough to stop any conversation on any occasion but top it with Dora's rudeness; well you have a floorshow for free.

"I'm sure there is but you may have to share a table."

"Share? We're not in the habit of sharing anything."

I bet you're not you miserable old bat except your terrible dress sense.

"Let me see what I can do." Fortunately, a young family are just leaving as we walk out into the garden, that's a relief. "I'll just clear this table; it won't take a moment. You can be deciding on what you want."

"What we want is to be able to sit down."

Then get back to your own garden you

miserable old devil. I'm getting angry but trying to look calm, smile just smile. Sally's mouthing to me asking if I need help but I'm shaking my head. Why should her break be ruined by such a horrible person.

Right, everything is on the tray and I'm just double checking so she can't have another snipe at me, that's fine, come on Kate out into the arena, face the foe.

"If you need any more milk just shout." Dora's eyebrow has shot up making her look even more like an evil witch in a Disney cartoon.

"Ah good afternoon, ladies," Mr Potter is saving the day bless him. "Will I be seeing you at the Gardening Club on Wednesday night?"

"Good afternoon, Mr Potter, of course we will be there." Dora is actually turning and smiling sweetly at Mr Potter the horrible old bat is smiling! She's evil that one but now she's showing a new side to her I'd never have believed, wow I'm really stunned.

Sally's come back inside and looks totally refreshed I really don't know how she does it, I feel like I need a week under the duvet.

"Did you see that outside, old dingy Dora smiling and drooling over Mr Potter?"

"Oh that, yes I did love but that was nothing you should see her in action at the Medical Centre, a real little vamp with the men she is."

"No! Tell me more; I need some good juicy gossip."

"Yes love, God's honest truth if she's dealing with women, she's what you see, a nasty old battle-axe but men!" Sally's shaking her head. "With men, her whole face changes, just melts, she smiles, her eyes open wider, and she tends to lean forward over the counter." Sally's laughing now as she demonstrates Dora's actions; they're quite something if Sally's not exaggerating then that woman's definitely got a dual personality.

I'm feeling quite strange, sort of lightheaded, not queasy as such more unsettled, sort of anxious but not anxious, disturbed that's it. I'm just working through my self-analysis as I slice some tomatoes. I don't understand but as soon as I've done this food, drink and a sit down should help.

"Kate my dear, are you alright my dear? I've called you a few times?"

Perhaps spinning round fast with a sharp knife pointing directly at a customer is not exactly the ideal thing to do given my recent circumstances.

"Oh, I'm sorry Mr Potter; I was away with the fairies there. You're wanting to pay, yes of course."

"Are you sure you're alright?" His eyes are on the knife still pointing at chest level. "I'm sorry my dear, you're having a tough old time at the moment aren't you what with poor Miss Taylor so soon after Rose? Can I help in anyway? Not with the baking of course, no goodness me, cooking and all that was never on my duty. I'm better now but then thank heavens for Marks and Spencer's I say." He's chuckling at his own thoughts.

"Mr Potter you're an angel I did want to ask you something."

"Ask away my dear, anything to set the tongues around here wagging is fine by me," gesturing towards the garden. "Life has been rather dull these past few years but there's life in the old dog yet."

"Too right there is, it's about your love of gardening. I did ask you to look at the roses; I was wondering if you have time to do more than that for me?"

"Only the Big Man knows how much time I have my dear but tell me what you had in mind."

"Perhaps coming in a couple of hours a week to keep up with the grass cutting and the fruit trees need sorting out, that kind of thing."

Mr Potter's smile is lighting up his whole face and suddenly it looks years younger. There's a twinkle in his eyes. "My dear it will be a considerable pleasure and one I will relish. May I ask a favour of you, something I've been trying to pluck up courage to ask?"

Oh no! It's about the tea leaves and what I stupidly blurted out, drat it, what the heck can I say?

"It's just my dear wife would never allow me to have a dog, all the dog hairs you know, well yes you do of course you do, will you allow me to take Flossie for the odd constitutional?"

Now that's a word I haven't heard in years, listen to me I sound ancient!

"Mr Potter you can walk Flossie whenever you have the time, just ask her."

Now he's looking a little confused at that.

"She barks once for yes and shakes her head for no."

"Well, I never, a little lady of extreme intelligence. May I?" pointing to the garden.

"Let me get her lead I know what the answer will be, oh there's just a little matter first though."

"Don't tell me I need a licence or dog walking lessons."

"No but you'd better take these just in case." Well, if he wants to do the job he needs the right tools doesn't he. With Flossie's lead I'm holding out some little "poopsie" bags and I've given him one of the disposable gloves from my stash.

"Oh yes, quite, best to be prepared my dear, boy scouts and all that, thank you."

He's really happy even with the prospect of poo scooping lurking around. I'm just hoping she holds fast till tonight, cross your legs, Flossie!

"Woof!"

This is funny really; I'm here waving them off as though she's my little girl going to play in the park. Can you believe it I'm actually smiling and waving from the kitchen door then wham Dora Passmore's pinched face is glaring at me from the corner table like a slap across my cheek. "Turn the other cheek" Gran would say, that's right dismal

Dora take this! I'm turning and grinning full on at her, holding her glare with my eyes, full beam like a car's headlights at night. She can't take it! I've zapped her good and proper! Hey ho, one to me.

4:00 PM couldn't come fast enough for me but it's been a great first Bank Holiday opening. It should be a lot easier this week as the love birds have more time to work here from now on. Sally is a real gem, but I have to remember she has a family and their needs come first. Cleaning is over and we're sitting having our usual drink and assassination session of the day.

"So, what's your next plan Kate love? I could tell you've been thinking about what to do all day."

"Don't tell me you've turned psychedelic too?"

"I wish."

By the time I've told her about the mystery man, shown her my notes and told her my theories her face has gone through several changes. Now it's showing concern.

"So, if you track him down on your laptop what are you going to do love? You can't go meeting him it could be dangerous."

"I can, I've got to, it's another piece of the jigsaw puzzle."

"Tell our Cameron love, please, promise me."

"I'm not bothering the police; they've got their own methods and for all we know they could have found something already. Besides what would I say? Just because a man ran into me doesn't mean he killed Miss Taylor. If he was her toyboy they'll find out."

"Then promise me you will tell me everything before you go anywhere love. So, I know where you're going and who you're with."

"And what time I'll be back, ok Mother I promise. Come on now, back to your family with you."

Sally's gone; Flossie is napping upstairs after her long walk with Mr Potter. It's great I may be able to get away with a short walk along by the river later; just I need to eat as thinking is making me ravenous.

"Music, now what shall I have on whilst I eat my chicken and pasta? That's it something Italian, aha Andrea Bocelli, perfectisimo, perfectisimo."

"Katerine, Katerine..." He's singing away, Italian is so romantic all I need is a good Italian wine or maybe just a good Italian would be better! Both will have to wait; the wine will make me sleepy and I've baking and "stalking" on the internet to do. A good Italian wow that would be great. Do they do takeaway men? If so, I can always ring my order in later, now hold that thought.

The kitchen clock says 8:13 PM, mission accomplished and not bad though I say so myself. Never underestimate the humble loaf cake; I adore them. It is my ambition to do a revival of all the old-fashioned family favourites. When I have time that is. By doubling the basic mixture and changing a few ingredients to my preference I now have cooling one large orange and chocolate chip loaf cake and a cinnamon, cherry and raisin one. My love of chocolate holds no boundaries; it's what we need to survive the stress of life, that's why I'm just waiting for my extra chocolatey speciality of Kate cakes to finish baking. Both chocolate cakes should be cool by 10ish, one I'll fill with buttercream and the other I'll put cream and fruit in tomorrow morning. Everyone loves chocolate cake. I've got one of Sally's light pastry cases defrosting which I'm filling tomorrow morning. Gran used to make a wonderful Manchester Tart with left over pastry; it's lovely on a warm day. A good spread of seedless raspberry jam along the bottom and up the sides then pour in very thick custard. The trick is to keep stirring it as it cools so it doesn't go lumpy. Then set it in the fridge and then sprinkle desiccated coconut all over the top. Kept refrigerated the slices of custardy pie served with fruit and a dollop of cream are ecstasy. Pure heaven on a plate, cheap and one any family can do together. Happy times Gran.

The blinds need to come down now it's starting to get dusky outside. This is the time I love and always did with Rose. Crumbs is warm and very cosy with all the delicious baking smells and the lights in the square twinkling through the windows. In my mind I can see ahead to Christmas with all the square lit up with small Christmas trees above each shop and a giant one at the end all glowing with coloured lights. Here I am practically planning my Christmas menu and we've only just gone into spring. After the bad winter we've had why on earth am I thinking of that? Because I am a dreamer.

There's the buzzer, the cakes are ready.

"You beauties, come to Mummy that's it. Mmm you smell divine, onto the racks to cool with you." One day I'll bottle the smell and call it "Kate's cakes for all". My dreams are being interrupted by the telephone.

"Hello Crumbs Tearooms."

"Good evening, Mrs Philips it's Sergeant Benson. Would it be possible to pop by for a chat?"

"Sure, what time in the morning were you thinking of?"

"I wasn't, I meant now."

"Oh, as in right now this minute?"

"If it's not a problem."

"No of course it isn't. I'll have the kettle on."

"See you soon."

Looking at the clock it's 8:35 PM, don't the police have a home to go to? Even in Midsomer Murders Inspector Barnaby goes home to Joyce and her dubious evening meals and he's always pouring out a glass of wine, I think to cover the taste of what she's cooked. The thought hasn't even left my mind and there's knocking on the door. I hope he's not with the Irish Hulk that will be too much.

"Come in, tea or coffee?"

Gosh he looks gorgeous and certainly is not dressed for work, slow down my beating heart don't be foolish. He's got jeans on that fit in all the right places, a soft looking V necked sweater in a delicate light mint green shade over what must be a white t-shirt, his shoes I notice are black, shiny and soft leather and not too pointy or squared off at the ends, just right, yummy, yummy. Calm down Kate, stop reacting like a teenager.

"Please sit down, sorry did you say coffee?" My ogling has totally blocked out whatever he said.

"Yes please, white no sugar."

Why would he need sweetening? Perish the thought.

"Is this formal, do I need my solicitor present?"

Well, when I'm sitting facing a hunk with only coffee cups to stop me devouring him what else can I foolishly say? A lot believe me. He's looking over at me as I'm preparing the coffee and without asking him, I'm warming some scones.

"Thank you, Mrs Philips." He's smiling as I give him his coffee and scone. "Please sit down, this is purely informal as you can see," his strong, brown hand is indicating his clothes, wow!

"I've just been over at Chris and Sally's for tea and please before you say anything I was invited a few weeks ago. We're a close family and it's what we do."

I can feel myself colouring up with the recollection of our last stormy meeting.

"Sally is very loyal to you, but I can read her like a book, I just want you to be able to talk to me off the record."

"Do it, do it Kitty, you've no idea what you're getting yourself involved in and I can't help you."

Why on earth does she always turn up when I don't need her, or do I? But then, does she? Actually turn up I mean. Oh Lord this is nutty. Rose's voice seems to be coming from the seat next to him so that's where my eyes are focussed but it's useless there's nothing.

"Mmm he smells nice Kitty, all showered and manly like in the adverts."

"Stop it!"

Cameron's hand which was just about to put the half of a scone up to his mouth is hovering, his eyes looking from me to the empty seat beside him.

"Excuse me? Shouldn't I be eating this?"

"Sorry, sorry, yes please do."

He's put it back down on the plate.

"Mrs Philips, come on now, what's going on? Let's not play games just tell me and about your list."

"My list, what list?"

"The one that's covered with names or is it an invitation list for a party because I'm afraid Miss Taylor will not be able to attend." He's pointing to the table next to us where I'd left the list and my laptop ready to work on.

"May I?" Cameron's picking up the list; it seems I don't have much choice. "Why is the Headingley Stadium listed, where does that come in?"

"Um a possible venue?" Why couldn't I have said

that with more conviction?

"For what?"

"My 30th birthday party plus divorce party all in one." Well to me it sounds plausible. His eyes are twinkling wickedly now.

"So much information, thank you."

"Pardon?"

"Oh for goodness sake Kitty now is not the time to go all coy on us, he likes you isn't that much obvious?" Rose is sounding cross.

"No, not for me," I'm muttering.

"Well, I don't expect so for you as you're the one organising this so-called party. Kate come on, come clean please."

"Kate, Kate there I told you. He likes you so get on with it now." Rose is excited, I'm glaring at the empty chair, how do you send foul looks to nothingness?

My mind's going into overdrive. I can tell him bits, the bits that anyone could have seen, in the garden, the bump. Surely the police have gone through the flowers, well if they haven't that's their fault. I'll just fudge my way through; after all I haven't found the mystery lover yet, have I? That's it, sorted, here goes.

His delicious, warm, fudge brown coloured eyes have held mine for what seems like a lifetime, ooh if only! In the end I've waffled my way through about the incidents and really come clean about Rose. I think it was a clever diversion and anyway it's true. He must know Chris had readings with

Rose if they're such a close family, so he'll know that's all true.

"Well, that's it, you've blown it my dear and you've made me out to be a raving headcase," Rose's voice is sarcastically chipping in.

"Says who? I'm talking to thin air" I'm trying hard to transfer my thoughts, so I don't look any worse than I have already.

"Kitty there's no need to take that tone, just be careful my dear."

It worked again; well at least now I know how to cover my ramblings up, just listen to me, is this truly happening? He's looking at his watch, maybe he has a date.

"I'm sorry I'm keeping you when you should be elsewhere. Sorry about the ramblings."

"Don't be, it's understandable what you've been through but please all I ask is don't go playing Miss Marple, talk to me. It's a big, bad world out there, believe me I know."

I'm just looking at him, I don't want to nod, I don't want to lie to him, best just stand up and give him the chance to escape to his date.

"Thank you, Sergeant, for listening." I'm now holding open the door.

"Take care; you know where to find me."

Ooh how I wish, then he's gone, and I can smell the fresh showery smell as he passed through the door. Lucky girl whoever she is.

Chapter Eleven

I've cut a deal with Flossie. Half an hour's playing ball down the full length of the garden instead of our usual walk. It's just after 9:00 PM and I'm really not feeling easy tonight about walking around so late, maybe it's what Cameron said but I'm also itching to get onto my laptop and do my search. Perhaps that's not fair to Flossie but she did have an extra long walk with Mr Potter, and she did shake her head in a "no" when asked if she minded not going out tonight. It's fine, the fruit trees thrive on her tiddles.

It seems Rose has gone back "upstairs" as she and Gran used to call the Spirit world, that's if of course she was even here in the first place, because I'm sitting browsing websites uninterrupted. Long may it remain that way! Not having names to go by is going to make my task harder but I'm getting there slowly but surely.

"OK that's more like it." Computers have never been my thing; I only used them for my work at the Ramada Jarvis and now for Crumbs' stock. To me, people get obsessed with spending hours looking up things they'd no interest in before. Let it be said they do have their uses, as of course in this instance. In everyday terms what I'm doing is pure stalking but it's essential to my investigation.

"Ooh hark at me, "investigation"!" Well essentially it is. Miss Marple, indeed I happen to like Miss Marple, she's quaint and canny and she gets results. There's only one thing wrong with her, she's not real either but I can still make her my role model.

Googling to me is a stupid name for it, like ogling which it is really in a way but with a "g" in front, anyway Leeds Sports Centre near the university is now displayed on my screen. Clicking on "Gallery" has brought up some photos.

"That's it, that's the one I need." I'm now clicking on "Awards Ceremony" which took place at the Headingley Stadium. Someone had been trigger happy that night, there's 87 of them. All the little squares are dancing in front of my eyes; they might as well have been taken in black and white because apart from the odd glimpse of carpet that's all I can see. If I were a man I'd want a coloured bow tie, too penguinesque for me, even the females are all in the Addams Family black attire.

"Whoa girl what was that?" Going back to photo 68 there is just a slight flash of red showing, just a few inches. How exciting, this could help if I enlarge the photo. Holding my breath, I'm clicking and immediately a larger version has appeared across my screen. The photographer must have been somewhere behind me to my right. He's got all of my mystery man's table in with him turned sideways looking at the speaker. That's him though, I'd swear to it, the whole of his right side is in the shot, my chair and a little of my back. There's a small mark on his cheek which will be his right cheek, it's not a mole it looks more like a scratch or scar. Shame it had been getting dark that night but then I didn't really look at him properly it was all so quick. "Coaches Table" is coming up on screen but coaches of what, don't give me half the information. This is why I don't spend time on my laptop, I'm too impatient.

Stalking the Sports Centre's photos, activities and all the other newssheets I can find is making me stronger in my gym phobic beliefs. There are some unquestionably good looking, fit men in front of me but to me, any man who spends more time thinking about his own body is sadly missing out on quality things, namely me. I couldn't have a man who daren't eat a piece of cake, come on get real that's a mortal sin in my eyes. Come to think of it Cameron never refuses, now that's a plus mark for him.

All this sportiness is making me peckish and a break from the screen won't do any harm. Looking at the clock it's 10:21 PM. I'll just have some warm milk and a biscuit; I need to find out more but I also need to be going to my bed. Scones and cakes to finish in the morning mean another early start and I can't fob Flossie off again.

"Just another half an hour then that's it, so please Rose, Gran, a little less interference and some more help please. Oh no, my laptop's lost its connection what's going on?" I'm frantically checking my sockets and switches; everything seems alright so what's the problem? Just when I thought I was getting somewhere. "I hate computers!"

I'm tired and I'm feeling so frustrated it's not fair. Waggling cables is about as technical as I get but you never know. "One more waggle and then that's it, bed." Not that I expect to sleep even with the warm milk I'm too worked up to relax. Closing my eyes, I waggle for all the good it will do and a metallic clashing noise is coming from it. Not daring to look I'm like a child opening just one eye.

"Oh my God, what's this?"

Figures in white with face shields are lunging at each other with foils, prancing around the screen like a scene from the Three Musketeers.

"Where on earth did this come from? I didn't click onto anything related to fencing." I can hear a voice in the background occasionally prompting them, it's not clear but something is telling me to turn up the volume.

There's a definite Southern accent there I know it is, yes, the voice is what I'd call educated rather than a "Ra" voice. Wowee it's him, it's got to be, I don't know how but thank you, just in case for helping me. So, fencing, let's see what comes up if I type in fencing at Leeds Sports Centre. Not being able to cross my fingers whilst typing I'm doing the next best thing, crossing my legs. Just another teeny-weeny fault of mine, I'm ever so superstitious about some things. I suppose I sit on the fence a bit but daren't chance it. Here goes.

Now at last, I have a name. Alex Granger, it sounds a strong name but whether it's him is a different matter. There hadn't been an awful lot of information about him but I'm sure I can fudge my way through a call tomorrow morning. Well, I'm looking at it this way; it would be a shame not to put to good use once more the skills I learnt at the Ramada Jarvis Hotel. Fudging your way out of a difficult situation when faced with awkward guests is an attribute quickly acquired in the trade.

Putting my laptop to sleep I'm feeling quite proud of myself. MI5 don't know what they're missing. Sleep, I need some sleep, tomorrow is going to be quite a day starting with baking, oh my goodness I've not put them in the cake boxes yet, I wonder if there are any other private investigators or government spies at this very moment masquerading as bakers, role reversal and all that. Too many deep and meaningful thoughts are not good for me before bedtime, tomorrow is another day.

Flossie is yanking my duvet off and I'm hanging onto it, someone has to give in before it rips.

"Oh, come on Flossie, just five more minutes lying here in the sun please, you can join me if you want."

Flossie is shaking her head.

"I guess that's a no then."

"Woof."

My bedroom is bathed in early morning sun and it's so warming on my face through the partially closed or indeed partially opened curtains. Whichever way you look at it it's wonderful. I don't want to move till I'm well and truly baked.

"Baked!" the magic word has me running starkers for the shower, wobbly bits unashamedly wobbling, nobody is perfect!

Not bad, I'm only 14 minutes behind my usual schedule and there are 48 beautifully well risen and crunchy topped scones sitting on the racks cooling down. They're calling out to me "eat me, eat me" but I'm resisting all temptations, only just as if I do it would leave an uneven number and I'm not keen on that. Sometimes my batch gives me 49 or even 48 and a baby one for tasters then I'm in there faster than a wasp on a jar of jam but not today. Well, it will save the wobbly bits getting wobblier. No such hope with all the other daily temptations...

I usually shower after my baking and Flossie's walk but today with the shock has been topsy turvy and in a way better, it certainly woke me up. I don't know why I just got used to having a quick wash, clean teeth and on with the baking first. "You're never too old to learn some new tricks" Gran would say, with me it's fast becoming a matter of time.

I've quickly brought Sally up to speed with my "stalking" and tried to reassure her that my next plan will be carried out carefully. She now knows I told Cameron the situation, what she doesn't know is that not everything was revealed. Perhaps that's not fair but I don't want her worrying and in my view he's the detective so let him detect. As soon as we get the "elevenses brigade" served I'll make my phone call to Alex Granger. Shoppers start to think of a rest and a cuppa around 9:30-10:30 AM so why it's called elevenses is beyond me. People no longer have huge breakfasts, so I suppose that hunger calls earlier. It's starting to cloud over a little but blue sky and sun keep peeping through and it's pleasantly warm, that's the main thing. Everyone seems content with their lot so now is as good a time as any. Boy I'm feeling so nervous, but I know I can do it, that's it some positive thinking, right here goes.

The young girl on reception who has just answered my call seems pleasant and too cheerful, she has to be new, that's one in my favour. I'm waiting for Alex Granger to answer his phone, "come on, come on, pick it up please." I'm nervous and that plays terrible tricks with my bladder.

"I'm sorry Mr Granger isn't answering his phone."

I know that I've just had it ringing in my ear for ages, one day I shall state the obvious back to the operator but not today as I need her help.

"Do you know..." my query is cut short by her

over excited voice.

"Alex, ooh Alex, call for you," she's shouting somewhere across the echoey room. "One moment please he's just coming."

What does she mean by that? Coming to the phone or going back to his office? He's not going to want to discuss anything with people in their sweaty gym clothes milling around him.

"He's just gone back to his office, putting you through now." She's gone before I can say thank you, but I say it anyway. "Manners cost nothing" was another Gran saying.

"Alex Granger."

His voice is the same as on my laptop I'm sure it is, educated and Southern but is it the same as the one who bumped into me that night, it was so brief? It suddenly occurs to me how little thought I've given to all this, that's typical of me, all action.

"Mr Granger you don't know me, but I believe you do know someone I know; I mean knew."

"Oh yes and who might that be?" His voice has a hint of amusement in it; maybe it's a chat up line he's used to hearing. Well, he is a man in an environment full of hot, sweaty, panting females and of course men, he could be gay after all.

"Miss Taylor of Wetherby." That's it straight in for the kill, oh my God I can't believe I just thought that! But then he could have so I'll excuse myself.

"Mr Granger?" He's not answering me, don't put the phone down, don't, please don't I'm mentally relaying.

"What do you want?" His voice has changed, not nastily more to a flat, saddened tone.

"Well, there's a few things I'd like to discuss with you. I knew and liked Miss Taylor very much." I can't say to him I was the one who found her body, that might freak him out and I need to find out more. He certainly doesn't sound like a murderer but what do I know it's just a feeling, there was something in his voice.

"Can you come here to my workplace tomorrow evening after my class at 8:00 PM, you obviously know where I am, just ask at reception and they'll call me?"

"Thank you I'll see you at 8:00 PM in ..." but he's put the phone down. At least there will be plenty of people around as it's a busy sports centre and what I've seen of the website the entrance is large and open plan with floor length windows and a clear view of the swimming pool in front of the reception area. If we stay at one of the café seats overlooking the pool, it will be safe. I just have to think of what I'm going to say, that's the tricky part. I can hardly ask if he was her lover and then murdered her, out of what? Passion? Not when her head was in the pool it's more likely to be an argument over money so blackmail? Why hadn't I thought all this before rushing in? Fools rush in where angels fear to tread. Gran's words not mine let's face it I've never been a full-time angel, but I certainly fit the fool category.

Sally bless her is trying her best to be supportive

but I know she's far from happy about my plans. I'm breaking the rules today out of necessity and we're sitting at a table on the patio for our late lunch as Mr Potter is busy amongst the fruit trees, at least he's happy snipping here and there. Flossie is treating it as a game of fetch and diving on any twig that's falling to the ground. She has quite a stack over by her shed.

I've been trying to keep my voice low as there are some customers at the next table, a mother and daughter here for a day's outing, I can tell how close they are, and it's brought back memories and a pang of loneliness to me. Next to them ever splendant in bright orange dresses, pure white knitted cardigans, white shoes and large handbags are Flora and Dora Passmore. The colour isn't bad on Flora as her skin is a little more olive toned with the sun, but Dora's skin has taken on a strange yellowish tinge, not made any better by the pink blusher and orange lipstick they're both wearing. Do they have their own? I can't see them sharing lipstick besides Dora has demonstrated more than once that she has a mean streak, she won't let Flora try a forkful of her cake on the rare occasion she chooses something different.

"Well love I'm not going to change your mind and I bet telling our Cameron is out of the question?"

"It is." I'm trying not to spray crumbs from my mouth as I answer.

"What time is your appointment tomorrow

with this Alex Granger and do you know where this sports centre is?"

"It's just at the back of Leeds General Infirmary, I'm meeting him after 8:00 PM. Oh Sally I know you're worried but it will be safer to meet there than anywhere else. What on earth can happen with so many sweaty hunks running around in their shorts?"

"Ooh maybe I should come and be your bodyguard, just in case love!" She's giggling now, that's a good sign. "Don't want any of them hunks practising their press ups on you love."

I'm sure I heard a tut but maybe I'm mistaken. I've far too much to do and think about before tomorrow.

Talk about being organised, I'm quite proud of myself planning everything like a military operation. It's not easy to take time off when there's just myself running the show but tomorrow's cakes are happily defrosting, pies ordered from Sally and Mr Potter is taking an evening's stroll with Flossie. I've given him a back door key so he can settle her in afterwards so here I am about to walk through the sports centre door.

I'm a self-confessed gym phobic but this looks great, very impressive and no sweaty trainer smell! A large reception area is ahead of me with only one girl staffing it and she appears to be run off her feet answering the phone and dealing with the students. Turning back around as I'm watching, I can see through the floor to ceiling glass to the pool which for this time of night is quite busy. There's some café seating and a large circular stand full of pre-packed cakes, sandwiches, crisps and bottles and cans of drinks. Starbucks coffee and cake seems to be doing well, I thought this was supposed to be a healthy place all blood, sweat and tears well not the blood. I must have the wrong idea about exercising it seems quite nice here except the girls all look too fit and gorgeous, I'd show myself up. No, I'm not up to bearing flesh and sharing my wobbly bits with all and sundry.

"Can I help?" The smartly dressed receptionist is talking to me.

"Oh, sorry I was miles away."

"Are you booking in or are you a member?" She's saying in a tired voice.

"Neither, I have an appointment with Alex Granger, my name is Kate Philips." I'm smiling at her but she's already trying his extension. He's not answering and I'm very aware of a queue forming behind me. This must be the last rush of sweaty ladies before closing time. Suddenly I'm feeling very old again, there doesn't seem to be anyone over the age of 25, well not until Mr Granger turns up that is. I'm willing her not to say the classic "no reply" line.

"He is here I know he is; the fencing class was over 30 minutes ago and he usually catches up on some paperwork afterwards unless he's needed for anything of course."

Do I detect a slight flush of her cheeks? Feet are impatiently shuffling behind me.

"If you direct me to his office, I'll just wait for him I don't want to hold everyone up."

"Thank you I'm sure he will be fine with that. Go past the cake area, there's a fire door on your left and a large sports hall ahead of you, just stick your head in there will you to make sure. That's where he does his coaching. If Alex isn't there walk down the corridor alongside it up the steps at the end to his office, in fact when you go in the sports hall look down to the bottom end of it, his office has a large window overlooking it and see if the light is on."

Hopefully I've taken all this in I'm a bit rusty on messages since not working at the hotel.

"Thank you I'll come back if he doesn't turn up." She hasn't heard me; she's far too busy with a crowd of fit looking young men. Pass the fire door she said, done that, this must be the sports hall. Just pushing open the large door is a test of strength alone and I've just failed, nearly cutting half my body off trying to squeeze through. Empty and in darkness but the lights are on in the office window high up overlooking the hall. Now that would be too much of a distraction for me, a little perverted in my way of thinking with all that potential ogling. Right show some strength here and pull that door in one and squeeze out quickly, that's better. This narrow corridor feels like a rabbit run there's not a soul along here, I wouldn't want to be the last out in this place. Up two steps there's his door on the left, should I knock? Better to be business like so I'll knock. OK so now what, try the handle? We do have an appointment and it's now 8:15 PM, I'm not messing about here, I don't have the time, I might chicken out if I don't. Tough, I'm going in.

"Kitty don't do it!" Rose's voice is loud in my ear, she sounds manic, that's if she's real of course, which she isn't either way.

"Don't be silly I'm going in for an appointment." Why do I keep doing this, talking to thin air?

"Please Kitty you're letting yourself in for more than you can handle."

"Jealous are you Rose? Clark Gable not taking you off on a cloud somewhere tonight?"

"No, I just don't like bodies."

"That's a good one, where you are it's full of them." Laughing I'm pushing the door open hoping Alex Granger didn't hear my one-sided rantings from inside his office.

My rantings were definitely unheard. The office is empty. It's bigger than I expected and very tidy. Only the one desk with two comfortable looking chairs in front. One of the chairs is pulled out at an angle and that makes me want to straighten it to make it all look neat again. There's another window which is still a little open at the far end behind the desk. It's an outside wall and I'm guessing it probably looks out onto the side where

I parked my beloved Clio. No harm in checking she's alright. This is the first time I've been back to Leeds since leaving the "Marital Mess" and student areas are notorious hot spots for crime.

"Kitty be careful!" Rose is shouting.

"Rose, will you quit shouting at me just show yourself and talk sensibly." I'm spinning my head at all angles hoping for a glimpse as I pass the desk to check on my car from the window.

I think I'm screaming, well in my head I am but my throat feels constricted like in the nightmares I've had through the years when I've tried to cry out for help, but nothing will come out. The sight on the floor before me is worse than any nightmare and far bloodier. No amount of calling Alex Granger would have contacted him when he's lying on the floor behind his desk with a fencing foil thrust into his abdomen. I can't take my eyes off him, I need to, I must. His look is of sheer terror, it's in his eyes and his contorted face, my God this poor man didn't know what was happening to him! One bloodstained hand is still half gripping the blade of the foil where it's penetrating his body. The bottom half of his white shirt is now bright red with the loss of blood and the floor is covered, there's a pool of blood under my shoes. I'm swaying, no I can't and a voice inside me is telling me not to sit on the chairs, breathe just breathe in the air. I'm at the window gulping in the little air I can suck in.

"Oh Lord, why me, why again?"

Running back out onto the corridor I just can't stay in that room I can't, my head's feeling fuzzy. I've got to ring the police but not from there, my phone, where the hell is it? My searching fingers feel the shiny smooth casing of my phone at the bottom of my bag.

The words "murder and body" seem to be echoing around in my head. I've had to sit on the floor in the corridor before I fall on it. My eyes are fixed on my soft, pale grey leather ballet pumps, the ones I love and can walk for miles in, but not anymore. The dark browny red blood stains are up the sides and it's seeped into the ridge where the sole is glued to the upper leather pump. I suddenly want to rip them off, throw them away where they can't be seen but I can't, not yet, not till, oh my God. Tears are flowing now, and I can hear sirens, running feet and loud voices. Please don't let them make me go back in there, I just can't. I've got my knees up to my chest and my head tucked down with my arms wrapped around them hugging, hiding my face from the nastiness like a child.

All the rush of police activity and me being escorted to another office seems dreamlike now but here I am cupping a latte and feeling the warmth from the disposable cup seeping through my icy fingers. At least my teeth have stopped chattering, the nice bald-headed man in white has pronounced me alive just in shock! It's probably sliced years off me! Ugh wrong word. I can see through the office window that I'm at the back of reception, the pool has been emptied and the few swimmers have been allowed to dress and are now being questioned. The receptionist is crying and giving her statement with a lot of exaggerated pointing in my direction. I know how it looks I'm not stupid and I don't suppose Leeds City Police are either, I can't really think clearly at the moment but one thing I know for sure is someone didn't want him talking to me, but who? My prime suspect has just been done in, does this mean he wasn't Miss Taylor's killer or was he and this was revenge, or was he doing it for someone else? Later not now, all this needs thinking about later, right now I need to think how much to tell them about my appointment.

Chief Inspector Harris seems nicer than DCI O'Donoghue, less of an edge about him but that could be his way of tackling a suspect in the early stages, reeling them in gently. I've given him the same amount of information as I gave "Cameron", Sergeant Benson that is, the truth just not the whole truth, he appears to be satisfied for now.

"You say you found all this information out because you thought you recognised him in the garden and when he bumped into you?" Inspector Harris isn't looking at me, he's reading my statement.

"That's right."

"It seems a lot of trouble to go to, were you and Miss Taylor close?"

"No but she's been a customer for years." I

daren't look into his eyes.

"But no relation?"

What's he on about? Here we go, trick question time.

"No."

"It would appear you have an interest in solving these, shall we say puzzles." Now he's fixing me with his glare, not icy blue like Doughnut, He's half smiling and his brown eyes are crinkling at the sides but there's no warmth in them.

"Yes." Well what else can I say, I've decided to keep it short and to the point. How much more is he going to ask?

"Right Mrs Philips that's all for now, please keep yourself available and Mrs Philips remember Miss Marple wasn't real, but this is and believe me it can get even nastier yet."

"Thank you can I go now?" I've heard it all before.

"Yes, you can, are you alright to drive I can get you taken home in a car?"

"No thank you I'm perfectly fine now." I'm not but I just don't want any more police around me. What does he mean "it can get even nastier yet"? I just want to get home and away from this place, now I know why I'm a gym phobic as it kills in more ways than one if you're not.

The cooling night air hits me and like an alcoholic I'm practically gulping it in trying to clear my nostrils of all the deathly smells.

"Mrs Philips we really have to stop meeting

like this," the soft Irish accent behind me makes me jump and drop my car keys, the shock blasts through my body and I suddenly feel very lightheaded. I'm vaguely aware of a voice saying, "Catch her Benson."

Strong arms are around me but I'm feeling a cold draining sensation from my head, my face, going downwards, so am I.

Chapter Twelve

Strong coffee smells under my nose have brought me back into the land of the living, should I think that? Ugh my mind is all jumbled but I can still see him, the foil's handle inviting someone to pull it back out, to save him, only it wouldn't have done he was too far gone, gone! I want to crawl back into the black oblivious state of my faint but that is not possible.

"Drink some of this it will help, there's sugar in it to give you a quick boost." His eyes are still icy blue and cold, but his voice sounds softer, warmer.

"Thank you."

"Benson you drive Mrs Philips home and make sure she is in safely; I can manage here."

"Yes sir, shall I come back?"

"When you can."

I don't like the sound of that. "Why are you here?" I think I have a right to know, I'm involved in all this, something is not right here.

"Mrs Philips, villains have no boundaries, and this is my old stomping ground. Goodnight."

If this were any other night and I was sitting closely to Cameron Benson being driven somewhere romantic for the evening I'd have wallowed in his male presence, it isn't so I'm faking sleep! Oh come on, it's a last resort and one women all over the world will be doing right now, it's one of the three top fakes, I can't even think about the first and a headache wouldn't wash.

"We're home."

"Mmm, are we? Thank you." You're such a good actress Kate; I'm just congratulating myself and mentally applying for RADA.

"I'll put the kettle on, you need something to eat and drink."

Now that's gone and spoilt it all. He's going to probe, of course he is you dummy. He's a policeman.

The kitchen and upstairs lights are on just as I asked Mr Potter to do. Flossie probably needs a wee, I'll let her out for a few minutes, anything to stall the questioning, I desperately need some time to think.

"I'll just have to let Flossie out, Flossie come on girl," no answer, no bounding down the stairs to greet me. Suddenly Chief Inspector Harris's words are ringing in my ears and I'm up the stairs two at a time as quick as lightening. Thank God she's safely curled up in her bed by the chair gently snoring away. Flossie is all I have left in this blackening world, and I couldn't bear anything to part us now.

Sergeant Benson or Cameron as I secretly think of him has been busy in my kitchen. Tea and hot buttered crumpets with, I notice, one of my little pots of jam on the side. He's even put a paper serviette on each plate, I'm impressed.

"If you want a change of job, I'll take you on anytime." I can feel a blush threatening so I'm jumping up for some sugar, which I don't take and neither does he but needs must.

"Mrs Philips please just sit and eat; you need something you've had a nasty shock."

"You forgot the "again" part." I'm looking straight into his beautiful eyes now.

"Just eat then we'll talk, you know I have to but why ruin a good old English hot buttered crumpet."

His eyes have a twinkle in them I love and he's putting food first, my kind of food. If this was not serious, if he wasn't a policeman, if he was unattached, there are too many ifs. That's my life always so iffy.

It's the old ruling that food always tastes better when someone else prepares it and boy is it true. I've eaten both the crumpets and plastered them in strawberry jam which I would never think of doing, it's sacrilege in my eyes, even though I serve jam if requested. Sometimes the simplest things are best.

"Thank you I enjoyed that you were right. I did need some food."

"Glad to be of service Ma'am," he's saying, saluting mockingly.

"Come on then let's get it over with before I blubber."

He's looking me straight in the eyes and it's very hard to not look back, I'm trying to look elsewhere but I'm caught like a rabbit in a car's headlamps.

"Mrs Philips."

My hand has shot up to stop him speaking.

"Please I really would feel more comfortable if you call me Kate." Well, it's true! It is.

"Alright Kate, tell me what happened please, all of it this time."

Before I know it, I've told him everything, how I found Alex Granger on the photos, everything. It's like a weight lifted from my shoulders.

"Apart from sitting in the same room at the Headingley Stadium and the two brief encounters here in Wetherby you'd never had anything else to do with him?"

"No that's the honest truth."

"You just had a feeling, how?"

"What do you mean, how?"

"At last, we're progressing tell him Kitty, you have him listening to you now tell him, about me my dear."

"No, I can't!" Why on earth has Rose had to reappear?

"What do you mean you can't? You don't know?" He's looking puzzled.

"Go on now Kitty, you may not get another chance," Rose's voice is twittering to my right side. I can't help it I'm tired and I've just about had enough of all this on top of the murder, correction murders.

"Please excuse me one moment." I'm looking at him and crossing my fingers he'll not put the handcuffs on me straight away. Turning to my right I can't see a damned thing, this could just be my imagination but OK here goes, I don't care anymore what he thinks, I can't live like this.

"Rose please just leave me alone, you pop up uninvited, cause havoc, when I needed you most you couldn't even stay and help me tonight. I don't believe it's you Rose, I can't see you and I don't believe you so go on, go away."

"Kitty I explained I don't like dead bodies."

"You don't like dead bodies, that's great, just great. Rose if it is you then get it into your head you are one, dead, finito, kaput, gone."

"Don't be so cruel Kitty, not in front of your young man."

"He's not my young man; He's a policeman now go!"

"Alright you're upset my dear, so I'll leave you alone. Don't forget I'm here if you need me, I'm only a thought away my dear, we all are, goodnight."

"Goodnight!" I'm afraid I may have been shouting a little; OK a lot well my voice was definitely louder. Turning back, I'm expecting him to read the riot act and cart me off for some psychological tests, I can hardly blame him if he suggests therapy sessions.

"Finished?"

"So sorry. Yes, I am but it had to be done. I don't believe it's Rose, but it just keeps happening." I'm looking at him now trying to read his expression but it's hard to! "Maybe it's all the stress of the move and the divorce, let alone the murders and mayhem on top. Two, no three, deaths with Rose's. That's nearly all the most stressful times rolled into one, well it's not good for anyone. All the magazines say so, don't they?"

"They do indeed."

"Well, there, you know it all now. I'm surprised Sally didn't warn you."

"Warn me?"

"That I've turned into a raving nutcase."

"The jury is out on that one yet and anyhow I told you Sally is a bad liar but she's fiercely loyal to those she thinks are worth her loyalty. If you think you're a raving nutcase, then most of my family must be the same."

"But not you?"

"I'm open to all my family tell me and believe me that's plenty but I'm a policeman and like you I need proof."

"Do you think we'll ever get it?"

"Maybe, maybe not but it doesn't stop the good memories and the hope that we are being watched over and protected by those who cared most about us."

"So where did Miss Taylor and Alex Granger fail?" Suddenly I just feel so deeply saddened by it all.

"You know I can't explain that, it happens but I have to cling onto the fact that good will always overcome evil."

Strong words from Sergeant Benson tinged with a little spiritualism there, he's not telling me everything, I know that because "good will always overcome evil" were Rose's words. This time it's me looking at him searching his face for clues.

"Kate I've got to get back to Leeds." His eyes are showing concern.

"Can I ask how you got to know so quickly about what happened and me?"

"Kate we're not far behind you only we have different methods of investigation. Look please just leave all this to us. Two people have been killed and that's two too many for Wetherby."

"Only one in Wetherby. Alex Granger is, was from Leeds."

"So were you but you're here now."

"Meaning?"

"Meaning please just keep doing what you're good at here at Crumbs and leave the detecting to the police. I don't want you to get hurt." His eyes are looking me over appealing to me but his mouth has, without realising, churned out just the kind of garbage any girl with enough go in her won't take so easily.

One and two and three, I'm counting to myself before answering. I think in this case I need to.

"Right Sergeant Benson you'd better get back to catching your killer then and I'll get on and do what I do best." I can't stem the edginess in my voice but that's for him to live with, tough!

He looks hurt but he's at the door and I'm

politely holding it open for him even though my tongue is fighting inside my mouth to say what I really think.

"Make sure you lock up and put the alarm on Kate, don't take any risks please, I'll see you tomorrow."

"Well, you know I'll be here, doing what I'm good at. Goodnight." Men! Why are they all the same? I'm not helpless and I'm certainly not a whimpering, no brain falling to pieces at the edges bimbo just because I've found two bodies!

Hell's bells two bodies in less than a week. If this carries on Wetherby will be tipping Midsomer Murders off the body finding ratings but why and who? Cameron Benson was right in one thing, no matter what's happened I need to carry on with my business. Tomorrow's cakes are already in their boxes, but he's hit a nerve and I need to do something other than simmer away. Anger isn't the best way to bake unless it's to pound bread, so I've made myself a nice large cappuccino and sprinkled lashings of cocoa powder on the top. The oven's heating up whilst I discover just how much hair is on my top lip, judging by all the froth clinging on there's plenty. So what, I've never tried to be a glamour puss. It can stay another few days besides if it grows anymore, I can use it as a disguise!

"That's more like it no man is going to tell me what to do ever again. I'm me, body hair and all."

Feeling stronger I'm going to whack in some

buns first; they won't take long then a couple of marble cakes. I love swirling the chocolate and pink into the mixture. When you slice them, it's fascinating to see what pattern has been made and it looks so pretty on my plate.

Two racks of buns are cooling, and the cakes will be ready in five minutes. I've all these little babies to build up my reserve stock. Tomorrow time is needed to sit and make lists of things to bake and check and write my shopping list, supplies must be running low. The clock is showing 12:02 AM and Flossie needs to stretch her legs in the garden and do her tiddles whilst I wash up.

"Flossie come down girl." I'm calling her from the bottom of the stairs. "Hello sleepy head, did you have a nice walk with Mr Potter?"

"Woof."

"Go on then into the garden and don't chase anything that's crawling around in the dark."

Flossie is shaking her head; bless her she's bounding down towards the fruit trees, but it is quite dark down there. Extra mental note to myself to ring "Sparky" as we all call him about my outside lights in the garden. A shiver has just run all the way down my spine, what was that for? Looking down the garden into the darkness I can only just make out the trees and occasionally a bit of Flossie's white shape dashing around.

"Now don't get all stupid after all you've said about strength and men," I chide myself. "Wash up, tidy up and bed, that's for me."

Every time I put on my yellow rubber gloves it reminds me of a scene from a TV drama I saw, not a murder as such, no this had some saucy bits and prostitutes in it. Gran sat watching it with Rose or me depending on where we were staying at the time. She loved it but tutted at the "naughty bits". I was absolutely fascinated by the true-life drama set in the red-light district of Bradford. Since then, I can never resist giving my gloves a twang as I pull them on but not for the same reasons as the actress of course. It makes me smile every time. Right now, I need reasons to smile no matter how trivial they are.

Tonight's twanging session seems to echo in my quiet tearoom that's because for once I've not felt like music on in the background. Somehow it just didn't seem right, a little irreverent even though I didn't know him. The other reason is my mind is more open and usually better when I'm baking. Not so sure this time. Maybe I'm going round in circles, all I've come up with is that someone knew both the victims and how to find the last one easier than me but why? What's the motive? My number one suspect is now dead; someone else knew one if not both of them so was that person also being blackmailed by Alex? Did he have another lover here in Wetherby? An irate spouse would have no reason to kill Miss Taylor, only Alex Granger. Surely if Alex had killed Miss Taylor, he wouldn't place flowers there unless it was an act of remorse. Did Miss Taylor have more than one man and he killed the other through jealousy? That's what duelling was all about in years gone by, honour and all that. To me someone had to have a pretty strong thrust to drive that foil home and I don't know of any females who know their way around a fencing foil. It would take strength or immense hatred to do such a deadly deed. There's one more thought going around my head, jealousy is a powerful motive and not only male partners get jealous. I've never known Miss Taylor to have any partners of either sex, but I know someone who will know. Sally.

My head is fit to bursting with thoughts and tiredness. Clearing everything away and putting all the baking into boxes and the freezer has taken twice as long as usual. The clock is screaming at me 1:18 AM that means I've only five hours in my precious bed before starting all over again, am I mad? Looking around my wonderful teashop is answer enough. Flossie is barking away outside, what's got into her she's never this doggie talkative, it's a good job I don't have neighbours the racket she's making, must be for a fox or a rat. My hand is on the door handle, but it doesn't open, it's locked. I don't remember locking it, but I know I should.

"Flossie stop it now,"

"No Kitty! NO! NO! NO!" Rose is shouting so loudly it's really stopped me in my tracks. "Turn the light off quickly and look out of the window."

For once in my life, I've actually done as I'm told

without arguing, fear is rushing through my veins at express speed. Peering out into the black garden isn't easy. It's taken a couple of seconds for my eyes to adjust. I can't make anything out. If there's danger out there I've no idea what it is except Flossie is making enough noise to wake the dead! That thought has just sent a shudder through my body, it's all death around me at the moment and whatever Flossie is fighting I'm praying she's bigger and fiercer than the creature. There she is running from behind the shed around the trees, what's she chasing? I can't see well enough from here but whatever it is it must be dark coloured. There's something at the very bottom and I can see Flossie's white backside running down the path, she's going berserk now her barking is so high pitched. "BANG" the sound is reaching me magnified in the night air, that unmistakable bang of my gate being frantically shut. I think Flossie just saw off a human!

I must have been standing here quite a few minutes gripping onto the edge of the kitchen sink, the realisation that no animal could let itself out through the gate had quickly hit my brain full force. I'm shaking, what do I do? He didn't get into my home, should I call the police? But that will take up most of my last precious hours of sleep, that's if I do sleep. Flossie has just seen off a burglar and tomorrow, correction today, I'll call Sparky about fitting the outside lights. Whoever it was is highly unlikely to try anything again in a hurry. That's it then there's nothing anyone can do tonight; he was probably wearing gloves so there wouldn't even be fingerprints on the gate. Whatever happened out there Flossie had it covered and I'm sure she will be alerted to anything else as that noisy scene proved. Good old Flossie and just in case it was you Rose, thank you. I don't know if it was or not but it's not something I want to think about right now, tonight's been one hell of a night.

"Come on Flossie, you good girl I think you deserve a treat for that you're my little Scrappy Doo alright. I love you my little guardian angel, do you fancy a nice bit of chicken before bed?"

"Woof!"

"I thought so, and you certainly deserve it. Serviette madame?"

Flossie is shaking her head and looking at me as though I'm the daft one. Maybe she's right after tonight's episode, I need my bed.

Chapter Thirteen

After double checking all the locks and leaving the downstairs lights on as a precaution I fully expected to toss and turn all night. A girl can only take so much excitement in one day, and night. Remembering what Rose had once told me when I couldn't sleep because of worrying over my school exams, mainly because I never took enough notice in class and I'm basically a thicko, anyway I tried again and it worked a treat.

Rose had explained the roles different angels play in helping us through our lives with our man-made problems. Me being me at the time let it in one ear and out through the other, Gran's saying again. Something must have stuck in the grey matter in between and last night I asked my angel of sleep to help me and she or perhaps he did. Worth trying again just to make sure.

I've managed to drink two beakers of coffee and do my shopping lists. That's one job out of the way whilst the scones are in the oven.

"Flossie let's get a quick walk by the river now before the customers are hammering on the door for their morning cuppas."

"Woof."

As usual Flossie is first out bounding down the

garden like a racehorse, but she's stopped by the gate and is sniffing around and making a growling noise.

"Let me lock up, don't be so impatient Flossie."

The sky is overcast but with the brightness that makes you think it will clear away later. My tubs of flowers are doing well. I must remember to buy some "feed" for them. Early mornings and early evenings to me are special in gardens, you get all the wonderful green, flowery scents, everything smells fresh.

"Stop being so noisy Flossie I'm the only one around here allowed to have PMT."

Flossie's growling is now interspersed with an excited bark and looking down at her I can see why; she's guarding a very large and nasty looking claw ended hammer! Clearly someone had been intent on hammering on my door late last night and they were not looking for a drink and a slice of fruit cake.

"Flossie don't touch it sweetheart; I need to call the police."

"Woof."

Picking up the phone I'm really hoping Detective Sergeant Benson is on duty but it's early yet, so I doubt he'll be in before 9:00 AM. Last night would have been a late one in Leeds. It's ringing.

"Could you put me through to Sergeant Benson please?"

"I'm sorry he's not on duty yet, can I help you Madam?"

Madam! I hate that, I'm not a Madam, they live in houses of ill repute!

"Please could you ask him to call Kate Philips as soon as he arrives, he knows the number, something has happened that he needs to know about."

I added the last bit because I really don't want the desk sergeant doing a nod, nod, wink, wink "He's got a bit calling him" session with the others in the station.

What now? I can't touch the hammer, that much I do know from all of my TV series, Sally, I'll call Sally, she'll be up getting the kids their breakfast.

Mornings in Sally's house have to start with a proper breakfast and I'm feeling guilty for the interruption I must be causing.

"Hang on love one sec, will you? Chris, Chris are you out of the shower?"

I can hear Chris laughing but can't make out what he's saying but knowing him it will be something with an adult meaning.

"Quickly love before breakfast burns."

"Sally it's a bad time I'm sorry but I really need to get hold of Cameron."

"Mum, can we have beans with the sausages and scrambled eggs; I like beans, please, please!"

Suddenly three voices are chorusing in the background "Please Mum!"

"Shush you lot or you'll go out on only a bowl of Cornflakes like all the other kids in these streets!

Sorry love, Chris is taking over the cooking. Right now is it his mobile number you want? Pen ready love?" She gives me the number. "So why do you want our Cameron so early?"

"There's too much to tell right now but I need to get hold of him straight away, someone tried to break in last night after the murder. I'll tell you everything when you get here!"

"Murder! What murder? Another one? Are you alright love?"

"Sally just see to your family and I'll tell you later, thanks for the number, bye."

I can hear Sally's kids in the background saying "Murder, wow!" Children have ears like sonic devices detecting at all pitches and distances and I can imagine the questions going on as they have their sausages, scrambled egg and beans. She'll handle it, Sally always does.

Cameron is looking at me over the rim of his cup. His eyes have dark rings and look very tired but there's also concern for me showing. The hammer has been bagged up and yet another statement taken. My file must be getting thicker than the files on some of Wetherby's villains. He's wearing the same bluey grey suit from last night. The shirt is different but I'm almost sure the tie is the same. I've seen them on the television just keeping a spare shirt in a locker at work, changing and having a shave in the office, no time for decencies when there are big cases ongoing. Is this one of those big cases? It seems like it to me. I'm just sure the two murders are somehow linked.

"Have you been out all night? You look tired, I feel guilty because despite everything I slept quite well."

"Pretty much all night I just crashed on the sofa for a couple of hours and barely had time to shower and change."

I can smell the faint smell of Imperial Leather soap he must use so he did manage that.

"Sorry I stopped you, but it was the hammer that unnerved me."

"I'm glad you called." His look is of genuine concern and I'm having to look into my Earl Grey tea, He's making my tummy turn somersaults. Right now, I don't need any more complications in my life.

"Have you come up with anything further after last night?"

"Like what exactly?"

I'm not in the mood for playing games, that's so typical of a policeman. My time is just as precious as his, so what if this time I called him; this isn't a drop-in centre for tea and doughnuts!

"Why do all policemen answer a question with a question? Have you lot no idea how infuriating it is?" There that's telling him.

"Do we?"

My hands are going up like a proper Italian but this time they're stopped mid-air. Cameron is clasping them, his warm, long fingers totally covering mine bringing them back down to rest on the table. Strong but gentle as though he were catching a butterfly. He's still holding onto my hands and his voice is softer in my ears but I daren't look up.

"Kate that could have been you at the Sports Centre last night."

"I didn't kill Alex Granger, why should I? My only reasons for going were to find out more!" My voice is getting a notch too high but I'm full of different emotions and it's difficult to control them.

"That's not what I meant Kate, you were the only other person walking along the corridor to Alex Granger's office within minutes of him being killed. Think about it, one corridor leading nowhere else but the sports hall one end and the office the other, it could have been nasty."

"But nobody else was walking down there. I would have heard them, and the sports hall was empty."

"Can you be totally sure of that? You said it was dark in there and the door was very heavy, so you only managed to open it a little."

"Yes, and I squeezed through, but it seemed empty. The lights were on in his office window at the far end which overlooked the sports hall. I just left quickly."

"Kate the sports hall and the fire door which you passed at the beginning were the only places the killer could have escaped through. The fire door you would have heard rattling as you approached it because the bars across which are used as handles bang as the door is opened and closed."

"No, I didn't hear any noises at all."

"So, if the killer had still been trying to get away the sports hall would have been the nearest place."

"He could have already left before I arrived."

"He could have done; did you see any cars leaving the car park?"

"No, what about CCTV, what's that showing?"

"A total blank, not working and it hadn't been for 2 weeks apparently. It's all down to cuts in funding as everything is at the moment."

"Don't get me on that subject, you wouldn't like my comments on this so called our so-called leader."

His eyebrows have lifted.

"Do we ever really know what someone is planning and doing? The answer is a big NO because human nature has a way of making most people want more for themselves and to look after Number One."

"Whoa there, not everybody is the same." He's smiling broadly at me.

"Sorry I do get a little carried away on certain subjects."

"I'm sure you have every right to your opinions, but my concern is for you and your safety so no more Miss Marple please."

I'm looking at him, gosh he is gorgeous, but I've

made a vow to myself on behalf of all females never to be ruled by a man again. Anyway, he never asked me to promise did he, that's one mistake to him.

"Thank you for your concern but my business calls and I need to get ready for opening." Phew! A genuine excuse, thank heavens for Crumbs.

"I'll see you soon."

"See you."

Watching him leave with the bagged up hammer, giving a smile and a wave from the doorway is doing serious things to my poor old neglected hormonal balance. "Another time, another place" keeps going through my mind, well maybe just another time.

The ringing of a phone is something I can't stand, not the actual sound it makes but the impelling urgency which overtakes me to answer it immediately. Perhaps it is a deep-rooted fear of being rejected which I have been twice now if you can count my so-called mother Carol and now my husband Matt the Rat. I have to answer it quickly before the caller gives up. That's why I was good at my job as receptionist at the Ramada Jarvis. My sprint from the door to the phone in the kitchen area is getting faster; all the walking is paying off.

"Good morning, Crumbs Teashop." I'm trying to sound chirpy.

"Kate my darling it's your mum, how are you?"

How am I? If I swore, then now would be a good time. I'm...shocked! For starters Carol rarely rises before nine in the morning unless they're jetting off somewhere and she never calls herself "mum". Why now?

"I'm absolutely fine, wonderful, just about to open up Crumbs, the sun has been shining forever and business is well, busy very busy. How are you two?"

"Fine darling I'm thinking of doing the shops in Paris if I can get a flight."

Doing the shops in Paris! My God, Carol makes it sound like she's looking up the number 98 bus timetable to go into Leeds for the afternoon. I can't even remember the last time I was able to do even that!

"Oh right."

"Darling I just needed to know you're alright."

"Oh Lord here we go she's ill, she must be, something's wrong this is not the Carol I know."

"Carol what's wrong, you're worrying me now, tell me are you ill?" There's no sense in beating about the bush.

"No darling I'm in top shape or so my private health check told me last week, we both are, no it's you, I know something is wrong."

"There isn't."

"Rose and your Gran came to me in a dream last night and I just couldn't settle till I spoke to you. Lawrence had me a special breakfast sent in from my favourite restaurant, but I just couldn't touch it until I knew you were alright."

How the other half live as Gran would have said.

"Well, you can put it in the microwave and eat it now you know I'm fine. Carol sorry but I've got to go and open up Crumbs. The locals will get tea and coffee withdrawal symptoms if I don't. Thanks for ringing I'll speak to you again soon, bye."

I've put the phone down before she says anything else, but the shock of our conversation is still with me. It's unbelievable, after almost 30 years of denial, well it was denial, I always felt I'd done something wrong daring to be born, the last thing I want is for her to become all mumsy on me. No, I've got used to the old Carol and I prefer it that way.

Carol's call has driven me to strong drink, strong coffee so early in the day is today a necessity and Sally is partaking with me. In between bites of toast, she has asked me more questions than the KGB.

"You're not going to do anything silly like that again, going off on your own, you could have been killed, I won't let you!"

"Don't get all melodramatic Sally I'm not going looking for any trouble but there's something you're forgetting."

"What's that?"

"Somebody out there thinks I know more otherwise why were they here last night? With a hammer?"

"Talk to the police love, leave it to them, couldn't

they put someone on guard outside?"

"I don't need anyone I've got Flossie; besides it wouldn't be good for business, would it?"

"Don't you believe it love, they're a rum lot here this murder has spiced up their lives alright. Everyone is talking about it. If they get a link between last night's and Miss Taylor's, you'd better get some more baking done as Crumbs will be the place to be in."

How right Sally is. I've had to turn the music off because every table inside and out is full of gossiping locals, men and women. Music is just making them talk louder to each other and I'm starting to get a headache with it all.

"Do you lot mind if I just have a few minutes fresh air and a paracetamol?"

Simon and Charlotte are busy pouring out more water into teapots and water jugs and people are re-ordering, afraid to go home in case they miss anything.

"No go on we can manage." Charlotte is giving me her sweet smile.

"Thanks, I won't be long."

Down at the bottom end Mr Potter is weeding around the fruit trees. He looks like he could do with a break so I'm taking him tea and a piece of cake. His kind eyes are studying me as I pour out tea for us both.

"Thank you, Kate, most kind of you."

"No thank you Mr Potter for everything and walking Flossie, I don't know how I'd have managed without you yesterday."

"Bad thing wasn't it my dear and then last night's attempted burglary on top too, bad, I don't know what's going on in this place. Wetherby is such a lovely little town; it's a wicked world Kate, a truly wicked world."

We've fallen into a comfortable silence sitting together on the rug drinking our tea. This must be what it would have been like having a dad, picnics, walking Flossie together, helping with the gardening, playing with the grandchildren. Well, none of them are possible but somewhere I do have a dad that at least is real, and I would hope he is like Mr Potter, perhaps he is but with his own family far away from here.

"Penny for them young Kate."

"Oh, it's nothing, just a little daydreaming." Mr Potter is looking at me in a kindly way. "If you fancy a walk with Flossie, you'd be doing me a tremendous favour and the kettle will be on for your return. That's if you're not going anywhere." I'd forgotten he may now have other plans for the afternoon.

"My dear you and Flossie would be doing me the favour; it gets lonely sitting on my balcony looking down at everyone walking by the river."

Oh my heart strings have just been pulled tight. He's such a lovely man and deserves to have a lot more pleasure in his life. Flossie has woken up; I love to see her stretching with her front paws hanging out of the shed. After going behind the shed to do what comes naturally, she's bounding towards us, her little legs striding out happily, she even looks like she's grinning at us.

"Did you hear that Flossie, Mr Potter is taking you out this afternoon, so you be a good girl for him, promise?"

"Woof."

"Wonderful, my little friend and I will stretch our legs together. Now if you don't mind my dear, I shall crack on with my tidying up then go home to wash, change and have a spot of lunch."

"Please stay and have some lunch here, it's the least I can do for all your kindness."

"Thank you but another time my dear, I have some quiche and salad already prepared and a little rest on my balcony afterwards will be in order." He's playfully tickling Flossie behind the ears and under the chin and she's almost sighing with delight, the little minx! "I need to be refreshed for my hot date with the best looking girl in town don't I, eh? Sorry Kate, no offence to you intended."

"None taken, I must get back in there and give someone else a break from the gossip. See you later, afternoon tea for you and your lady friend is on me."

"Woof."

Sparky has rung to say in Great British workman tradition that he's running late, and he'll be coming to start on the outside lights tomorrow. Fridays are part of the mad weekend but what else can I say besides OK. My business head is saying good, I'm far too busy for interruptions but then there never will be a good time with the new Sunday openings. My own head is screaming out for it doing immediately, I hadn't realised till now how timid last night has left me. Don't be such a wuss Kate.

Market day in Wetherby always brings more people out and about and today being Thursday they're here in the square. I know the stall holders and Charlotte and Simon have had their work cut out popping out with take away orders for them. They don't mind, it gets them outside and I'm pleased to say neither of them have taken any liberties with the little spurts of freedom. They're good kids and I'm lucky to have them. It's after 2:30 PM now and the market square is quieter. Soon the stall holders will be dismantling their stands and we'll be able to see right across the square again. Flossie has gone out on her "date" and the kids are having their lunch at the bottom of the garden.

"Joseph, Mary my pins are playing up today love I've got a corn the size of a pea on top of my toe." Sally's standing on one leg like a stork. "My dad takes my mum's off with a razor blade. Just the top of it of course but that doesn't get the whole thing out now does it love? There's no way I'm letting my Chris loose on my feet."

"Why don't you nip out to Superdrug and get some corn plasters, you could do with a stretch and some air Sally."

"Thanks love I won't be long; do you need anything?"

"A good man, a life, a chance to wear some nice clothes and a chance to lie in bed on a morning, how am I doing?"

"Not good, I'll be off love and I'll get us a nice ice cream each will that do?"

I'm heading for the till. "Here take this and get us all one, the love birds could do with cooling down."

"Spoilsport."

My most favourite ice cream is the simplest and one I can never get anywhere except at the seaside, they've probably stopped making them now it's so long since I went to Scarborough. Rose, Gran and I used to walk through the town and sometimes come down in the "lift" to the sea front. The long way was walking down through the gardens, well I used to run when I was little as the winding paths seemed so steep. Fun days. The sweet shop that sold all the tacky seaside souvenirs was always our destination for three Wall's ice cream sandwiches. Gran insisted on unwrapping my block of vanilla ice cream and putting it together with the thin wafers in case I dropped it all. "There's a knack to doing this properly Kate" she used to say, handing me the paper to lick clean before binning it. The way I looked at it was an ice cream in my hand was worth more than one on the floor-my young adaptation of one of Gran's sayings.

Sally shot back into Crumbs all excited waving

two boxes of Cornetto's, not quite the same as my dream ice cream but still yummy.

"You'll never guess what I've just seen."

"Ok I'll give in straight away before the Cornetto melts." Hint, hint.

"Oh, sorry love here you are a nice strawberry one I'll just take these to the kids and bung the rest in the freezer for another time."

"Thanks Sally." I've soon got the wrapper off and all on my own, that just goes to show what a big girl I am now Gran. I'm still smiling at the thought when Sally barges back into the kitchen.

"Did you get your corn plasters?"

"Yes, love but that's not it, listen, guess who was walking along past Boots looking very chirpy and pink faced."

"Go on then who?" I've just had the gooey strawberry bit.

"Mr Potter and a female." Sally's voice has lowered a touch.

"Mr Potter took Flossie out on a date."

"Lord save us love keep up will you! I know he took Flossie out, but he's met a lady and he looked pretty pleased with himself too. They're coming here for tea later."

"How do you know that have you gone all psychic on me too?"

"Because I heard him ask her if she wanted to take tea with him."

"He might take her back to his apartment."

"To see his etchings love?" Sally's giggling.

“No, you’re right, Mr Potter is a gentleman and he’ll bring her here when he comes back with Flossie. Check we’ve got some good well risen and crunchy topped scones left will you Sally please. Mr Potter enjoys his cream teas. I’ll wash some strawberries to put on the side.”

“Stop fussing love you’ll give the game away, act naturally, shall I use that pretty china cake stand that was Rose’s?”

“Stop fussing Sally, act naturally.”

We look at each other and burst into fits of giggles.

“Right, you wash the strawberries love and I’ll give the cake stand a once over, just in case we have a visitor.”

“Agreed.”

Chapter Fourteen

Two quick barks, Flossie's way of shouting "I'm home", sounded from the garden and like any mum I rushed to the kitchen door to greet them. Flossie of course knows she has to stay at the bottom end but she's wagging her tail and has found her coming home treat I left by her water, she's happy and looks tired out. I know the feeling.

"Ah Kate may I introduce an old friend, a very dear old friend Peggy Dawson or Ferguson as I knew her. Peggy meet Kate, the best baker in Wetherby."

"Pleased to meet you Kate, Howard has told me such lovely things about you and Crumbs." Peggy has held her hand out to shake and she has covered mine with her other hand, so soft and warm and in a split-second I feel so much love and sadness all mixed up together being transferred from her to me. This lady is kind and caring I can feel it.

"Please take a seat, what would you like to drink Peggy?"

"Earl Grey please Kate."

"Oh, the same as Mr Potter."

Her smile has lit up her lovely oval face; she's petite with just a little roundness to her. I'd say she's younger than Mr Potter but that may be down to the girlish feather cut short hair framing her face. Glints of natural red hair are shining in the sun; if it's not natural I'd like to know what she uses. I really like this lady, I don't know how I feel so strongly about her, but I do, she radiates calm and love.

"Kate my dear may I use your facilities please before we eat?" He's holding up his hands.

"Oh yes of course, it's the door just through the kitchen."

"Thank you."

Mr Potter seems different, more relaxed and his already handsome features look younger if that's at all possible. His tanned face and arms are complimented by his pale lemon and blue striped short sleeved shirt and light beige trousers, even his white, thick hair looks different, trendier but that's impossible unless he'd been to the hairdressers en route. As he walks away from me towards the darker doorway, I've suddenly caught sight of a deep circle of light around his head, He's totally glowing, I've just seen his aura! This is becoming a habit.

Back in Crumbs, Sally is like a cat on hot bricks itching to know what's going on.

"Well come on, I can't wait, who is she?" At least it's fairly discreet whispering which is good for Sally.

"Wait till Mr Potter is out of the loo," I whisper back.

The door to the side of us opens and Mr Potter

appears smiling. Two pairs of eyes are on him, poor man he must feel like a teenager on his first date.

"I'll be out in a moment Mr Potter; cream teas alright for you both are they?"

"Splendid my dear and Peggy has Earl Grey tea."

"I know, just like you."

"Yes, thank you."

Sally is in with her questions faster than a greyhound at the dog track as soon as he's gone through the door.

"Well I never love it just goes to show there's always hope. I'm sure he looks years younger, go on out you go and find out some more."

"Shh! Be careful, they will hear us."

"Not them love I reckon they've got a lot of years to catch up on, let's hope we've not lost our gardener, he could be needing all his energy for better things."

"Sally! You're awful but I hope you're right, not about losing him though."

So much has happened in less than a week with the murders and my burglar it's nice to see something happier taking place. Peggy's light laughter and Mr Potter's deeper tones keep drifting into the kitchen; I'll take them some more tea as all that talking is bound to make them thirsty.

"Sorry to interrupt but I thought you might like some more tea; would you like anything else to eat?"

Mr Potter is looking towards Peggy, and I can see

the admiration in his eyes.

"Kate this has been so delicious thank you, but my waistband isn't elastic much to my regret, tea will be just perfect. I'm afraid we've taken up your table for a long time already but it's so wonderful being here catching up, it takes time at our ages."

Peggy's eyes are twinkling, and her face is slightly flushed with the sun and excitement.

"Please stay as long as you wish to, it's quieter now the market's packed up for the day."

"So much has changed since I was last here but it's still very peaceful".

"I don't know about that with all our recent events, when were you last in Wetherby?"

"I grew up here, but my family and I moved away over 30 years ago." Her head has gone slightly down, and a brief look of sadness has taken away the lovely smile. She's looking up again, smiling and trying to gain her composure. "It's so awful, Howard has told me about Betty Taylor, truly unbelievable. We went to the same school, Brownies, Girl Guides and then the occasional disco. I remember she loved to dance, so did Flora Passmore."

"Flora Passmore dancing at discos!" This is riveting stuff.

"We were young and carefree once Kate!" Peggy's laughing again and looking up into Mr Potter's eye. "Flora had quite a following of young men in those days. Dora used to go as well. I seem to remember Flora was keen on a handsome young man at one time. Did she marry him?" Peggy is asking Mr Potter.

"No, none of them married Peggy; they are all spinsters of the parish."

"That's a shame she seemed so in love with him but then Dora was always the one to get the men. I'm so surprised she never married either, love 'em and leave 'em was her motto. When did Betty Taylor come back from her travels? I'd left Wetherby just after she set off. Travelling around Italy with her aunt wasn't she, lucky girl."

"She was gone about 6 months altogether then her parents died tragically, and she came back and lived in the bungalow until her own tragic death."

This may seem rude but the old matchmaker instinct in me is twitching, I need to know more about these two. There's such a spark between them it has to be more than just nostalgia. OK here goes.

"So did you put your white flares on and do your John Travolta impersonations Mr Potter, I suppose that's where you two met?"

Peggy is flushing upwards!

"Err yes my dear I did occasionally go to the discos when I could, but I was working in Leeds at the time, dashing between the two places in my old Triumph Herald."

"Oh, your beloved white Triumph with the dodgy boot I remember it so well." Peggy's eyes have misted over. There's definitely a clue there.

"Is that where you met your wife Mr Potter?"

"Yes, I lodged with her parents for a while in Leeds. Peggy started work with the same building society and occasionally filled in duties in Leeds, but I knew her from home before that." He's covering his tracks I can tell, best leave it at that, no more embarrassment for these two lovely people.

"You're not leaving it just when it's getting juicy are you Kitty? Now I am disappointed in you," Rose is twittering away in my ear.

"Excuse me I have to clear some tables." I move away. "For goodness sake Rose, don't you pick your moments," I'm hissing back into thin air from what I hope is a safe distance two tables away. This is ludicrous. Rose's so called "voice" had left me alone for a little while and I'm in no hurry to hear it again, if it is her of course.

"Well, you could find out more, call yourself a detective, go on ask more questions it's rather juicy, you'll enjoy it."

"I'm not a detective and if you already know the answers then tell me. There that's a test for you, if you're real then tell me! I'm not upsetting two happy people for a figment of my imagination. You know all the answers so you should be helping people, remember what you said, "only do it for the good of others." Now if you're not going to be truly spiritual then please leave me alone."

"Kitty I'm always here to protect you but you must do the work, one day you will believe."

"And pigs may fly."

"Oh they do, well up here anyway."

"Goodbye Rose I've work to do, and I won't listen to any more silly words in my ears."

"Alright Kitty but I'll be back when the police come around."

"What police? When?"

She's gone, well I think she's gone, at least the voice or whatever it is has stopped. I can see Sally and the kids clearing and cleaning the now empty tearoom. It won't harm to close a little earlier today. Mr Potter and Peggy can always leave through the garden.

Now everyone's left for the night I can either sit in front of the television for an hour or crack on with tomorrow's cakes, it's so tempting to relax but the way my days are going I'd better crack on. If I'm quick I can get a walk in with Flossie and be back before it's dark although I wouldn't admit it to Sally last night has left me very nervous. At least Sparky will be here tomorrow.

Victoria sponges are quick and very easy to make, and the golden cakes are now fanning themselves on my cooling racks, two are for titivating in the morning and two are for the freezer. One will be a traditional Victoria sponge cake with jam and fresh cream filling and liberally dusted with icing sugar on top. The other will get filled with cream and raspberries with extra raspberries on top, lovely. Sally's pies will be locally grown rhubarb and a lemon meringue, something she has just perfected with a beautiful thick topping of meringue. Strawberries! I need some extra punnets for tomorrow, it's a good job Morrisons stays open at night. All this planning and baking and I haven't even thought about my own food. Right now, I'm just full to the top with all the gorgeous smells from the cakes. The easiest thing is to make an omelette and salad but that's keeping me here longer and I need to walk and get back. OK so I'm lazy but I'm feeling worn out mentally and physically so I figure a trip to Madge at the Wetherby Whaler is in order and I can eat whilst I'm walking. I solemnly promise to be more organised tomorrow and to eat a load of fresh fruit for dessert when I get back in, minus the cream of course.

Madge is as cheerful as ever and just as generous. Flossie is waiting outside wagging her tail in appreciation. The wafts of fish and chips as we walked over reached her nostrils before mine and she almost had me running the last bit of the way to the shop.

"You heard when Betty Taylor's funeral is yet love?" Madge's face is pink with the heat from cooking the fish and chips.

"No not yet Madge the police don't seem any nearer to finding her killer, I don't know what will happen."

"Shame, a right shame it is still I saw someone with Mr Potter today, a right nice surprise that was. Peggy Ferguson as she was then, I thought she'd come back for the funeral seeing as they were all pally together when they were young, her and those Passmore girls went to school together. "

"Yes, I've met Peggy, she's lovely."

"Howard Potter certainly thought so and between you and me she was head over heels in love with him, everyone could see the way that was going." Madge is leaning forward onto the counter her face all warm and glowing, happy to reminisce about old times. I'm praying another customer doesn't come in, I want to find out more about this, well it is interesting.

"Really, why didn't they marry?"

"He was from here, a bit older than her but lived and worked in Leeds. He used to come back to fill in occasionally at the branch here in Wetherby, that's where they must have started it."

"Started what?"

"Love, bless me what happens when two people click?" She's laughing.

"An affair?" So why didn't he marry her?"

"That's called bigamy love."

It took a few seconds for that to sink in.

"No!"

"Yes. Suddenly her parents, right proper churchy people they were, well they sold up and that was that till today."

"Poor old Mr Potter."

"He came back with that miserable wife of his, no children but he stuck with her pandering to her every need."

"Did his wife know?"

"Can't have done otherwise she wouldn't have let him come back to work at the building society branch here, by all accounts she never took a liking to these parts. She should have made friends with that Dora Passmore, two miserable devils together."

"How sad."

"Nowt so strange as folk love, who'd have guessed them Passmores would be spinsters. That Dora was a right "flighty piece". We all expected her to be the one to get caught."

Get caught, you mean married?"

"No love I mean pregnant but then them kind never do. It's always the innocent ones, isn't it? I mean look at..."

"Three haddock, two lots of chips and two pots of mushy peas please Madge."

Oh drat a stream of customers has arrived just as I am sure Madge was going to tell me something else I didn't already know. Still, I have learnt a few bits of my jigsaw puzzle concerning Mr Potter and Peggy. Her parents must have whisked her away to avoid a scandal, small town, loose tongues but she came back eventually and found him. How sweet, not many people get a second chance and I hope they do. "Don't go looking for love it will find you" I said that when I looked into Mr Potter's tea leaves. Could Peggy be the love finding him? Spooky!

Chief Inspector O'Donoghue and Sergeant

Benson are sitting in a car outside the back of Crumbs when I return, my heart has just sunk down to my boots. I almost feel like turning and running back around the street corner and hiding. Now I know what criminals feel like. Even Flossie has stopped in her tracks.

"Shall we run Flossie, leg it to the river?"

Flossie is looking at me and shaking her head in a "no".

"You're right we've done nothing wrong." Flossie is whimpering. "OK I mean I've done nothing wrong; they've probably seen us in their car mirror anyway."

"Woof."

Both car doors are opening. I can't look at Cameron, here goes, once more into battle.

"Good evening, gentlemen, please come in." One to me, I got the greeting in first, but this isn't a game, this is serious. "Tea or coffee?"

"Neither thank you Mrs Philips, I need to ask you a few questions."

This is serious, Doughnut's icy blue eyes are chilling me through.

"Fine, if you'll sit a few moments whilst I see to Flossie then I will see you."

Flossie is nicely settled upstairs, and I've put her the television on for a bit of company. She's happily watching Coronation Street curled up in her basket. I'll be blowed if he's going to stop me having a drink in front of me during his questioning, besides it will give me something to hold onto and stop my hands fidgeting. Back downstairs Cameron is seated but DCI O'Donoghue is pacing the floor looking at the menus then over to the shop window.

"Excuse me but I need a drink. I won't be a moment." I'll have a chamomile tea and hope it does the trick.

"A watched kettle never boils" was Gran's saying and how true it is, I've even poured a little out, so it's got less to boil and I'm still waiting. The palms of my hands feel moist, this is ridiculous I'm getting into a real tizz, and nothing's been said yet. That's the problem, the silence in the tearoom is only being cut by the bubbling of the water in the kettle. A quick glance over my shoulder has shown the large figure of DCI O'Donoghue still dominating my shop windows, staring out at goodness knows what with both hands in his pockets. I can almost see the whirring wheels going around in his head. My eyes look onto Cameron who is sitting facing the kitchen in his usual seat, his back to his boss and he's giving me a quick smile to reassure me, if only it did!

"Right Mrs Philips are you quite sure you're ready now, please be seated." His Irish accent holds a hint of sarcasm, how dare he say, "please be seated", this is my shop and I'll sit when I want to!

"Kitty calm down, don't let the brute get to you."

I've still got my back to them holding onto the kitchen surface. Why now of all times is Rose back, well the voice is. I'm mouthing, "go away, just go away please."

"Kitty grow up. I told you I'd be back when the police came now go and sit down and try to behave properly."

"Why don't you go swing on a star!"

Walking back to sit at the table I notice Cameron has his pen and writing pad in front of him. Doughnut is still looking out of the window, that's extremely rude of him, I don't have to put up with that.

"Inspector if you would kindly be seated, I was brought up to look at a person whilst talking to them as it's far more polite!"

There I have said it. How dare he try and intimidate me in such a manner. Cameron is smiling at me, but my eyes are fixed on DCI O'Donoghue. His hands have dropped from his pockets, and he has turned his head and body halfway around, one eyebrow is arched in a quizzical look. I can see he was going to say something and quickly corrected himself, there's no love lost between the two of us that's for certain.

"Whatever you do Kitty just answer the man, no messing just straight answers," she's twittering in my right ear and my hand has gone up to it and I'm pressing my forefinger against my ear canal, pushing it inwards trying to stop the voice. Cameron hasn't missed this and is looking at me and to the side with concern in his eyes. Now DCI O'Donoghue is seated in front of me his eyes piercing into mine. I wish I could spirit him back to the window.

"Mrs Philips apart from the two brief encounters with Alex Granger, you have never met him before, is that correct?"

"No, I had met him without knowing it at an event at Headingley Stadium."

"Ah yes so you did and because of this you suddenly set about to find him and arrange a meeting."

"Well yes I suppose so."

"You suppose so? Then were you or were you not at a meeting with him?"

"Yes, but I didn't meet him, not alive at any rate."

"And this meeting was all because of a whim. Female curiosity?"

Cameron has to have told him everything as it's a murder investigation and my betting is they've no leads yet so that's why he's back here with me.

"Yes."

The eyebrow has gone up again.

"Where did you park your car at the sports centre?"

"I drove down the side, the barrier was up, and I parked practically under Alex Granger's office window."

"Did you see his light on then?"

"No how could I? Until later I didn't even know which one was his office."

"So, you're not familiar with the sports centre?"

"I'm not familiar with any sports centres.

Walking Flossie is the only exercise I do."

"That is since you moved to Wetherby and what about when you lived in Leeds? You seem to have had a totally different lifestyle then. Correct me if I'm wrong Mrs Philips but that's how you first met Alex Granger, whilst living in Leeds with your sports journalist husband?"

"I never actually "met" him, he just happened to have the table behind us at the event."

"And there were awards and acknowledgments to do with fencing?"

"Yes."

"Be careful now Kitty, you're doing well."

I'm pressing my ear again and I can feel the heat from my cheek burning my hand.

"So, you're a fan of fencing, know the rules and how to fence, correct?"

"No, it isn't correct. I don't know anything about it."

"You know what is used."

"Yes, a foil."

"Kitty!" Rose's voice is so loud she's hurting my ear.

He's staring at me and not speaking and to steady my nerves I'm sipping my chamomile tea looking down into the soothing liquid.

"Ah I see you know what's good to stay calm and focused Mrs Philips, you probably needed one of those before setting out for your meeting."

"I can't remember." The pig!

"Do you remember which way you walked when

leaving your car?"

"Around to the entrance."

"Yes, but which way if you parked facing Mr Granger's office, left or right?"

The only way I can ever retrace my steps on anything is to close my eyes and work through my actions. I'm past caring what this big Irish bully thinks. My hands are manoeuvring the parking and I'm aware I'm pointing to the left and right but who cares he's getting his answer. As I open my eyes Cameron is giving me a smile.

"I turned right which was wrong if you see what I mean."

"Why?" O'Donoghue's face is serious.

"Because it took me all the way round the back of the sports centre, and I had to walk further."

"There were no doors you could have used?"

"There was a fire door, but I didn't try it."

Cameron seems to be shifting uneasily in his chair but he's not looking up.

"Did you see anything, or anyone parked around there?"

"There were a few cars parked there but it was fairly dark and there was a skip just to the side of the cars."

"Careful Kitty my dear don't say any more!" Rose's voice sounds different, agitated, I'm trying to press my ear again.

DCI O' Donoghue is leaning back in his chair. If he breaks it by leaning too far, I've a good mind to charge him. This man is really getting up my nose.

"Look I don't see how I can help you any further Inspector, I don't know why Alex Granger was killed or what the connection between the two murders is. Do you have a connection?"

"Oh, to be sure we do Mrs Philips. You." His Irish twang noticeably stronger with his answer.

Now I'm angry and fighting to control it which isn't easy with Rose twittering away at the same time full of warnings. My mouth is open to retaliate but he's beaten me to it.

"Benson, show Mrs Philips the photos."

Cameron is putting two photos on the table in front of me.

"Do you know what they are Mrs Philips?"

"Fencing foils, I've told you I know nothing about the sport."

DCI O'Donoghue's big finger with a well-manicured nail is pointing to the first photo. Ponce, I bet he's a Mason and in with all the big boys.

"So, you're not familiar with a foil used for practice, this particular one is a maraging blade foil."

"No, I'm not."

"This foil," He's pointing to the second photo. "You can see this foil has been broken leaving roughly 30cm of blade length from the guard."

"Guard?"

"Handle to you Mrs Philips. Foils can get broken in practice as did this one and unfortunately for Alex Granger they just threw the broken guard and the thinner "foilable" end of the blade into the skip outside."

"You mean this is the same foil that killed Alex Granger." My eyes are glued to the picture. Last time I'd only seen the guard sticking out of his body, seeing what actually killed him is making me feel a little queasy.

"The very one."

"I can't help you Inspector I don't know anything other than what I've told you. Where did Alex Granger fit into all this?"

"We were hoping you would tell us, there's nothing on him at the moment, we're trying to trace any family."

"He must have had a mother somewhere; everyone has a mother."

"Yes Mrs Philips, even me." DCI O'Donoghue's eyes are fixed straight onto mine as he scrapes back his chair and walks to the door with Sergeant Benson silently following. "Goodnight Mrs Philips, lock up securely and don't do anymore meddling, my force is stretched very thinly at the moment."

They've gone and I've locked the door and pulled down all the blinds. Flossie has had her tiddle at the bottom of the garden and a good sniff around. It's been another long and tough day but it's not over yet. I need to relax up to my neck in bubbles. I've some thinking to do before bed.

Chapter Fifteen

Visions and snippets of conversations I've had over the last few days keep drifting in and out of my mind. I've tried to block out the ones of Miss Taylor and Alex Granger but it's impossible. My water in the bath needs topping up, it's amazing how quickly it's cooling down. This is the third time I've had to put some more in. I've bought myself one of those little cushions to put on the back of the bath for my head. I'm not sure about it maybe it would be better a little higher up now my water level has risen.

"That's better Kate, now concentrate, what's the connection between the two deaths?" I'm getting weirdly used to talking to myself. Everything I'm trying to work through keeps bringing me back to the same two things: love and hate, the strongest emotions we can ever feel and where there's one there's always the other, they just manifest in different forms.

My pulse feels like it's quickening, and it is not due to the water because it's going tepid yet again. OK so one more topping up and then I'm through with trying to shrivel my body for the sake of detection plus it's getting very late, one more shot at it right here goes.

Love, how many kinds are there? I've personally done the passionate kind and know what that's all about. Somehow the idea of Miss Taylor and a toyboy, especially now I've seen Alex Granger face to face, horrific as it was, just doesn't feel right to me.

"Use the dictionary Kitty and before you start shouting at me that's all I can give you."

If Rose really is in this room, then I've drowned her with the amount of water that's just flown over the side of the bath as my arms and legs flew up.

"Don't do that, you nearly drowned me, stop popping up like that!"

"You're shouting at me." Rose sounds hurt again.

"Hell's bells what do you expect?"

"Kitty my dear don't swear it isn't ladylike and I've got it on good authority that there are no bells ringing in hell, such a dreadful expression and most unladylike."

"I'm not swearing you know I don't, just stop doing this to me, please if you are real show me yourself, if not just leave me alone."

"Kitty we've had this conversation before now don't be tiresome, that's a good girl. I'm always here to protect you and now and again to give you advice but you're on your own for now anyhow."

"Great! Thanks a lot, as they say in America, "You're blowing my mind." In other words, in this case you're making me appear to be bonkers.

Dictionary indeed, what good will that do? I'll get it sopping wet in the bath."

"Visualise the words from the dictionary to go with love Kitty and don't be too long dear; you're getting waterlogged. Toodle pip Kitty."

"Toodle pip! She's mad! No, on second thoughts I am for even listening."

Like a New Year's resolution my will has been broken and the water level topped up again. It's not my fault, it's Rose's, I think. That's better at least I'm warm again now where was I with the love angle or even triangle. OK words, I'll try it why not? Eyes closed and visualise.

"Young love." No, it wasn't exactly young.

"Passionate love." Yuck! Don't want to think about that one.

"Undying love." Wrong on that one, they're both dead!

"Unrequited love." No evidence yet that it wasn't.

"Unconditional love." Ditto.

"Motherly love." Well, the age gap is right for that one.

Suddenly Carol is coming into my mind and her strange, uncharacteristic phone call. Carol my mother, not that anyone else would know that when I don't and never have called her "mum"-her choice not mine.

"Hell's bells!" Unconditional love, motherly love, that's certainly another angle and if so, why would anyone kill a mother and son? This is giving me something new to work on but for tonight I'm pooped and my bed is calling, no shouting at me.

4:12 AM and the stupid birds are acting like they're at a rave all singing at once in the market square. I've been trying for the last 20 minutes to get back to sleep. It's my own fault for having an overactive mind. It must be dreadful having a child genius; do they ever sleep? Not that I'm putting myself in the genius category of course, I'm more the "nosy, inquisitive, once I get my teeth into something I don't let go" category. Same difference but without all the certificates. Gran used to say those types were "all textbook knowledge and no common sense". I've not done the textbooks and if I had any common sense surely I'd back off now!

4:28 AM and I'm sitting wrapped up in my faithful Primark dressing gown which is lilac coloured with little penguins all over it and a large hood I bury myself into when I want to hide from the world. Sometimes it works, it's up now as a precaution as I'm on "Rose" alert. So far so good but I may have to put the hood down because the bowl of cornflakes I'm eating is extremely crunchy and it's quite deafening. Yes, it's got to go down. When I've finished slurping up the sugary milk in the bottom of my bowl, I'll be ready to think some more.

The ever-growing list of suspects and notes is in front of me, and I've decided to be a bit more professional and get it all entered onto my laptop. I've added my latest theories to both lists and done a bit of delving into another possibility my brain is churning over and that's adoption. Situations surrounding the finding of your birth mother have now changed. By what I can gather to go down any legal channels it's now up to the parents to find the child if they wanted to.

Little by little I'm recalling what has been said to me by various people about Miss Taylor, but she didn't really seem the type. Good job, well liked and respected, a very pleasant lady it's so sad. The scene in the garden had to be some kind of confrontation as it certainly knocked her for six. I know Alex Granger was from the South by his accent, the police must have a lead on him by now. I'm probably wasting my time here. DCI O'Donoghue is a very clever man with all the resources at his fingertips but it's niggling me. I saw how upset Miss Taylor was in my tearoom garden and how Alex Granger had reacted on the phone to me. I may have been charging off to meet him that night for all the wrong reasons, but someone wanted to stop him talking to anybody. Why? If I am on the right track of a son suddenly turning up out of the blue, then how can I be sure he was Miss Taylor's? Peggy and Madge have talked about the then "Girls" of Wetherby, the discos and social events of over thirty years ago and by what everyone has said, Dora Passmore was a real one. A "flighty piece" as Gran would have called her and yet she never married. It must have been a Wetherby curse or did all the available young men suddenly leave the area, there are too many spinsters, why?

Stirring my herbal tea bag and watching the water turn a lovely deep blackcurrant colour I'm trying to imagine either of the Passmores as the mother. Alex Granger could have been trying to make contact with his mother through Miss Taylor and she didn't want to reveal anything. Flora Passmore was in the crowd, she was madly in love, a love that was snatched away from her. She could have had a baby. Dora the flighty piece, what about her? Madge said those kind never get caught out. I need to speak to Madge again and find out what she was going to tell me, it may just give me a lead. At last, I could be onto something. I'd love to know if old Doughnut is on the same track but that's impossible to find out.

It's light outside now the sun is just coming into the square. Lovely as it is we desperately need some rain. If I could I'd make it rain through the night for the farmers' crops and gardens and pleasantly warm, not too hot, during the day. There's nothing wrong with that system, everybody would be happy then. All the blinds are up I may as well get my shower and start on the scones and finish the cakes.

For a Friday it is a lot quieter than usual. All the good weather could have many of the locals packing up and heading off for the coast before the weekend rush. Holidays abroad are a lot cheaper in this part of the season, some could have booked for a package tour and now be walking the streets of Benidorm along with all the other Brits, total madness. I've been to a Spanish resort and lovely as it was, we never heard a Spaniard for three days, plenty of Welsh, Liverpudlians and Cockneys. Rule Britannia!

With just a steady stream of customers through the morning it's been good to be able to have longer breaks ourselves for once. Charlotte and Simon are playing ball with Flossie between the fruit trees, her little tail is wagging faster than my car windscreen wipers. Sally has gone to do a bit of food shopping at Morrisons and then she'll nip home with it as she lives close to the supermarket. I don't mind how long she takes, the hours she puts in for me. What does niggle me is that there is no sign of Sparky the electrician. It's well after 2:00 PM and today would have been perfect to get on with the job. The lull has given me chance to get on with a few jobs myself whilst it's been quiet. I've cleaned out some cupboards and the oven and made my own shopping list for more ingredients. I must ring the farm and place an order for the free-range eggs.

"Hello, my dear, it's another wonderful day isn't it?"

Mr Potter's chirpy voice is ringing through the almost empty tearooms. He sure looks happy with himself. If he was a female, I'd say he was lit up with love. He's smitten alright, good and proper as Yorkshire folk and Gran would say. Tucked under his arm are three books so no prizes for guessing where he's come from.

"Hello Mr Potter looks like you're in for a quiet weekend on your balcony," I'm pointing to the books under his arm.

"Far from it my dear I intend to be very busy indeed if you don't mind that is, there are a few ideas I'd like to discuss with you."

"I'm all ears once Charlotte and Simon come in from their break. Why not go outside and I'll bring some refreshments, how about a nice piece of cake with your Earl Grey?"

"You spoil me my dear."

Aaaw sweet! He's so lovely, such a gentleman and I'm dying to know about him and Peggy. Has love been rekindled or have the years taken their toll?

Mr Potter has his books spread out on the table and I can't help but see that one is about Stratford on Avon and the surrounding areas.

"Thinking of a holiday Mr Potter?"

"Perhaps a short break or a day excursion is on the cards my dear. Peggy mentioned she's always wanted to visit there so I thought I'd do some research." He's smiling deeply.

Now that sounds promising and an opening for me so here goes.

"That's wonderful, so you two are going to keep in touch, are you? Peggy is a lovely lady Mr Potter."

"Oh, I know it Kate, I've always known it and I'm not going to let her slip away this time my dear. Loneliness is not a recommended pastime, that's what brought her back here."

"No family then?"

"She had a son once."

No! Now stop it Kate, don't get carried away, I'm telling myself, just act casually.

"She doesn't see him then, that's a shame, families can be like that."

"No, he was killed in an aircraft accident with her husband ten years ago, she's like me, no family to speak of and plenty of time on her hands."

"How sad, well I hope you bring her here again soon. You enjoy your tea and cake and I'll be out when I can."

So that's it, poor Peggy I feel dreadful for thinking she could have been on my list of possible mothers. Well, she could have been, couldn't she? Why am I trying to justify myself to myself!

If it continues to be this quiet Charlotte and Simon can get off early and do a bit of cavorting down by the river. That's not really what young ones do anymore they'll more than likely sit in the beer garden of one of the many pubs here with a soft drink.

"Hi Sally, get everything done you wanted to?"

Sally's flushed face from rushing around is beaming at me.

"Oh, thanks love I owe you one, it's saved me going straight after work. The kids hate trailing around the supermarket and it's my Chris's night out with his lot."

His "lot" could mean anything from two to ten or even more of the Benson clan, being that they are so close to one another.

"Is Cameron going too, I'd have thought any time he had off he'd be with his girlfriend?"

"Cameron? He's going if he can get the time off, but this is a BTN night love. He's no girlfriend our Cameron, who'd put up with the hours he works?"

Given half the chance I would! But with his hours and my hours that's a nonstarter if ever there was one.

"What's a BTN?"

"A Benson Testosterone Night love. There's only me and our Laura, that's Richard Benson's wife, put up with them all."

"What do you mean?"

"Afterwards love, they all pile back to our houses for coffee. Tonight, it's mine but I don't mind, they're a good lot and no trouble. Who can ever boast of having so many handsome men in one night eh?"

That's true if they're all like Cameron and Chris.

"You'd better take some Viagra then Sally, don't want you disappointing them all."

"Disgusting! Is there any chance of being served without being subjected to all this vile, disgusting smut?"

With all the good humoured banter neither of us had heard the Passmore sisters creep into the tearooms. Turning around I can see why we never heard as Sally had left the door open for a through draft and we'd had our backs to it.

"We'll be in the garden when you decide to take our orders."

Sweeping haughtily passed us is a blur of lime green and yellow with Flora identically dressed and obediently following, her head bowed. Sally is looking at me laughing silently.

"What a sight! They remind me of those lollies you can buy, those Twisters that are striped lime green and yellow, did you see the slime green handbag? Call the fashion police for those two!"

"No love she reminds me of one of them poisonous snakes in a jungle silently slithering in and out of doors like that. Nasty old bat! Anyhow she's no room to talk with her youthful carrying on, she was a real one she was, me Mum and Chris's Mum remember her alright."

"So I've heard, ok I'll take their orders then can you hold the fort whilst I have a word with Mr Potter?"

"Can do."

I'd best just wait in the doorway whilst Mr Potter finishes his conversation with them, Dora Passmore's glare could turn me into stone.

"Well, I'm sorry you were indisposed Miss Passmore you missed a very good talk on pruning and taking cuttings but then I'm sure Miss Flora told you all about it.

So, the old bat was indisposed, she'd better not

try and blame it on my baking, but I wouldn't put it past her, she's a viper that one and I hate snakes.

"OK ladies, are you ready to give me your orders now?"

"I've been ready for a full five minutes and at this rate we'll be here till closing time."

Smile Kate, you can always trip her up on the way out after she's paid up of course- business is business!

Nothing gets past the two Passmores sitting so primly drinking their Darjeeling tea and cutting up their cake into miniscule squares. Use the cake forks! That's what I gave you them for is what I want to scream at Dora. Why do they bother to come out together, they seldom have a conversation with each other, but they zoom in on everyone else's for sure. Dora Passmore's ears must be fine-tuned towards the juiciest conversations.

"Now Mr Potter I'm all ears." I'm giving a sickly-sweet smile to Dora Passmore, no harm in letting her know I'm onto her snooping. With a bit of luck, she'll take offence and leave.

"Yes, Kate my dear I've been giving a little thought, well a lot actually to your lovely garden and wondered if you would be open to a few changes?"

"What kind of changes?" My divorce and the settlement will be through soon, but I don't want to go wild just yet.

"Don't worry dear Kate, just moving the roses and making another seating area, an English rose garden to one side of the path. Tables and chairs under the shade of climbing roses. There are some lovely old English varieties, lavender and roses to compliment your afternoon tea and pretty crockery. I've drawn up some plans if you would care to see them?"

"Yes please it sounds wonderful."

"Oh good, well here they are, just rough sketches of course."

Mr Potter has pulled out two A4 pieces of paper which had been folded and put inside a large book called "Rose Growing".

"You call these rough sketches; they are beautiful works of art Mr Potter."

"Thank you my dear."

The pictures are so pretty, one of them is on a slightly larger scale than the other but both sketches have been touched up with watercolours. A bit like the old wedding photos when they added colour to faces and flowers only more so on these.

"Which side of the garden do you think is best?"

"The sun moves that way and by afternoon and evening it's still on that side so it will be perfect. You're lucky to have such a long garden."

Mr Potter is pointing to the left side as we sit on the patio, he's right I can almost smell the lavender and roses in the early evening sun. When they have grown up all the wooden frames the climbing roses will give natural shade for part of the day. I love it. It's simple and very pretty, very Rose and me too.

"I love it, as long as you promise not to work yourself too hard, just price it all up and let me know. When can you start the project Mr Potter?"

"As soon as you want me to."

"Oh, thank you Mr Potter, this is so exciting, it's me putting my own stamp on Crumbs, isn't it?"

"I think you've already done that my dear." Mr Potter's eyes are twinkling.

"Tut, tut, tut." Dora Passmore's obvious disapproval is reaching my ears but who cares, the old bat shouldn't be eavesdropping on our conversation, she can always go elsewhere.

Chapter Sixteen

Mr Potter is so thrilled to be able to create a new small garden in Crumbs and he's making me feel like his Fairy Godmother granting his wish. It's not going to cost very much but I'm not going to let him do it for such a small sum even with Crumbs providing all his food. Mr Potter deserves a better fee than he has asked for. I don't want to discuss that with Dora Passmore's ears flapping like an elephant's, I'll wait until we're alone. This is so exciting and it's not going to cause too much interruption, besides my customers will be able to "look and learn" with their own gardening expert whilst they take tea.

"Sorry I'm so late, last job took longer than I expected love."

At last Sparky has arrived. I'd given up hope of ever seeing him today.

"Now I can either do the job when you've closed or come back in the morning. What's best for you?"

Yes, I've heard that one before.

"Well, you're here now Sparky and we close in half an hour so you may as well crack on with the job. Have a drink and some cake first though, you look like you've been on the go all day."

"Thanks love."

Sparky is sitting happily chatting to Mr Potter and looking at his plans. He's really looked different the last few days, I'm glad as it's hard being on your own.

"There you are Sparky, sit back for a while and have a break. I know how busy you are, Sally tells me."

Another branch of the Benson family, an extended branch but still close as they all seem to be.

"Our Sal has told me how busy you are too Miss Marple. You don't do things by halves do you now, I mean two bodies! Poor souls, doesn't bear thinking about. I tell you it's putting the fear of God into the lasses around these parts and that's why I'm so busy putting security lights and alarm systems in."

Now I understand more.

"You got any theories then?" Sparky is asking in between mouthfuls of cake.

"A few."

"Reckon that the young fellow that's been murdered did poor Miss Taylor in, don't they?"

"Do they? If he did then who murdered him, it sure wasn't suicide."

"True but who'd want to go all them miles to Leeds to pop someone off?"

"Someone who didn't want him to say what he knew Sparky. Maybe he knew too much or witnessed something to do with the killer."

I'm suddenly aware of what I've just said, it

could be true I'm not sure how but it's something I can work on later.

"How come you was in Leeds then love; you got some clues have you?"

Sparky's voice is louder than I want it to be, probably from years of drinking and loud music blaring out of his transistor radio. The Passmore sisters seem to be lingering a little too long on their tea, surely it must be cold by now. Right, this calls for some action Kate.

"Was everything alright ladies, I'm sorry but we're closing now, I wouldn't want you getting covered in brick dust from Sparky's drilling."

Flora is getting flustered gathering her hideous bag and her shopping together and Dora is glaring at me silently. The flash in her eyes is anger, her lips are tightly pursed. I'm half expecting her to rip me apart with one of her sarcastic comments but no, she's moving away, just upped and gone without a single word. Now that's totally uncharacteristic of her but right now I'm just relieved she has. I'm starting to feel edgy, there are a few things whizzing around inside my mind. What I need is time and a quiet room to sit and work them out in but at the moment that's like asking for a date with Brad Pitt. Scrub that last wish out for now, I look a mess and I only managed to shave my legs halfway up. So! Who sees anything but the bottom bits when trousers are being worn, anyway I've baking to do later, sorry Brad.

Sparky is drilling and singing away to his transistor and I'm just praying he hurries up with the job so I can do what I want to later.

Sally keeps laughing at me for pulling faces at all the noise. The truth is I really don't like dentists and their drills. This constant whining sound is really starting to get me on edge, it's like having my own dentist in every room all drilling together. Singing they wouldn't be doing; mine hardly ever speaks to me, only enough to scare me to death about what he's about to do and that's fine by me. No conversation = more action = less time in the chair.

The cleaning is all done in the tearoom, everything is nice and tidy for the Saturday shoppers.

"These flowers could do with a change love," Sally's not looking impressed with the little vases that she's putting back on the tables.

"You're right they do look a bit brown at the edges. Sling them all out Sally, I'll wash the vases and Flossie and I will walk you home then call in at Morrisons for some fresh ones." Fresh air and some exercise will help me to think a few things through.

"You know where everything is Sparky if you want a drink, help yourself, I'll only be an hour tops. You've got my mobile number, haven't you?"

"No probs love, get yourself off and keep an eye on them there clouds building up I reckon we're in for some'at."

"They haven't forecast rain, have they? When I listened this morning there wasn't a mention of it but that doesn't mean anything."

"No, they didn't but I can tell and me corn's twitching, it never fails me love."

"Sally is your corn twitching? Sparky's is and so rain is on its way, so he says." I'm shouting above the drilling.

"Wouldn't know about that love, mine was zapped with that stuff I bought and it's as right as rain now!"

I'm getting lost in all this rain and corn stuff and Sally and Sparky are sharing the joke and laughing.

"Ta ra have a good walk. Give my love to the kids and Chris, tell him I'll be along later for a pint, will you?"

"Will do Sparky, bye love."

These Bensons and the branches of their clan are so good humoured and lovely, just how they should be. There must be loads of them dotted around Wetherby and the outskirts never straying too far away from the nest.

Sally has decided a walk along the river with us before going home will help her to face the rowdy but happy homecoming and the even rowdier evening ahead. I don't know how she does it all, I'm torn between wanting to belong and be part of it all and absolutely revelling in my own peaceful (apart from the Rose thing) haven. Am I getting too old and set in my ways? In just over a week, I'll be 30 years old, now I'm almost there it seems quite young to me, the only snag being the divorce tag which will go with it.

"Penny for them love," Sally is looking at me closely.

"Oh, it's nothing Sally, honestly, just contemplating life."

"Sounds serious, whose life?"

"Mine."

"Are you worried love about the murders? Leave it to our Cameron's lot, that's best. You've had enough shocks recently; you'll start turning grey at this rate. Anyways love you've told the police all you know so that's that."

She's looking at me in her "Mum can see if you're telling fibs" way and I'm just about to shake my head so as not to worry her. Flossie beats me to it.

"Kate, what's going on?" Sally says looking down at Flossie.

"Nothing's going on." Well not yet it isn't.

"Do you know something else? Come on love this is me asking not old Doughnut O'Donoghue."

"Woof."

"Flossie! Who asked you to butt in?" That's the trouble with having a dog that's half human with a conscience, they snitch on you. "Sally, I don't know, honestly it's just lots of things have been going around my head. Little bits said by others and at the back of it all something is niggling me and I've no idea what."

"You need one of them hypnotists love to get you on the couch and unlock your depths." She's going all theatrical on me.

"No, I already know my mother abandoned me, my choice of man is pathetic and that has led to my mistrust in the species. No need to pay to be told all that thank you."

"No love I meant that regression thingame, you know see what's hidden."

"All I need is a drink, some music and to get stuck into my baking. That usually sets my brain working."

"It's the ironing with me love but seriously promise me no more charging off detecting, it's too dangerous. Ring me if you want to talk things through, OK? Hey, watch out you idiots, this is a path for walking not riding bikes!" Sally's shouting after some boys on bikes. "You ok love he's a tearaway that young Fletcher's boy. Mark my words He's got his prison number tattooed on his forehead already that one. Pinched old Mrs Webster's knickers off the line last Tuesday just for a dare he said. She caught him red-handed. He's always nicking fruit from the Greengrocers in the market square, I'm surprised you've not seen him."

"No, I haven't but then so many people walk through."

"Not wearing that stupid bright coloured baseball cap they don't. Stands out a mile that does. Right, this is me love, night night and take care."

"Bye Sally, thanks for everything, see you tomorrow morning. Come on Flossie we need some eggs and a tin of condensed milk from Morrisons then home before these clouds empty everything on our heads."

"Woof."

It may be another odd thing about me, but I do love a good storm, as long as everyone is safe that is. I love to watch the lightning in the distance and count how far away it is. Gran was terrified but Rose and I used to watch together as the back garden was lit up and the thunder crashed overhead. We had some really spectacular summer storms whilst I was still living in Headingley. Rushing along with two dozen free-range eggs in a carrier bag and Flossie running ahead I'm just hoping I make it before the heavens open. My baking will have to wait till it passes over, I'm not chancing it.

"Nowt much more I can do tonight, sorry love. I'll be back in the morning, these cables alright left inside your shed? I'll take my tools home with me."

"Yes, put them in the shed and I'll lock it when this has passed over. Get yourself home Sparky, hope it doesn't stop your pint with the boys."

"Takes more than a storm to stop that love, ta ra."

"Bye Sparky."

Flossie doesn't seem to mind a storm either.

We've both eaten and are now in the bedroom waiting for nature's display to begin. It's dark but so far nothing is happening, very disappointing I must say. I can see flashes in the distance but can't judge which way this one's going, and my counting keeps shifting from 7 to 6 to 8. What's going on, this is turning out to be a waste of time for me, I've got Madeira cakes and caramel shortcakes to make tonight and a heap of thinking to do. All this is knocking my plans skew-whiff.

"That's it Flossie I'm going to make a start on the baking, let me know when the show begins girl."

"Woof."

Downstairs it's really dark in the tearoom now I've turned the lights on but I don't want to pull the blinds down yet so I can see how the storm is going. I can turn the gas oven on to warm up and get all the ingredients weighed out in readiness for baking. Phew the air is getting very muggy, it's about time the downpour came then at least the air will feel fresher after it. Grating the lemons is working up a real sweat on me. It's airless in here and I'm starting to feel sticky and uncomfortable. This isn't good, surely the storm is about to break. I'm nervous about turning on my mixer if the lightning is clattering overhead, Gran used to run around unplugging everything in sight bless her. No sense in getting myself all worked up over a silly storm I can either down tools and go back upstairs to Flossie or have a drink and get my paper list of suspects out. My laptop will have to stay in its case, I'm not risking blowing it up. I can just imagine me sitting there, my face blackened and hair all frazzled like in a cartoon. No, there have been enough casualties in the last week, two too many. Air is what's needed, cool fresh air.

Chapter Seventeen

Standing on the kitchen doorstep a semi cool breeze is wafting across my face, it's fantastically refreshing. If anybody walks past the garden now, they'll think a zombie has taken up residence in Crumbs because I'm on the patio with my arms up arched like bat wings to let the breeze waft around my armpits and it's heaven.

The garden has taken on that dark eeriness we get just prior to all the banging and clattering. There's nothing to hear but the occasional rumble miles away, there aren't even any birds doing their evening calls to each other. This is thrilling, my first real storm in my new home, just me alone with Flossie. It's so exciting, scary but exciting, bring it on!

Big blobs of rain the size of two pence coins are aiming at me on the patio, warm and salty tasting big blobs. The pattern it's making on the flagstones is great and there could be a market for this! Oh, oh here it comes it's cooler and breezier and the rain is starting to pelt down now. The leaves of the rose bushes sound like drums as the downpour hits them, my tubs! I never thought of them I'm too busy acting like a child. The few I can lift onto the patio will be more protected there and the others are far too heavy for me to budge. My hanging baskets are spinning like tops in the wind and torrential downpour. This must be it; the full force of the storm is almost here now; I'll be safer inside.

All the lights are off and everything is unplugged downstairs. Flossie is standing on the chair I've pulled to the bedroom window, her front paws resting on the windowsill. I've just stepped out of my wet clothes and thrown on a t-shirt and linen skirt but not a clean bra as it's only us after all. I wouldn't feel right without my knickers though, blame it on my Gran.

The Heavenly Big Band is playing well tonight with almighty cracks and very loud big bangs. It's quite a spectacular show and it's lasting longer than usual. Just as I think it is moving off in the direction of Leeds it comes back for another encore.

"Now that was really something Flossie wasn't it girl?" She's certainly a storm lover, she's had a silly grin on her face all the way through. "Did you enjoy it?"

"Woof!"

"Good, well I've got to get on with some work now, so I'll see you later sweetheart. Would you like the television on Flossie?"

"Woof."

Flossie is nicely settled watching "The Mentalist" on Channel 5. Now he's a dish if ever there was one but I'm not sure I'd like a man who always knows what I'm thinking or doing. Too

Big Brotherish for my liking, not that I'd stand a chance with him in a month of Sundays.

The lovely, tangy, fresh lemon smell from the grated lemons is so strong it's seeping through the closed door at the bottom and up the stairs. Now I'm in the tearoom it's really pungent. No wonder they put it in cleaning products as it is so refreshing.

"Mmm wonderful this is my little piece of heaven, right to work, follow the system girl and go for it."

I have to have a system worked out when I'm baking so:

Bake shortcake part of caramel shortcakes first.

Prepare Madeira cake mixture whilst shortcake is baking.

Bring out shortcakes to cool and whack Madeira cakes into the ovens for approximately 1½ hours.

Prepare caramel and put on cooled shortcake, leave to cool.

Cover with melted plain chocolate and leave to set.

Perfect, all is going to plan. Two cakes are in, and two trays of caramel coated shortcakes are almost ready to spread with chocolate, most of the washing up is dried and put away and it's time for a breather and a drink.

Now the storm has cleared the air it's a little cooler outside. Everything smells fresh, green and earthy after the heavy rain which is still falling but more gently now. We really needed this and

I'm just glad I managed to get the tubs of flowers under cover and I'm sure the ones I didn't will survive. After I've finished, I'll put these back in their places to get some of the rain. It's still darker outside than it should be for this time of night and there aren't any stars out because of all the clouds. Never mind, tomorrow night I should be able to sit out here if it's fine and I have my outside lights on, it'll be great for parties. Why not, that's what I need, a good knees up of my own to celebrate my 30th and divorce. I like it, Mr Potter could bring Peggy, the Benson clan I know and including Cameron of course, some of my good customers and shopkeepers around me. This is exciting, something to plan and to look forward to. I've a lot of planning to do and not much time but what's new?

"Beep, beep, beep."

My Madeira cakes are baked, back to it. Two beautifully risen and buttery Madeira cakes with a candied citrus slice on top of each of them are now out of their tins and standing tall on the cooling rack. I just love loaf cakes, to me the easiest and most versatile type of cake. They always bring out the country girl in me which there isn't any such thing really but it's so farmer's wifeish and homely, they slice well too. Dark, delicious, smooth chocolate smells are now fighting with the lemony baking ones. Chocolate is so naughty but so nice and I get to lick out the bowl!

All done and I'm tempted to bring the chocolate

bowl to the table to scrape it with my fingers whilst I study the notes on my laptop. Knowing me I'll get it all over the keyboard. Just one more teeny-weeny bit at the bottom, got you. That's it, pigging time over. It's a known fact you should eat chocolate before an exam or anything mentally taxing, or was it an egg? Anyhow it helped to fill a little gap and I'm about to test my chocolate theory out. Agatha Christie always had Poirot drinking chocolate and wiping his moustache on a crisp white serviette and look how clever his little grey cells were, plus I'm sure I've got the makings of a moustache. Life can be cruel for a female. Enough of this, time to work.

Flossie is mooching around in the garden; she needs her bedtime wee. I just need my bed, but I can't give in, it's there I know it is, hidden somewhere in a corner of my over cluttered mind is the bit needed, the niggle that's niggling me but won't let me remember it.

"Come on Flossie now girl. It's your bedtime, stop playing with my fairies at the bottom of the garden. On second thoughts ask them to help me solve these murders please."

"Woof."

"Oh yes I'll believe that one when I see it."

Flossie is having one last charge around but all I can see is an occasional flash of white. Here she comes.

"Good girl, tired now, are you?"

"Woof."

"In you go, I've turned the television off so straight to sleep and hopefully with a little inspiration from above I won't be too far behind you."

"Woof."

All the juicy titbits people have given me I've entered onto my laptop, what else is there to list? One thing I haven't got is where everyone worked, it's all information after all. Looking at what's already written up is fairly impressive so far, well to me anyway. Let's hope nobody sees it or I'll look more than a little suspicious especially in DCI O'Donoghue's eyes. Speaking of eyes, mine are starting to ache with the glare of the screen.

"Kettle on, time for one last drink and look then bed, come on Rose I thought you'd want to be in on the action, a little help wouldn't go amiss. Hell's bells I've got the pots to put back outside, I nearly forgot."

I'm fully aware how senseless it is but I still do it, that is I argue with myself. The pots need to go back in place, they could wait till morning I know that but the more I tell myself "Leave them they're fine for now", there's another small voice saying, "it will only take a moment". Less to do in the morning, well that's how I justify my actions. The last one to replace is the pot that I have nearest to the patio. With the lights from inside the kitchen stretching to where I'm placing it, I can see the lovely bright orange of the geraniums and their petals starting to open up. What a vivid splash of colour these beauties will give all through summer. It's a shame the leaves have such a horrible smell, that's why Rose wouldn't have them.

I've had a craving for a Horlicks drink all day but to me it just doesn't seem right to drink it any other time than bedtime, not that it does anything for me like the adverts say. Horlicks actually gives me nightmares instead of peaceful slumber as advertised but I love the stuff so now and again I risk it. Tonight I feel like taking a risk or two.

"Okey dokey if you're listening Gran and Rose or anyone else that's free, I've got my drink and I'm going to study my facts one more time. Please feel free to guide me."

Names and occupations are all in front of me and something is bugging me but it's still not bouncing out at me. Going with the "mother's love" theme why would someone want to kill because of it? How cruel if Miss Taylor and Alex Granger were related then why would someone need to punish her because she had a son, then go all the way to Leeds and kill again?

Without realising it I've been writing on my pad whilst concentrating on the names displayed on my laptop screen. In big black letters and underlined several times are the words LOVE and HATE. Two of the strongest emotions we can ever feel and the cause of many a battle through the centuries. I loved Matt my soon to be ex-husband, he was my life, my whole world revolved around him. That was until I left him to nurse Rose. He had turned out to be a lying toad and a cheat, but I can honestly say I don't hate him or the blonde bimbo from McDonald's and I certainly wouldn't have killed because of him. No man is worth my freedom for a lifetime in one of Her Majesty's lower grade hotels. Here is a case of love and hate that's been dormant for a very long time.

The information is all in front of me but it's hard to piece the jigsaw together. Means, motive and opportunity all the great detectives always harp on about. The only chilling fact I'm getting is my suspect was a woman but from my list one is dead and much as it bothers me, I'm not yet ruling Peggy out. She was part of the "Wetherby Girls" and the one I have practically no background information on. They all went to the local discos, idiot I should have been asking about the men! How stupid of me, it takes two to tango Gran would have said but in this case boogey or whatever they called dancing back then. Mr Potter may know, that's if he's not too embarrassed, he seems to have been leading a bit of a double life at the time. Hell's bells! No definitely not, I refuse to think he is involved in this, oh this is getting worse.

"Rose, please where are you?"

Rose has obviously taken the hump, that's if she was ever floating around me in the first place. It's late, I'm tired and I was going to get a shower. Tomorrow's cakes need boxing up before I forget.

At least they haven't failed me, they all look well, what can I say. Good enough to eat. Oh no you don't, not at this late hour. My inner conscience is telling me off and winning.

"There you are my beauties safely tucked up in your boxes till tomorrow. Right laptop off and bed next." Talking to myself doesn't seem so mad no I really must be getting old.

"What's going on, how did that get here?" Obviously, nobody is going to tell me but I'm absolutely shocked. On the bit of table in front of my laptop is a big orange. I mean big. Mr Jaffa would be proud of this one. I buy oranges, don't often eat them but I use them for baking orange cakes, this one would make several.

"Oranges and Lemons say the bells of St Clements," Rose is singing in my ear.

"Rose? Come on don't play games please, I'm tired. What's this all about? Please come on Rose, don't be awkward."

"When have you ever known me to be awkward Kitty my dear?"

"Well, I'm not sure but if it's you then how did you bring this orange, can you carry things?"

"Don't be a silly girl Kitty of course I don't carry things, why would I need to?"

"Then how?"

"Don't ask tiresome questions it's wasting time."

"So you're going to help me now then, are you?"

"Help you? No of course not, you don't believe in me. No, you're to help yourself, you have the clues so work it out, visualise my dear Kitty, visualise. Oranges and Lemons say the bells of St Clements."

"Rose, Rose?"

She's gone again, at least I think she has. The only proof I have is the big orange in my hand, I can't understand all this, is it possible to suddenly have something materialise that wasn't there before? Well, it has. Oranges and lemons. My mind is racing and not getting far. Sweet and bitter, what's all that got to do with the murders?

Ten minutes of thinking and staring at the screen hasn't sparked anything off, no sudden lights are switching on in this brain, once a dummy always a dummy.

Chair pushed back a little I've closed my eyes and offered a small prayer for help, guidance and protection and I'm sitting with my hands open on my knees with my palms upwards.

"Don't forget to breathe Kitty, steady that's it. In and out, in and out, in and out."

Rose's voice is gentle but starting to fade away, phew in, out, in, out. Suddenly it's like a TV channel has been turned on in my head, almost an action replay, I'm looking at the orange geraniums. Orange again, OK so maybe it's showing me the last thing first. In, out, phew in, out there's Sally, we're out walking, and the young tearaway is charging past wearing a bright orange baseball cap! The lights have been switched on at last, steady now don't lose it, I've got to keep calm, in, out, in, out. Orange is significant I know it is. What do I do now? Keep breathing, keep trying to clear my mind.

Nothing is happening now, the last thing I want to do is give in after getting a peak at something. I'll ask again for some help.

At home, Gran and Rose used to sit around doing all this, I always thought they were potty but I'm willing to give it a go. Done, oddly enough I'm feeling very calm and relaxed in, out, in, out slowly, eyes closed to the outside influences. Here we go again I'm getting out of my car, looking which way to walk. A door is just closing, I can hear the bang, I'm going the wrong way never mind just passed some cars, someone is getting into one of them I can see them out of my right eye corner. Not getting which car just the glint of the driver's door window in the security light and some orange clothing! Orange again, a clue, it's there, has been all this time but who?

I could continue but I'm afraid of being shown any of the goriness that followed, it's that car that's significant. The Leeds police will have asked for the CCTV footage so that's something I could ask Cameron tomorrow, a genuine reason to speak to him, better still to meet him.

"Thank you Rose and everybody for opening my eyes, well you know what I mean they weren't open, but I was seeing, wow I was."

The kitchen clock is telling me it's 10:43 PM, early yet for the Friday night revellers but for my new spinster, workaholic lifestyle it is getting past my comfy bed and sleep time. I'm still wide awake though, fired up and raring to go now. Go where? What can I do now? Music that's what's missing, a bit of Simply Red will do and another drink, what the heck if I get up for the loo in the night, I'm not exactly going to disturb anyone.

Kettle's on, the music is on, time for a quick wee and then back to my laptop for some more inspiration. I'm feeling really positive and fired up, there could be something in all this meditation stuff after all.

10:48 PM. What's wrong with texting Cameron and asking him to pop by really early in the morning for breakfast and a chat? He's going to be either still in the pub or on his way to Sally's.

"No harm in keeping him informed is there now." I'm talking myself into writing the text. There, it's sent, the wonders of the mobile phone. It's up to him now if he wants to know my new information he'll be here for coffee. Mmm dreamy music. I could always play it again in the morning as background music. "Kate my love you're becoming a real little schemer in your old age, back to work girl." I'm whispering, why the heck am I whispering there's only me and the laptop and of course Mick Hucknall crooning in my ears.

Oranges and lemons. I've had a brief flash of orange but lemons, what's the significance of that? There's nothing on either of my lists with a connection. No names or information given to me suggesting anything remotely connected. Sweet and bitter. Could it be a reference to characters? It's a very long shot but I can't think of anything else so it's worth a try. Of all the people I know and have on my list, to me it fits the description of the Passmores. How appropriate; poor sweet Flora and sour faced Dora, hey could that be true? Why the orange though, that's what I don't fully understand. Fruit, fruity, no I'm going off track. It's got to be the colour, the boy's baseball cap, the geranium, the flash of orange, what else was orange?

"Oh my God! Sorry, everyone upstairs." I do seem to be shouting. "The only orange that has been around me was when the Passmores flounced in wearing those hideous bright orange dresses. When? When was that? Quickly, think. Which day was it? Let me see they were in over the holidays together, naturally, Flora follows Dora like a scared mouse, they must go everywhere together."

"Kitty my dear please," Rose's voice is interrupting my waves of thought. "Kitty I insist! Be careful, tell your young man now, now. I'm telling you don't delay there's danger. Kitty for once will you listen to me!"

"Rose it's alright I know who did it. The orange was throwing me a little you see because that wasn't quite then, but I know who did it."

Chapter Eighteen

I'm tip tapping away on my keyboard, my thoughts need to be put down before I lose them. Rose is practically screaming in my ears, and it isn't helping. Seeing everything on my laptop screen will help me to fill in the gaps. I just know I'm right.

"Kitty for pity's sake pick up the phone and call someone before this gets out of hand."

"No, Rose I need to be totally sure of this."

"Why?"

"Because I'm going to be accusing someone of murder that's why. Rose if it is you then you should know who it is, just let me do this my way, I've come this far without you."

"Don't be childish Kitty I've explained the rules."

"Rules! That's pathetic."

"And you're in danger please Kitty listen to me."

"Shh Rose I'm concentrating. Always together my foot! Not according to what Mr Potter said, not that night!"

My whole body feels recharged, it's a feeling like no other I've ever had. All the pain that's been caused, why? I'm still not sure but the cold-hearted person who inflicted it, that I'm 100% positive of. My fingers are flying over the keys, now the killer's name, that's it in bold print and underlined.

"Rose if you can hear aaaagh, help aaaagh! Rose!"

Oh my God something is cutting deep into my throat, please stop, please I can't breathe. My fingers are trying to get underneath what feels like plastic cable, my eyes are going to pop out don't, don't, I'm being pulled backwards tighter and tighter. Please don't let it end like this. Rose!

I can't get a grip it's too tight, this is it, no not now, no! My nails are cutting away at my own flesh. Noise so loud in my head choking, gargling, pressure, blood, upwards and bursting, eyes, up, up, up it's going up in my head I can't, I can't it's hurting I don't want this pain.

"Kitty stop struggling hang on, stop struggling, struggling, struggling." Why is Rose's voice echoing?

I'm falling, Gran's smiling at me and shaking her head but I've come this far, and I don't want to go back, so peaceful, pain free and floaty. My Gran, my lovely, lovely, motherly Gran. No don't do that Gran, don't turn me away please don't turn me away I love you Gran.

I feel heavy, something is stopping me and anchoring me down. With all my strength I want to push it away, but I can't. My body feels in two parts.

"Gran help me, please I'm coming with you."

Nothing is moving the anchor. "Gran!" I'm screaming but she's gone. I'm falling into darkness, down, down, down.

Wherever I am is incredibly noisy and by the sound of it a very busy place. I can hear voices, some louder than others, some seem to be whispering. I hate that, I want to shout out "If you're talking about me speak up!" but I can't, I'm voiceless. My eyes won't open, my whole body feels like a dead weight. DEAD!! I'm dead, where am I? Heaven? Hell? No what have I done to deserve hell, not that much, no only kids' stuff. The other place, maybe it's the other place that's it that's where I am. No please not limbo, the Nuns told us about limbo, that's just awful. No, I'm on one of the resting plains that Gran and Rose talked of. Are they here, coming for me later when I feel better? Why can't I move and see things? At the Spiritualist Church they always said when we pass over, we get back the use of any limbs lost.

"Hello, I'm here, you can make me whole again now as soon as you're able to of course, I know I'm in a queue errr thank you." Maybe they've sedated me with some spiritual type drugs to help me for the healing process in readiness for the next stage. Fine, OK I'll go along with that, catch up on some sleep I think I deserve it after all that has happened, see you all soon.

If that's what passes for a hand massage up here it's a bit rubbish, they'd do better tackling the hard bits on my feet with whatever spiritual implement is being used. Ugh! It's warm and slightly rough on my hand and I want this to stop. Just let me get those eyes open, why won't they open? Steady now be polite, you're a long time dead. Strewth what Gran used to say is now for real! This is really going to take some getting used to and chocolate, will I get chocolate? I can't live without chocolate oops well I am a new girl here. There's probably some kind of pep talk later and then it's anyone's guess as to what happens for the next eternity, I'm so tired.

Someone's whispering I know they are somewhere nearby. Oh, that's it, I've had enough of this so called pampering it's too strange, this time if I really try hard my eyes may open. My head feels like it's been chopped off and stuck on incorrectly, my throat is on fire, burning and extremely painful, hurry up with the healing sessions, sorry manners Kate, please hurry up. I'll ask whoever is whispering to show me where to go. Here goes, just a little bit at a time, wow they're so heavy, every part of me feels lead weighted, not good.

"She's conscious, what should I do?" A voice so like Sally's it's uncanny is talking. I miss everybody so much and my Flossie. Oh, Flossie I'm so sorry I had to leave you, but I'll be back, promise.

"Woof."

They've got dogs here! I can just make out a shape next to me through the slit of my eyes. Flossie? Impossible, unless they have lookalikes in this place. I can't speak it's just a painful croak, I'm so weak and it's painful.

"Woof."

This time I'm able to feel the dog's breath on my hand. Only a doggie person would appreciate how I feel, it's bringing tears to my eyes, the loss is so great, my heart is beating, all my friends, everything left behind.

"She's getting distressed, she needs to sleep. I'll stay tonight Sally you get home to the family."

What's going on? I feel so pained and confused I'm drifting into the darkness again, down, down.

My eyes have decided to work again. All those articles I've read on near death experiences, and nothing prepared me for this but then I had to go all the way and find out the hard way didn't I. Slowly my eyelids are starting to lift like blinds at windows. My blinds! I never put them down in Crumbs! Oh well it's hardly going to matter anymore is it. Just trying to lift them a bit more, the tears are blurring my vision but there's certainly a welcoming committee in the room I can make out two shapes, maybe three. Blinking is working, do I have all the same bodily functions here because I really need the loo? It's building up I can feel it. Oh crikey if that's the case then all the rest is the same and at that time of the month I always need chocolate, bars of the stuff. One, two, three, open, oh my G...

Cameron is asleep in Rose's chair with Flossie sprawled across him, gently snoring. Sally is sitting on another chair, eyes down looking tearfully into her favourite beaker. How can this be? The room looks the same with sunlight peeping through the gap in the curtains. They've done a good job of replicating my bedroom to make me feel welcome, this is so confusing, are they really my three friends or lookalikes? I don't want them all dead too.

"Kate love, you're coming round. Cameron quick wake up."

His chin has dark, designer style stubble, his t-shirt is all crumpled, but he looks gorgeous, ouch my throat! I can't swallow, it really hurts.

"Shh love don't try to speak, you're alright, you're safe now, sip this water through a straw, that's a good girl."

"Woof."

The water is icy cold and is wonderful if only I could swallow it properly. It's dribbling out of the side of my mouth. Lookalike Sally is gently wiping my face and chin with a tissue. My hand has found Flossie lookalike's head, I'm stroking her, and it feels good, comforting. I can't stop the tears. They're streaming down my cheeks into my mouth and are warm and salty.

"Oh love, shh now you're safe, it's all over now."

I want to shout, "I know" and I want to go home but I can't speak so I'm crying and flooding the duvet in fact.

"Kate please try to relax, we're here and nobody is going to leave you alone. Thanks to you we have the killer and just in time." The Cameron lookalike's gorgeous, chocolate brown eyes are looking into mine full of tenderness. Is he real? Is all this real, my room, my dog, my friends? Please, please let it be real. I'm not ready yet, think of all those lovely cakes I've yet to bake, the garden to change, so much, so much, so...

"That's it love, just sleep. I'll be here with you so close your eyes and sleep."

This time my eyes have opened fully, and I know for sure I'm still alive. Hallelujah! Thank you, Lord. How do I know? Simple, because Sally's silently scoffing! Cameron's not here but Sally is tucking into a huge sandwich, and I can see a piece of Madeira cake on another plate, bless her, my Madeira cake I baked.

"Tisss good?" I'm trying to croak, and it hurts.

"Oh love welcome back, no don't try to talk just nod love. Sorry to tease you with all this, it's soup for you I'm afraid, doctor's orders. Oh love you had us so worried."

Sally's crying now and giving me a hug, her salty tears are mingling with mine on the duvet. I'll need a new one if this continues.

"Don't speak love," she's smiling. "Doctor's orders and there's a lot of them. Our Cameron left a pen and notepad for you to write down what you want, here you are love."

She's given me the blue pen I've seen him use and the notebook and I'm trying to pull myself up so I can scribble a message. Sally's plumping up the pillows behind me, that's better.

"Thank you." I'm writing, she's squeezing my hand. "Where's Flossie?"

"Mr Potter's taken her out love, of course Crumbs is closed and there's police tape and dirty size 11 boot marks all over the floor, but don't you worry I'll sort that out soon as I can. Anything you want right now love before I get your soup?

I'm scribbling "a wee please". My bladder feels the size of a space hopper.

"Come on love, steady now you were sedated, enough to knock a horse out so you'll feel wobbly, hold onto me."

My knees are buckling, my head feels woozy, just let me make it before the space hopper bursts. Sally's got me to the bathroom!

"I'll leave the door open a little love, call me if you need help."

All I can do is grunt my thanks. It's just dawned on me I'm in my t-shirt I sleep in, oh the shame, Cameron's seen me. The relief of being able to let everything out is fast taking over the other shock. If I could sigh properly with the relief then I would. There's no way of describing the utter bliss, only those having been in this situation will know.

Standing at the sink to wash my hands and try to throw some water over my face is a real effort. This could be a cross channel cabin in a force 9 gale the amount of swaying I'm doing. Whoa there, steady at the helm Captain. At least my sense of humour is still intact.

"You OK in there love? There's nothing I haven't done or seen before with my lot, including Chris."

"Yes," I'm trying to croak.

Well, I was alright, only just, until I looked up into the mirror that is. Forget the hair sticking to my forehead and out at all angles as that's normal for me. What's shocked me is my face and neck. My eyes, normally a sparkly grey, are a dull metal colour with heavy, blue and black tinged with maroon coloured circles underneath them. My neck is horrific! The deep, bruised line around my throat is a sickly reminder of what happened and how close I was to death. My tongue is so swollen where I bit into it and dried blood is still in the corners of my enlarged lips. And they pay good money to have lips like these, total and utter madness! I feel sick, loo quick, quick.

It's getting darker outside and Flossie is asleep in her basket. She looks so peaceful I just want to cuddle and play with her, but I haven't the energy. Sally's bringing in another drink with a straw and another bowl of her lovely vegetable soup that she's liquidated for me. I do feel hungry now, but I hope I can keep it down after all the trouble she's going to. There are three vases of beautiful flowers on different surfaces making my room look like a star's dressing room, well it was almost my final curtain I suppose.

"Sally you're so kind what about your family? Who are all the flowers from please?" I'm writing on my pad.

"Don't you worry about my lot, there's enough help for my Chris with my family and his all mucking in. He's more than likely down the pub now whilst his mum or mine babysits. The flowers are beautiful aren't they love? The big bouquet is from your mum, pink carnations from our Cameron and the roses are from Mr Potter."

Carnations from Cameron, wow they are beautiful all of them but how did Carol get to know? I'm busy writing down the question and grunting at the same time.

"Lord love I don't know she just rang up whilst you were asleep saying she couldn't stop thinking and worrying about you. I've told her I'm staying with you; she's trying to get a flight first thing Monday morning to look after you."

Carol coming here to look after me! I'm in shock.

The phone has never stopped ringing with well-wishers and of course reporters. Sally's a brick, she's dealing with it all like a Personal Assistant to the rich and famous, well for now I suppose I am famous. All of Wetherby and around will know by now. Soup I need food, here goes.

"Just take sips love, I put nutmeg in just as you like it."

My thumb's going up, apart from the burning sensation as it first goes down it's delicious. I never could go without food for long.

Chapter Nineteen

For weeks I've been longing for the chance to stay in bed and do nothing and now it's been enforced on me I hate it. I'm bored and frustrated. Sally filled the bath for me with water. "Not too hot love, can't have you flaking out on me," and lots of bubble bath. She's brought a chair from downstairs into the bathroom in case I need to sit down whilst getting dried. At the moment she's perched on it keeping watch over me as I soak. It didn't feel right at first, I'm not prudish just a little shy but she insisted, and I understand her reasons.

Sitting up in bed in one of my "holiday strappy nighties" with my hair washed thanks to Sally, I feel more human and respectable.

"Now love you look better already."

I must be as I've just managed a very deep and manly sounding "thanks", but it hurts. Sally's laughing at me. I'm reaching for my pad and writing quickly, "Sally you need a break and to see your family, please go to them for a little while. I'm fine now I can just rest."

Sally's just about to protest when the door downstairs being banged on loudly interrupts her.

"I won't be a mo love, if it's them reporters I'll soon see them off."

Flossie has gone down with her as a bodyguard. My mouth is open to shout "let Flossie out into the garden please" but it's too much of a painful strain and I'm writing it on my pad instead. Reporters even I could have handled but the Irish twang of DCI O'Donoghue is drifting up the stairs. Oh well it's going to happen so I might as well get it over with.

DCI O'Donoghue has moved my dressing gown from Rose's chair to the end of my bed and has eased his bulk into it. Cameron has taken the extra chair from downstairs that Sally brought into my bedroom for visitors. I'm just thankful I managed a bath and with Sally's help had my hair washed. The normally icy, cold blue eyes appear softer and there's a smile trying to emerge from the usually hardened face.

"Mrs Philips I'm glad to see you, shall we say, awake."

I have a feeling he wanted to say, "alive and kicking". OK hit me with it, there's another lecture coming on I know he's not going to let me off easily, wait for it. Cameron's eyes are holding mine, ooh!

"You're a very lucky lady, sure you are indeed. Some would say you have the angels on your side." His eyes are twinkling. "I'm glad anyhow, don't look so Mrs Philips, sure I know you're not up to much at the moment, so I'll leave DS Benson here to go through a few things with you. Him being one of your guardian angels so to speak."

Now I am puzzled, what's with the niceness and all the angels bits? He's leaning forward now. I hope the chair can cope, by the change in his body language I hope I can cope. Here it comes.

"Mrs Philips, we have your laptop."

Why? I'm thinking what's my laptop got to do with this?

"Very interesting your line of thought, I wish some of my staff could have the imagination you have shown." He's fixing me with his eyes. "If only you had come to us with your information instead of still playing at Miss Marple, no matter we have the killers thanks to you and DS Benson."

My mouth is dry now and I'm croaking out my question, maybe I'm not hearing him properly but "killers" as in two of them? I only had one.

"Killers, who?"

"Why the Passmores of course."

Did I hear him correctly? Passmores as in both Dora and Flora? No, I can believe it of Dora but poor timid Flora there has to be a mistake. Dora's name was written all over my screen, that's what I was doing when I was nearly strangled. Which one was trying to kill me then? There's so much I need to know but I can't ask. Without realizing it my hand has gone to my throat and even touching my skin lightly is causing me pain. Dora and Flora!

"Mrs Philips it was Dora trying to kill you. Sure a few seconds more and she'd have succeeded. As I understand it you had texted my Sergeant here and for some reason best known to himself, he decided to come along last night and not this morning."

I didn't miss the look DCI O'Donoghue flashed Cameron nor the heavier Irish tone of voice. Whatever his reasons for coming late last night I'm glad he did. I can smile my thanks, sort of lopsided because of the bruising.

"Well now I'd best be getting back to the station. Sergeant Benson will tell you the rest and ask the relevant questions, if you're up to it. Benson?"

"Yes sir."

"Only one cup of coffee, you've a lot of reports to write up and Mrs Philips this time you were lucky with your detecting, but it almost cost you your life. No more Miss Marple behaviour please, the population of Wetherby has gone down by three and you nearly made it four."

I'm looking at him and mouthing three.

"Sure, those sisters won't be back here for a long time. Trouble follows some people even the innocent ones, I hope you're not one of those types. Goodbye for now Mrs Philips."

The room looks so much more spacious now his large presence has gone. I just feel embarrassed, He's right but I don't want to admit it and on top of all that I feel and look a wreck. Hell's bells if Cameron rescued me, I looked a bigger mess last night, old t-shirt, no bra, hairy legs. Ooh life's cruel, how could he have not seen all that, at least I kept my knickers on!

Sally has made Cameron one of my M&S

lasagnes with salad and some buttered French bread on the side.

"I thought the big one would never go love. Here our Cameron seeing as you're having to work late, you'll be missing your tea."

"Thanks Sally if you weren't already hooked up to my wayward cousin, I'd snap you up for myself."

"Mmm now there's a thought love but there's plenty left like me just open your eyes love, I'll just bring up the drinks."

Sally's winking at me as she sways passed us both and out of the door.

"You sure you're alright? I can come back tomorrow if not." Cameron has stopped eating and is looking at me. I can feel his eyes on me and my glorious full technicolour Halloween horror look. Great! Ten easy ways of how not to attract a hunk. I'm writing on my pad so as not to have to look back at him.

"I'm fine honestly, just concerned about keeping Sally here. Please eat then tell me what you can." My writing is a bit shaky, but it will do.

"Sally's staying the night, there's nothing she loves more than being mother to someone. Chris and the kids are fine, his mum and Sally's are helping. Don't forget this is very exciting for all the clan. It will give them a celebrity status for quite some time believe me."

I'm trying to smile. Sally's here again with drinks for us all, goodie goodie, I've got a pink straw this time, sorry but that's how I feel inside.

I need a cuddle and I can't get one from Cameron, not yet. My arms are up in the air and soft, sweet-smelling Sally has downed her tray and is wrapped up in my arms giving me her gentle motherly rock from side to side.

"There there love, it's alright, it's over now and your mum will be here on Monday. That's it love cry, you need to cry and get it all out, that's it."

That's better, I needed a good blubber, I'm not bothered that Cameron witnessed it, the tension has been released and I feel calm again.

"Come on our Cameron, you tell her what's what and don't ask too many questions, not tonight. I'll just go wash these up."

I don't want her to go downstairs, I suddenly feel so scared, my hand has caught Sally's and I'm hanging on. I need her here. My mouth is saying, "Please" to Cameron, He's nodding so Sally is easing herself onto my bed beside me, her arm around my shoulders is warm and protective and that is what I need right now. There's so much I want to talk to her about, apart from what happened with Dora, so much I need to understand. The confusing journey I almost took but Gran wouldn't allow me. She knew I wasn't ready to be with her yet.

"You sure you're up to this Kate?" Cameron sounds concerned.

"Yes." I'm determined to not be such a wimp and to help him all I can.

"I'll keep it short for now but if you want me to

stop just say." He's smiling his wonderful, dazzling white smile. "No, on second thoughts hold your hand up, that's less painful for you."

Listening to Cameron telling me how Alex had first approached Flora at the Council Offices looking for the whereabouts of a Miss Taylor is strange. Almost like a book you feel you have read before, some of the story is familiar but the rest you don't know. Flora had gone home and told Dora who used her position at the Medical Centre to check Miss Taylor's records. It seems all the jealousy of years ago had run deeper than anyone knew. Alex was the image of his father which was a great shock to poor Flora when he approached her. Losing the man she loved to Dora was bad enough, but she hadn't known about Miss Taylor's fling or indeed the end results, the child she could have had, a proper family and a different way of life. Jealousy turned into rage the day in the tea garden when he found her, and the Passmores overheard. Miss Taylor was rejecting her son once again and it pained Flora greatly. She confronted her that evening in her garden only to be humiliated again. Miss Taylor laughed at Flora; poor weak, timid, mousey Flora bullied by her sister retaliated for the first time in her life with drastic results.

Running out of the bungalow down the street she almost bumped into Alex Granger who most certainly would have recognised her. Arriving home deeply distressed, Dora then took control as usual. She wasn't going to allow their position in

Wetherby to be ruined by a so called "trollop" and her illegitimate son, not now after all these years. Ringing the contact number Alex Granger had left with Flora at the Council Offices she made an appointment knowing she had to silence him in some way.

Parking her car around the back of the sports hall Alex Granger was to meet her at the fire door and take her along the empty corridor to his office. Dora saw the discarded broken foil sticking out of the skip that she had parked next to. Concealing it in her overly large handbag was to her just a back-up plan, combine that with desperation and a quick violent temper and the end results were inevitable.

Enter Miss Marple, stupid little me trying to sort everything out on my own. The orange flash and all my visualisations last night that had taken time to work out. I'm writing the question down.

"The orange dress, why did she change?"

"We found the dress splattered in blood under some garden rubbish ready for burning." Cameron is smiling at me. "She changed because everyone had seen them in an outfit together that day. Flora had gone to the gardening club that night still in the outfit. How she ever thought she was going to be conspicuous by changing is beyond me, that dress is hideous."

Sally is giving me another hug.

"Well love you were right. Who'd have thought it of poor Flora though? Dora always was a nasty piece of work even when she was young, my mum says so. Now what I'd like to know is did she kill out of love for her sister or just self-preservation?"

"Get you Sally Benson getting all clever with your words, does Chris know you're reading a dictionary?" Cameron mocking Sally is bringing a little lightness back into the room.

"Well one thing's for sure they'll be wearing identical outfits where they're going, along with everyone else in there. Right our Cameron I'm going downstairs now to wash up, ten minutes only to ask questions then be off with you."

"Right you are Matron." He's standing and saluting her mockingly.

It must be very early yet as there's no light coming through the gap in my curtains, where's my clock? Sally's moved it so the ticking didn't disturb me, she's so kind. The birds are singing so it's got to be somewhere between 3:00 and 4:00 AM. Somewhere in the streets beyond there is a clunking noise ever so often, that's probably Bob the milkman on his rounds. He usually gets to me between 4:00 and 4:30 AM and I haven't heard him yet. My mouth feels like the bottom of a budgie's birdcage as Gran said, well in Leeds there are other sayings more on the lines of wrestlers and their jockstraps, but the budgie will do today. Now my feet are on the ground and in my penguin slippers gravity has taken over and I am desperate for the loo. Sally's in the back bedroom, it's better if I creep downstairs and use the shop loo, I don't want to disturb her, she deserves a good sleep and a lie in for all she's done for me. When I'm on my feet as they say, which I am now, I'm going to make sure she gets something nice for all her kindness. A bit of pampering for her would be good, I could go with her and have a girlie day, that's it yes, I likey very much.

At least my head has cleared now all the drugs good old Doc gave me to sleep have worn off. Switching on the lights of Crumbs and breathing in the coffee and residual baking smells is heavenly. I wonder what all the gossips of Wetherby will be making of all this? Business will be booming when I manage to reopen but when? Oh, I don't know just not yet, I can't. Loo! That's what I crept down for and then a drink, oh but which colour straw today Kate, that's exciting isn't it?

It was a tough decision when faced with so many drinks which one to have. The coffee smells soooo good but I've made an Earl Grey tea, light and refreshing. I'm sitting in my usual chair because I'm a fighter and I refuse to be dogged by the bad memories. This is my home and my business, and no murderer is going to turn me into a quivering mess. Besides it's all over now and never again will I be so stupid. Miss Marple indeed, what was I thinking of?

Some of the swelling has gone down, my Botox

lips can slowly drink from the beaker without too many drips, that's good I'm on the mend. I've put too many lights on in the tearoom, it is a lot cosier with just a few. Rose and I used to sit here early in the morning over a drink before she started on her scones, me in my dressing gown and Rose in her comfy, baggy pants and a jumper. Well here I am in my penguin dressing gown and slippers with my drink but no Rose and no scones today. Crumbs can stay closed for a while, I couldn't do much baking like this, I'd scare the customers away who are just visiting Wetherby. Can't say it will scare some of the locals, ghouls that they are they'll lap it up along with their tea and cake. Hey ho, that's the way the cookie crumbles and Carol suddenly descending upon me is enough to handle in one day. Lights dimmed that's much better I might try a coffee and a nibble of something. There must be some Madeira cake left.

Some cakes are better left to rest for a day or two, so my Madeira cake is lovely and moist with just a smudging of a hint of the lemon used. Now I feel terribly guilty, maybe Crumbs could be open tomorrow, I'll discuss it with Sally although she needs some time off too. This is crazy the more I think about it guiltier I feel, don't be ridiculous, stop it, this can all wait, can't it?

"My dear, dear Kitty tomorrow is another day."

Rose's voice is back in my right ear, is it though? Or am I just hoping it's her? Tears are welling up behind my eyes. The last time I heard her voice her words were words of warning and then desperate pleas asking me to hold on. Oh Rose, oh Gran. I can't help it the floodgates have opened again; great heaving sobs are echoing around Crumbs.

"There there Kitty, my dear calm yourself everything will be alright, I'm here and I'll always protect you."

I'm feeling low, really low and sad and my shoulders feel strange sort of tingly, there's a smell, so nice and so comforting that I just want to keep breathing it in. It's Rose's smell.

"Kitty my darling, look up, please, for me, look up."

My hair is wet and hanging in strands in front of my eyes as I try with all my might to do as I'm asked and lift my head from my soggy sleeve. Through my tears I can see what looks like my beloved Rose smiling at me from the other side of my table just as she used to. A warm smile crinkling the corners of her lovely brown eyes, her round cheeks pink from the heat of the oven. My hand has gone up to move the floppy curl of hair that always fell towards her eyes when she was hot from baking. It's stopped mid-air.

"Don't be afraid Kitty, do it."

Through my tears I'm doing what I'm told, I have to just this once. Rose's grey hair feels so soft in my fingers just as it always did, I'm moving it back to where it should be, but I don't want to let go. My fingers are going through her hair, oh Rose, Rose.

"Well, my darling Kitty, now do you understand I'm always here for you when you need me most?"

"I do Rose, thank you. Seeing is believing and from now on I always will."

Rose has gone, faded away slowly this time whilst blowing me a kiss. Unlike all the old times she's left me feeling calm and happy. When Rose does decide to return, I'll have the kettle on!

Books In This Series

The Crumbs Mysteries

1. Seeing is Believing
2. Murder at Café Miro
3. When the Tea Leaves Spell Murder (Coming soon in Autumn 2023)

Murder At Café Miro

Kate continues to build a reputation running the café she inherited from her godmother, Rose. This reputation is not just for her baking but also for her sleuthing, much to the annoyance of Rose and her ghostly interference. Kate gets involved even deeper in murder when a body is found at her friends' café in Leeds. She soon realises that the people around her are not quite what they seem but revealing this to catch a killer could hurt so many.

Books By This Author

292 Albion Place

When Nigel and Lorraine take on a new venture little do they realise just how much 292 Albion Place has in store for them. Launching two businesses within the same Victorian building on a street of trendy coffee shops in Leeds isn't so easy. Nigel struggles with his new café 'Hot Stuff!' on the floors below whereas upstairs 'Chic', Lorraine's hairdressing salon, prospers and she expands into beauty therapy. Their working days are far from mundane as 'Hot Stuff!' gets involved in a police stake out whilst 'Chic' salon is plagued by ghostly hauntings. Lorraine however is determined to let nothing stop her future plans. She has a colourful past accepted by Nigel and never spoken of. Secrets have a way of catching up with you, so does the past. Will the activities of a new member of staff threaten to put Lorraine's businesses and private life in jeopardy?

Angels Can Be Hairy Too!: Flossie's First Case

Flossie may be small for a Jack Russell but she is no ordinary dog. She has just landed back on Earth for her first assignment as a Dog Angel with these instructions:

1. FOLLOW YOUR NOSE FLOSSIE

2. DON'T TRY TO FLY TOO SOON

3. REMEMBER THE ANIMAL ANGEL ACADEMY'S MOTTO: "ONLY FOR THE GOOD OF OTHERS"

She will try her best to follow them, whatever lies ahead. Join Flossie on her first adventure in England and see how she uses her special powers to solve the case.

Printed in Great Britain
by Amazon